CONTENTS

Chapter One
Valedictory

Chapter Two
Super Constitution

Chapter Three
Standoff

Chapter Four
Armed Forces

SUPER

CONSTITUTION

Charles Kim

Copyright @ 2009 by Charlestone Publishing Co., Inc., L.A., Ca., U.S.A.

Printed in China.

Library of Congress Catalog Card Number: could be presented by request.
ISBN:978-1-60725-876-6

Article 1

Genius

This story begins in the early summer of year 2016. Any event or story before the summer of 2016, therefore, is in the past.

At the office of the President of China in Beijing on one morning of the early summer of 2016, a strange mechanical voice became audible to the ear of the President from the northern corner of the room.

"Mr. President, how are you this morning? My name is Miss Ohara from the star Ohara, twenty-one light-years away from the earth."

The voice was so clear. The President wondered whether there was a misplaced talking toy around the corner. And he looked around the corner. But he could not find anything.

"Mr. President, you could not see me. But that does not matter. The important thing is a serious communication between you and me."

1

Super Constitution

Accordingly, being a bit puzzled, the President responded in a joking manner.

"What kind of communication are you talking about?"

"Well, Mr. President, you have to listen to me and follow my instruction to save this beautiful earth."

The President adjusted his sitting posture, and talked to the stranger Miss Ohara.

"Miss Ohara, please wait a moment."

He became a little serious, and pushed a button to call his secretary. The secretary appeared swiftly, and asked the President what to do, as she approached the president's desk.

Still in a joking manner, the President directed his pretty young secretary to have a seat.

"Well," the President went on, "Miss Ohara, please go ahead with your instruction."

The secretary wondered whom the hell the President was talking to.

"Mr. President, your first instruction is to decommission all the weapons systems of nuclear, biological, and chemical arms of your country within a designated time."

This time, the mechanical voice startled the young secretary, and got on Mr. President's nerves.

"Is this an electronic game on behalf of Russia or the U.S.?"

"No, Mr. President," the mechanical voice continued as if a person talked right from the close corner, "I gave the same

Article 1: Genius

instruction to both countries' Presidents. Please confirm with them."

"What is going to happen if I disregard your instruction?"

"Then, your important people will be killed one by one until the instruction is fulfilled."

More than 6 billion people are living on this earth. Several nations possessed over-killing arsenals that not only could wipe out human being's civilization but also destroy the earth. Those countries' leadership could not catch the point in a tensed-up situation for anyone to be slipped into triggering a dangerous wire. Great human civilization had been achieved through the work of geniuses. Accordingly, a few geniuses or even one genius could make it different in bringing about a critical turning point to usher a safety pin for the world's peace and prosperity.

Dictionary says that genius means an exceptional capacity of intellect in creative and original work in science, art, music, etc.

Genius makes things different, very much different from ordinary person's work. Everybody wants to be a genius, but God does not give a chance. God gives it only to somebody very discriminatorily. Nobody can complain, nor can anybody sue it. We only admire it. We envy their performance that dominates our daily life. People benefit from the work done by genius of which work they appreciate from the bottom of their heart and enthusiastically pay attention to the work.

One out of 2,500 people shows above 130 of IQ, only one out of 100,000 goes beyond 140, and one out of 10 million births may reach over 160, which can memorize a book of 300 pages in a day and understand labyrinthine consequences that ordinary people cannot catch.

3

Super Constitution

No matter how hard you work, you never can imitate genius or compete with her. We had been born in this world the way God had given. If you are not genius, it is not your fault and it is not your parents' intention either. The gene splicing has been twisted that manner which we cannot change or alter yet.

A flea can jump 300 times of its height. An ordinary dog smells several times sharper than ordinary human; a rattle snake moves its tail more than a dozen times faster than short track runner's fastest running legs; migratory birds keep flying in the air several days without meal and rest, and etc. There are countless examples and existences for an extraordinary talent in the living world.

Ecologically, all living things benefit from each other even though a natural enemy rambles around without a cause or warning; however, all living things except human being have no big deal in helping their peers. The human ecology deals entirely different distinction in terms of helping each other among the peers: civilization, invention, education, and improvement that come from the work of genius. Only human world has the effect of other people's talented workmanship: thus the civilization came on the human being and it keeps going on to make and maintain the human as the lord of all creations.

On our daily life, time and again, we often talk about a moron who has an IQ of around below eighty. But he can be a super genius at the world of chimpanzee, which exhibits an outstanding mental power among monkeys. Of course, we could have never achieved the culture and civilization of nowadays with moron's status. Vice versa, if we had a very highly intelligent brain which would supersede a couple of times better than the present human being's average one, perhaps we would live in a world that we could travel at the speed of light.

Article 1: Genius

Surprisingly enough, human intelligence picks up its velocity of evolution by a pace of geometric progress. Man's existence on the earth has been traced back to at least a quarter of million years. Yet, up until about 5,000 years ago, man had no trace of using a letter, which was a key development recognized as the turning point for modern intelligent people. The modern technology we now enjoy only emerged in last couple of hundred years; furthermore, the speed of producing higher and better performing genius is gaining a momentum, becoming faster with an increase in their number.

Why is it happening at modern age after all those long periods of tens of thousands of years? Most of scholars agree that certain degree of quantity and quality provides turning points: the appropriate environment to live in, the betterment of stronger nutrient supply alongside vitamins and drugs, flexible organization of modern social fabric, and school system of which enables genius to meet genius naturally and easily. The gene splicing of talented or gifted people enhances the chance to produce more and better geniuses. In this way, sooner or later, human society can face deeply troubled social problems: formation of a class of higher IQ groups so much different from ordinary average one as the same as ordinary one so much different from the one of chimpanzee.

Anyway, let's disregard the worry of a future development of the human being's intelligent capacity. Let's talk about an imminent peculiar development of a unique technology, which is going to change our modern world drastically by making one sovereign power possible that would govern our whole world as a single nation. This staggering undertaking is going to be accomplished, not by armies and bombs and political twist, but by three geniuses.

Brenda Chen was born in Hong Kong on August 15, 1988, as the first and only child of Mr. Tao Chen, who was practicing acupuncture. While a nervous situation of the hand-over of Hong Kong to China was approaching, many Chinese people left the prosperous city to immigrate to Canada, the U.S., and New Zealand. Brenda Chen's family was one of the families that immigrated to the U.S. in 1993, four years before the hand-over event. By the way, Brenda revealed her extraordinary brilliance from the early age of three, startling her parents, neighbors, and distant relatives.

Most of psychologists say that genius originates from heredity and environment. Nevertheless, genius is born everywhere regardless of a family tree, time and again, embarrasing evolutionists. One's hereditary roots in the splice of DNA, however, prevail in the behavior of producing genius.

Brenda Chen had been quickly recognized throughout all classes she attended in New York City, as a gifted child. Even though she faced a language barrier in the beginning, she soon overcame it, advancing far ahead of her peers in every subject and amusing classmates and teachers highly. Before entering college, she skipped a year and entered ahead of her class. In 2006, she went on to attend Brown University in Providence, Rhode Island to major in biology, having been keenly interested in molecular biology.

Despite such an academic triumph, Brenda began to grow baffled and frustrated in dealing human relationship at the start of sophomoric year in college, recognizing some trouble spot formulating in her personality. She felt urging hot temper whenever she waited for somebody or something. She could not exercise patience; some unknown melancholy all of a sudden wrapped her to throw off her composure. Finally she lost control of her character: she acted like a stupid child. The behavior went on repeatedly. When she stayed alone quietly and calmly, she was surprised at her realizing her behavior. She could not understand. She went to her school councilor to discuss the matter; however, the councilor and she had failed

Article 1: Genius

to grasp the reason. After all, she had an appointment with a psychiatrist.

As usual, the psychiatrist provided a snug corner of the office with her. The psychiatrist generated a cozy dialogue of simple questions and narrations about Brenda's life, gently prompting her to recount everything from infancy onwards through her puerility, puberty, high teens and up until now.

When Brenda Chen entered Brown University, a thunderous topic about her fascinating appearance and gifted talent already rumbled on through the campus: her soaring IQ; her well matured behavior; her extraordinarily charming face; and her strikingly attractive and sexy figure. The campus news reported on a big title: no exaggeration was possible to describe her outstanding attractiveness. The paper extolled her beyond a common sense. But nobody went cynical. They rather echoed the paper's words and fell in with the topic.

The campus students went crazy when they confronted her. They looked on her with a mere infatuation, some crowd leisurely followed her, and some students vociferously expressed great enthusiasm. She instantly became a big star upon setting her first foot on campus. She had been used to her peers' glare and general public's attention from early days of her schooling. At the University's exciting reception, she was embarrassingly elated. She felt so great. She responded positively. She glowed and bloomed; though, as always, gracefully maintained her composure.

The psychiatrist whose name was Christine Fox listened to Brenda's narrative story carefully through questions and answers. Brenda had been well pampered by her eager parents all the way up to now. Also, her teachers and classmates had pleasantly treated her all the time. Therefore, there was no chance to inlay any stigma on her life's backdrop. Even the growth of her sexual sensitiveness had been retarded because she did not have much time or occasions to be exposed to pornography.

Psychiatrist Dr. Christine Fox, however, learned a sudden upsurge of sexual behavior, which seemed to implode in Brenda at the time of her entrance to the college and on. Brenda started masturbation by the time she entered college. It was a delayed happening for Brenda. A start of masturbation usually occurs much earlier than her age. But Dr. Fox quickly realized she had come across an unexpected medical jackpot in the form of a peculiar pattern of Brenda Chen's sexual behavior.

Masturbation illustrates a common sexual practice and maybe helps an ordinary maintenance of sound health for the grown-ups. Because Brenda Chen had been barred from ordinary phenomena of getting pleasure or getting relieved by masturbation, she did not have an idea of its normal frequency and the degree of the pleasure. In the beginning, she just startled on her pleasantly shocking ricochet of her body relieving her uptight nervous system. Upon her repeated action, she felt good and relaxed to do her homework. Eventually, she voluntarily approached porn magazine and video, increased the frequency of her self-gratification, and found that the action gave her unprecedented, spellbinding pleasure and stark stamina in pursuing her scholar work. It fascinated her, totally arresting her mind.

Nevertheless, she began to feel suffering from an unspecified urge that permeated into her body and mind. She could not tell whether the delicate suffering originated from her body system or her mental equipment. She wandered around amid a murky borderline of mind-body problem. The masturbation gave her unparalleled, outstanding pleasure she never experienced before in her life, and she enjoyed indulging herself every morning and every night, as well as during the

Article 1: Genius

day from time to time. She thought it reflected a normal behavior. Actually, her inner private life had gone isolated. Her extraordinarily popular stance made her so aloof among her intimate family and friends while she led her life without noticing her exceeding oddity on the process of producing her sex hormone.

Psychiatrist Dr. Fox asked some professional question to Brenda Chen, after listening to Brenda's long narration on her past up to nowadays' hidden activity of her self-gratification.

"Brenda, have you heard about a word of nymphomania?"

"Of course, do you mean abnormally excessive and uncontrollable sexual desire in woman?"

"Yes, do you know how it happens?"

"No."

Brenda's eyes twinkled with curiosity as she looked at her psychiatrist's mildly dubious face. Dr. Fox explained some biological phenomena of nymphomania briefly while maintaining a subdued countenance.

"Well, Brenda, every human being has a secreting organ of sex hormone. While some people have a very slowly secreting process, certain people have a very fast one. The gap between the slow and the fast takes place in a very wide range. When the secretion reaches to an enough level and begins to overflow back into the bloodstream, it triggers an urge of sexual desire. With this, the degree of feeling an urge of sexual desire also varies according to an inborn individual biological condition. The time frame between a slow and fast secreting hormone can range from several months to a couple of hours. More than ninety-nine percent of all people fall in the range of one week to a half-day. Of course, even in the same person, according to the situation, it varies."

"Brenda, I know you have such an exceedingly high-powered intelligence along with such a fantastic sex appeal. No one doubts that you are going to achieve a great scholastic performance and most feel you would become an indomitable contender for Miss Universe. However, Brenda, it seems to me you have an unexpected challenge you have to grapple with. You appear to have an incredibly high degree of sexual desire in addition to possessing an unusually rapidly secreting organism of sexual hormone. That means that you have to relieve the overflowing rapid of your sex hormone not to bother your normal nervous system: at least 2 or 3 times a day."

"Brenda, 2 or 3 times a day everyday mean that you need at least 2 or 3 satyrs to keep your emotion at peace. Otherwise, your normal emotional wave would be compressed by the rapidly flowing-over of excess hormone. The over-compressed emotion would at last gradually shift and reposition your normal emotional wave to thrust the crust of your emotion. That means destroying your normal behavior and disturbing your normal judging sense. And also the masturbation has its own limit. You cannot go on forever with it only. The natural instinct of inexorable and inexplicable urge will grip you, finally requiring real coitus to get out of its grip."

"On this matter, we have a problem to solve and a challenge to overcome. Brenda, I have an idea to correct the situation. But I need time to check with a gynecologist and endocrinologist to find out the exact degree of your urge and the appropriate frequency of your relieving cycle."

Brenda felt that a trouble spot innate in her body was not a small one. Now she could trace the source of suffering and

Article 1: Genius

vexation that had recently enveloped her. Brenda smiled at the patiently waiting psychiatrist.

"Well, thank you, Christine, how should I cooperate with you in solving the problem?"

"Actually, until we diagnose the exact course of your symptoms, you have nothing to do."

The Nature's laws are full of mysteries and wonders, which have produced superstition, religion, and philosophy. Human being longs for good luck, and so indulges in wishful thinking. After all, human bursts joy on a success that resulted in only a natural course as a good luck, and suffers acutely amid agony on a failure as a bad luck of which course has moved on as a natural result too. Remarkable questions confronting our daily life arise from that humanity does know something alongside something we cannot figure it out, on top of mysterious urging factors in body's chemical reaction.

Brenda Chen was born with an extraordinarily activating mental equipment, further blessed with charm and striking beauty. She grew up in a happy environment, which allowed her to cultivate a most gentle and moderate character without dysfunctional emotional-habits.

However, since her first experience of her self-gratification at her freshman's days, and along with the crescendo of a number of frequencies in masturbation over time, anxiety began to burn her every day. One day as usual, she practiced her extra-class exercise of parallel-bars play at the college gymnasium. She started the exercises of parallel bars from her early junior high school days. Even though she did not practice it for Olympic championship, her skill almost approached to the champion level. It was only her hobby for fun. And she did not want to spend too much time on it to be

Super Constitution

an Olympic champion. Meantime, she happened to annoy on her unusual unbalance of her body movement during the exercise at the college gym first time on one day. That marked the beginning of her normal character's slow deterioration.

Since that occasion, Brenda Chen often experienced unexpected flares of irritability, which shot through her mind and emotions and spread throughout her entire body. That irritation really bothered her. She could not understand it at all; where it was coming from; why it was coming on. Anyhow, it gripped her mind to bungle up awkwardly. She noticed her self-gratification tranquilized her internal chaos and allowed her peace for the time being.

As Christine Fox diagnosed temporarily and Brenda Chen vaguely learned a new phenomenon on her body structure, Brenda could summarize a new chapter of her newly developing characteristics. The best solution hung on to retain meeting some male who would match her mentality, her appearance, and her excessive physical condition of extraordinary sexual desire. It seemed impossible, in reality, to find such a man.

To fix her situation in a snug countermeasure, she had to take some action. The action would mean very quiet, deeply private, and intimately secretive movement with her positive initial and creative relationship. To hunt a man who could fulfill her at 100% from the start was out of the question. She wondered what type and how many men it would take to balance her odd situation.

In the next article, through Brenda Chen's gyratory violent movement inside her mind under strangely calm surface during her sophomore and junior, we would see a peculiar development of Brenda Chen's idiosyncrasy.

Article 2

Idiosyncracy

Human mentality plays a core-dynamism of human civilization. Human instinct, however, carves out, hardens up, and niches the basic human mentality to formulate its general character, which shapes up culture and civilization. Throughout human history, civilization and ordinary people's life organization, we could see colorful characters pit our daily lifestyles, giving birth to heroines and heroes and great eras and deluge of undulating emotions.

Several weeks later, after Brenda Chen checked up with the designated gynecologist and endocrinologist arranged by psychiatrist Christine Fox, Brenda sat across Christine's desk facing each other to talk about Brenda's problem.

As Brenda and Christine guessed, the factors reported from the gynecologist and endocrinologist had uncovered some somber problems. Christine opened her mouth first for the dialogue.

"Brenda, we have a much bigger challenge than we had thought."

Super Constitution

"I thought so. What is the detail?"

"Well, this case is not an ordinary one. I have only heard about it several times so far, and I never imagined I could face this reality."

Nevertheless, Brenda kept her composure normal as she listened to other person's story. Christine explained.

"The volume and the speed of secreting sex hormone in your sexual organism turned up in tremendously surpassing any recorded point thus far throughout the medical institutional history. And what's more, according to the gynecologist's unusual remark, you have not only an exceedingly well-controlled autonomic nervous system in the muscle tissue of your vagina, but also a 'fascinating skin-formation' on the wall of your vagina."

Changing her leg's position on the comfortable chair, Brenda questioned Christine in a calm tone of her clear, ringing voice.

"What do you mean by a fascinating skin-formation and how does the autonomic nervous system affect every thing?"

"Those are exactly what I am trying to clarify to you now."

According to Christine's plain explanation of the professional terminology about a peculiar skin-formation and the well-controlled autonomic nervous system on top of the exceeding volume and speed of secreting sex hormone, Brenda had too many fantastic functions in her sexual organ, which happened in one out of ten thousand women. The detail was as followed:

Usually the wall skin of ordinary woman's vagina has a smooth tissue. But a scant few women develop gristles the size of a grain of rice, similar to octopus's sucker-bearing

Article 2: Idiosyncrasy

arms, which engender extremely exciting sensation to male partner at intercourse. In addition to these odd moles on the wall skin, the autonomic nerves in the area of the muscles of such women's vagina are directly connected to the heteronymous nervous system which means she can move her muscle either way for contraction or expansion by her will: so called contractile muscle. A temptation for the action of contraction and expansion naturally augments according to the increasing arousal. The repeating and increasing activities of the contraction and expansion along with sensational touching of stimulating moles mesmerize any sensual man.

In the case of Brenda, the combination of her extremely strong sexual desire and her incredible muscle tissue and the peculiar skin-formation along with her fabulous intelligence and beauty, created extraordinary troublesomeness in her still burgeoning personality. Her fledgling adolescence slowly began to drive her gushing carnal desire up to her neck.

Christine, further, informed that, by confining Brenda's overwhelming natural forces, she would become so torrentially bombarded by its intensity, causing to blur her judgment and shattering her emotional stability. She would undergo deteriorated in agony. She would go crazy to damage her healthy personality. Why then, should she suffer from forcibly entering her own mental imprisonment and bind herself from satisfying herself? Does it make any contribution for the public's generalization of individual moral standard? Or does it satisfy for the simple conformity of the social norm?

Following the detailed explanations of Brenda's typical physical condition, Dr. Fox advised her on the best recourse of treatment.

"Brenda, I guess the best way to cope with your biological demands does not exist in subterfuge but exists on a positive response. In other words, you'd better square off the steadily rising urge rather than suffocate it."

"You mean I should try to establish a certain steady relationship, don't you?"

"Yes, I mean it. Of course, you are going to need maybe more than half a dozen steady partners. It is going to shoulder a hectic extra-curriculum on you to keep up each relationship for an appropriate balance."

"But Christine, it is going to bring forward a hell of a job to maintain about a dozen men in a pen of punctuality and secret. I have to line up those dates in a fixed sequence, which would present conflicting overlaps. And what's more, there goes no long lasting secret in human lifestyle."

"You are right, Brenda, it could rear its clumsy head in this intimate and private matter. But to let it expose by itself spontaneously is not bad at all. I think people will implicitly believe in you and accept your biological phenomenon as a natural development by that time."

The dialogue of private and personal matters between psychiatrist Christine and rather odd genius Brenda went on long hours further. They contemplated unwelcome but probably looming subjects such as how to gauge the major opinions, what sort of moral stance to approach, and how to deal with Brenda's personal characterization in case of a severe blunder on Brenda's behavior.

After all, Brenda and Christine agreed that Brenda would risk a scandalous adventure rather than suppress Brenda's potentially harmful urges. It could instead later mark out a rather widely considered bravery for Brenda to take such an adventure, and it could provide a great momentum for Christine's experiment in her empirical psychology.

Article 2: Idiosyncrasy

Brenda made a detailed plan to select her dates from two areas.
The first one preferred the campus of Brown University. The second one, of course, designated Air Force Academy of the United States of America.

When Brenda entered Brown University, she applied to Air Force Academy to be trained to be a special woman pilot of fighter-interceptor as a guest student. It greatly agitated the administration of Air Force Academy pro and con just because of her name of outstanding genius and her enchanting beauty. After all, the administration made a decision to test her physical and mental fitness. The result of the test favored her with a great score. Her champion-like parallel-bars practice helped her physical score. So, Air Force Academy accepted Brenda's application to be trained as an honorary guest for being one of "Tomcat Aces." The cadet's welcome-remark roared. During her freshman's summer vacation, she joined Air Force cadets, and she enjoyed the program so much. As her extra curriculum, she easily mastered all the textbooks of Air Force Academy, and she demonstrated an excellent performance to handle the topnotch fighter plane. That incident had attracted an unusual attention from Air Force generals, staffs, and cadets.

A few dozen candidates from each area appeared in the consideration. She made a list alphabetically first, then marked her favorite partners in the number of 10 from each area totaling to 20 men. She figured that maybe less than one third of twenty partners would remain as her steady counterparts. Maybe, only one or two could stay as for her satisfaction; in that case, she had to go to the next list on and on until she would have an enough pack.

She also made a plan of how to contact the candidate, how to engage in the coitus, and how to routine the affairs.

Super Constitution

She took the first choice from her school campus because the Air Force one had to be done during her coming summer season. She wondered who could exert a high level of sexual stamina for the long length of time duration and more frequent engagements of the session. She could not figure it out at all. She thought about some physiognomic interpretation from a candidate's appearance. Maybe she had to study some sort of phrenology. She felt she became a kind of fortuneteller, attempting to read sexual potential and personal compatibility in the face and frame of the candidate she put up as the first batter.

The name of the first contender was Harry Trumbull. He had a moderate frame, a little bit of handsome face, soft low voice, blithe smile and a glitter of eyes. He also marked brilliance at the school record. Brenda favored Harry as her first tool of prey to her odd phenomenon. Brenda approached Harry one day after a morning class.

"How are you, Harry?"
"What's up Brenda?"

Harry could tell that Brenda was approaching him with something in mind. It deviated a bit from her usual behavior. Normally she did not take an assertive manner of approach. Nonetheless, it engendered a terribly desirable experience for him. Not only Harry but also every student on campus would consider being approached by Brenda as an enjoyable surprise.

"Harry, will you do me a favor?"
"What favor?"

Harry gazed at Brenda's smiling face; he felt fascinated, but puzzled.

Article 2: Idiosyncrasy

"Harry, can you come to my apartment after dinner, say, around 8 o'clock? I have something to discuss with you alone."

Some puzzled question rang Harry's heart, but he kept himself calm, and simply responded "yes." In this way, Brenda's contact had been made, and around 8 p.m. Brenda gave a warm reception to Harry at the door of her apartment. Harry felt proud at Brenda's coquettish pose. But he never imagined Brenda's beautiful, bold offer at all, of course. Brenda confessed her attraction to Harry and asked him a permission to embrace him. Harry startled. He was embarrassed, shocked, and mesmerized. He kept silent for a while. Brenda took an initiative. She took his hand and pulled him and embraced and kissed him. Harry began to respond positively. They finally stumbled eagerly into Brenda's bed.

However, when the time came, Harry was unable to perform. At the crucial moment, they discovered that his erection became too soft. Brenda and Harry tried their best to revive Harry's stuff, but the stuff went on and off in half the erection. After all, two hours in strenuous caress had exhausted them without reaching any orgasm.

Brenda's first action of preying on the coitus with her favorite man failed as psychiatrist Christine predicted. Christine told Brenda that a man usually would fail on his first engagement if the man were excited too much or engaged in with much more powerful counterpart. Christine said that the function of human body's nervous system has a limit like muscle; we feel muscle exhaustion but usually we do not feel neuron's wear-off: neurolysis.

Excitement, anxiety, emotion, and mental turmoil can burn out body's nervous system. The more rapidly the mechanism moves, the much more the neuron burns off. When the neuron's delivery system wears off, the brain's order to fill the penis sponge with bloodstream and lock up the entryway, could not reach its destination through the neuron because it had been exhausted and lost its transmitting function. Not only brain's order, but also the sensation originated from penis could not hit the brain fully and on time. Brenda experimented through Christine's theory.

Brenda stroked Harry's arm reassuringly, attempting to alleviate his annoyance.

"Harry, today, I was too excited, and so were you. I think next time if we just take things slowly and discard our anxieties, then, we'll be able to enjoy ourselves."

"I am really surprised. I never had this kind of impotence. God, I am really glad you want to give another chance."

Several days later, Brenda and Harry met again. This time they made it but Harry could not hold more than three minutes, which Brenda could have the come only one time. She needed at least two or three times. She felt half-filled. For the full blast she needed five or six times of orgasms. Some irritated emotion disturbed her. She had no choice. She went to the next list immediately according to the plan she made. She contacted second man, third man, and finally 10th man.

Only one man made it at first engagement, and only two sessions out of forty ones during the first month gave her more than ten minutes, which gave her minimum satisfaction. Those forty sessions, though, brought about a hectic month with a long list of appointments, sometimes, squeezing in two sessions a day. Forty engagements in a month definitely noted a hell of sessions, but for Brenda, the number of satisfied sessions dropped way below her desired standard.

Article 2: Idiosyncrasy

Over the frustration by her disastrous attempts to satisfy her relentlessly raging desire, Brenda had slowly hardened her aggressive preying behavior. While she was increasing her dates and decreasing the gap between the demand of her desire and the supply of the satisfaction, she realized that her aggressive preying behavior had been shaped into a certain niche and been refined. Her gushing desire pushed her to the wall to activate her innate fighting spirit, which sharpened her preying behavior. Her overpowering intelligence, which well understood the delicate social norms and consequences of her behavior, however, guided her to the logic to placate her inborn sympathetic emotion, which refined her social manner.

Her refined social manner emerged and floated on the surface. Her sharpened preying aggressiveness submerged and crawled through on the bottom of her mind. Alongside her sweeping swing at Air Force Academy on the following summer school with a few dozen cadets in much more satisfaction, some trait of Brenda's general character had been crystallized throughout her swirling promiscuous activities on the dates with more than sixty athletic and intelligent elite so far. Most of them prided themselves upon their extolled performance in their field. They used to enjoy respect from their peers. They used to ride on high spirit.

No one refused Brenda's wondrous offer. Everybody watered his mouth on Brenda's approach and overture. Brenda's beauty and name fascinated everyone. There was no exception. Thus far, however, no one could match her desire in full swing even a once. Only a few could barely fill Brenda's vessel only half the brim. Brenda experienced the proud elite paraded as a dwarf in front of her giant stature. Brenda refined her dates into the number of around ten out of more than sixty, and still she continued exploring the possibilities for a new jewel, on the other hand, hoping she could hit a jackpot some day.

Super Constitution

Brenda could have sympathy on the big hiatus between her powerful intelligence and other's normal one. But she could not tolerate the torrid thirst her dates could not quench. Sometimes she felt angry. Sometimes she ferociously growled quietly.

She started to look down on her dates. Even though her dates provided some relief with her, she despised their caliber instead of appreciating their small contribution. To her, muscular and intelligent elite looked like a puerile cub.

Actually those boys were transfixed in front of Brenda's charm and name like a rabbit fascinated by a snake. Brenda wanted their strength of extinguishing her wild fire rather than their good will of condoling with her unfinished climax. She importuned her dates' power to wrap her up and flail her down to tatters. She begged for somebody to trample on her ever-gushing libido.

But the situation developed forlorn so far. Brenda's augmenting aggressiveness, her repeated frustration, her growing despise on her dates, and her surging boldness to prey for the sake of her inexorable libido had finally shifted the crust of her genuine and gentle character. Her sarcastic side of her ordinary character bulged under the careful guidance of her composed intelligence. The appearance of her behavior still stilled like a giant river's quiet flowing.

The underneath of her calm surface had formed swirling torrents, which unfolded spectacular dizzy canyons with colorful sheer cliffs. Her inside went wrinkled, rippled, and echoed torrentially kicking and screaming–desperate to free her from the bond of her poignant libido. Accordingly, this sardonic, forceful nature of her body's chemical reaction demanded a firm resolution of her agonizing internal chaos only through enough strength to satiate her gushing sexual desire: the justice of the strong, not the good will, nor the right.

Article 2: Idiosyncrasy

The good will or the right without matching strength implied meaningless.

When people suffer from hunger or foreign invasion, the state or the ruler's justice is the strength to feed and to protect. A crescendo of Brenda's aggressiveness along with her powerful intelligence to exercise her well-balanced discretion had formed a phenomenon of her dual personality: so-called phenomenal idiosyncrasy.

Dictionary describes idiosyncrasy as "a characteristic, habit, mannerism, or the like that is peculiar to an individual." The idiosyncrasy in Brenda's case, in particular, suggests not only a peculiar behavior of an individual, but also another peculiar behavior creating a perfect harmony or compromise.

We can site it as a sacred ritual in human life to feed hunger. But it makes an evil to exploit or plunder its peers to feed hunger. Anybody can justify it as a consecrated practice of private life to relieve sexual desire. But it can make a crime or an evil for us to rape or force or cheat an unwilling partner.

Brenda continued with her bustling swinger's lifestyle as usual, acquiescing to psychiatrist Christine's advice. Nonetheless, no matter how secretive or reserved it behaved, a rumor about her sexual daring finally began to spread. It ran an inevitable collision course. Brenda had been braced herself for its impact. A gossip about her sexual behavior drifted in the whispers, picked up its momentum, and raced wildly all over the campus.

As far as the gossip goes, it did not come out that malicious. It reflected rather like celebrity's news or curious everyday chitchatting. The talk centered on how such a wonderful genius with so unusual charm like Brenda had a peculiar strong lustfulness: such a promiscuous drive for nakedly carnal, lascivious undertaking.

23

Super Constitution

Speculations ran rampant, feeding the proliferation of such words throughout campus: goddess of sex symbol, tantalizing seductress, super multi-orgasm, and never-ending black hole. All those words undulated from mouth to mouth with half envy and half satire. All the words of the gossip actually did not intend defamatory or degrading mischief. They indicated a surprising secrete they confronted, a super peculiarity they happen to find, and one fascinating vulgarity of that genius-beauty queen.

Whatever direction their credulous intentions flashed on, Brenda could not help feeling awkward whenever she mingled with classmates. Brenda felt as if a thin veil fluttered down, separating her from her classmates. She exerted all her energy into preserving her placid, natural, and gentle demeanor. Inwardly, however, she found herself analyzing her surroundings in cold-blooded objectivity. Her inner life sank deeper and deeper into isolation while her socialization floated higher and higher into popularity, amid awkward complexity.

Brenda felt a distinguished dual line on her basic attitude of her moral stance. When she socialized in the campus life or general social matters, her outstanding, plausible performance ran through her usual snug style. That style smartly avoided prickly friction with her associates or companions for the activities or debates. Her classmates and professors alike were always amused at her brilliant wit. Her exceedingly quick ability to grasp the solution to a problem enchanted them all, as usual.

When she engaged in her utmost private matter of mating her dates, her overwhelming sexual performance bewildered her dates. That bewilderment, after all, tore down her dates' self-praised pride. Also, it totally irritated her half-filled ecstasy. In the end, it drove her aggressive preying-behavior further and further sophisticated.

Article 2: Idiosyncrasy

With every sexual encounter, she felt her body struggling to sweep her burning ecstasy up into her bosom from her loin. But always the burning ecstasy from her loin did not reach to her heart. In most of cases, the solidly glowing ecstasy dissipated all direction before it thrust its way into her impatiently waiting heart. The repeated frustrations with rare occasional successes had only hardened a cruel fighting spirit. The frustration eliminated her sympathetic emotion into a callosity, which drove her to a cold-hearted, carnivorous beast in acquiring anything to feed her hunger.

To feed her hunger or fulfill her gushing desire, she conducted cool analyzing power, she undertook a cruel preying behavior on the action of the coitus, and she developed a penchant for considering her dates as just a toll. To achieve her hidden ego, she justified her intelligent power to reach a target in the cold manners, which disregarded any sympathy or compassion. Her reason nullified her sentimental affections.

Herewith, Brenda's personality developed into two parallel lines of distinct tendency: highly gregarious socialization of her outer life; and deeply hidden isolation of her inner life.

The two lines could never meet compatibly, and never mingle either. The two lines have to be compromised by the person's intellectual power. The well-balanced harmony of the two lines requires even greater intelligence. The bigger the gap between the outer life and the inner one, the much higher intelligence is being required. Otherwise, the face of the dual personality closes up bigger and clearer: ugly confusion and stinking stupidity. The good examples: frequently lying politicians; stupid liar's grave mistakes; insidious double-crossers; and etc.

Super Constitution

Brenda's idiosyncrasy had come into existence as a spellbinding vista by her towering intelligence, by her phenomenal sexuality, and by her nympholeptic beauty.

Brenda's abnormal, super idiosyncrasy grew bigger and bigger. Her existence became a colorful monster: a mystic puzzle to her dates; wondrous amusement to her teachers; and an enlarged bizarre example of psychology to Christine. She gobbled up knowledge, bewildered her dates, tortured her mind, and shaped up her giant stature alongside her academic advancement. In the meantime, all of a sudden, she saw she was heading into her senior year.

Brenda would meet her matching partners at her senior days in the following article. That event would signal the actual beginning of the "Super Constitution" written by three geniuses.

Article 3

Freshman's Icon

By the time Brenda was promoted to the senior class, her reputation on her scholastic performance, her personal popularity, and her bizarre sex-power had long provided a zest with every gossip around the campus. Such talk permeated into every student's conversation, and made a heavy contribution to everyone's preconceptions. Consequently, these preconceptions molded a typical perception on the idiosyncratic behavior among the American Ivy League universities. Brenda's dynamic presence and its vibrations had marked some animation on the character of the American campus. She dynamically influenced Brown University's pep talk on its chitchatty behavior with significant effect to the incoming freshman class.

In the freshman class, two phenomenal characters made their appearances to match Brenda Chen. One was John Smith, and the other was James Leigh.

John Smith had a typical phenotype of Caucasian male, tracing his WASP roots back to the first Smith's arrival with the founding Pilgrim settlers in Massachusetts, some 400 years ago. He was borne in 1992 in Houston, Texas.

He developed a conspicuous figure from the early infant years both physically and mentally. When he entered an infant school at the age of five, he startled a young lady teacher by demonstrating enormous conversational ability. He spoke with articulate awareness, discussing general social affairs on equal standing with his teacher; his grasp of language was incomprehensible by his peers, and wholly unexpected by his teacher. His mental acumen approached high teen-ager at the tender age of five. The young woman teacher, speechless after their first conversation, was even more stunned when she discovered that John could do push-ups 100 times straight without feeling an exhaustion. John's physical condition of the muscle fiber had a queer trait much disparate from an ordinary condition. Migratory birds can continuously fly a couple of days without rest, eating, and drinking because those birds developed a crazy muscle sense not to be fatigued in a certain length of an extraordinary duration of time.

John made quite a stir everywhere he went. He began a practice of karate from the age of five at entering an infant school. He disclosed not only astonishing physical endurance during exercises but also prodigious athletic skill and accuracy in a variety of fields: jumping, tumbling, running, and motioning with lightning quick judgment. He mastered all the sophisticated forms of karate in body motions of attacking and defending. (In Korea: taekwondo; in Japan: karate.) He also did develop an enormous crushing power to break a brick, roof tiles, and thick wooden panels with his open hand, bare front or back fist, front kick, swing kick, side kick, and back kick in a terrible speed and a sharp accuracy. Whenever he demonstrated his weirdly powerful and accurate performance in public, he looked like a super, acrobatic stunt man, who gave onlookers a pleasant surprise.

Article 3: Freshman's Icon

An unusual event happened when John promoted himself to senior class of his high school. His reputation on the taekwondo (karate) had soared as a stark monolith around his hometown Houston, Texas. The president of local judoists association in Houston offered a bout between taekwondo and judo. But John refused it flat because judo banned dangerous throws and blows only stressing the athletic or sports element. What's more, judo started from holding or contact. And karate (taekwondo) aimed at finishing by a blowing contact on a vital point in the human body.

Originally the president proposed ten judoists competing against John one-on-one until either one of the competitors would throw him into the air or John would knock out ten judoists one by one in turn. In addition to John's refusal reasons, John, politely, mentioned that he could knock out even 100 judoists if they sparred one-on-one. An allusion to 100 knockouts furiously irritated the pride of the president and members alike. So, after all, the bout had been set at the sports arena: 100 anxious judoists versus stunting crackerjack John. All the concerned people figured John might last twenty or thirty judoists even though John had an excellent marshal art

The rules had been set. The two umpires had been selected. The knockout count was five seconds. Audience filled the arena into capacity full. Reporters and cameramen of local media lined up. Most of audience of high school girls and boys expressed sympathy to John because he faced up to 100 expert judoists and he was a hero in the marshal arts, a prominent genius in class, and a good-looking guy.

The two umpires had a casual chat. One umpire talked to another umpire.

"Rick, what do you think about the taekwondo-champ John Smith?"

Super Constitution

"I think the karate-champ brags his reckless courage. I heard he was distinguished as a genius in the class. I guess he does not understand human body's biological limit."

"But Rick, time to time, we hear about some unusual saga such as Samson and Delilah."

"Are you kidding? Those things only inflate an unrealistic legend as a real story to draw out some attention."

"But Rick, you never know. I feel some hunch in this guy John."

Girls and boys chitchatted, giggled, exclaimed quietly, and sporadically burst into laughing. The audience was excited. A tightly cushioned judo-play plate was rolled out and straightened firmly. 100 judoists lined up on the eastern side, and John stood up on the western side. John determined that he would not crack or break any bone but hit the vital point of the body's front and back in the up or down part. Two ambulances parked outside and a dozen local policemen secured the place.

The first ten best judoists poised to throw John into the air, way ahead before the ten-man count. All of the audience wondered how many men John would knock out before John was thrown out in the air. As a practical athlete, 100 judoists were confident of that human being's continuous exercise would drain body's energy to debilitate body's muscular strength and motor neuron (muscular movement).

The first man from the poised ten best judoists on the front line walked to the center of the judo plate, clad by judo uniform, and confronted John in the distance of five feet. The umpire signaled the start of the bout by his voice. Soon, John's nimble front-kick struck a sensitive part below the

Article 3: Freshman's Icon

judoist's navel before the man held John's foot. The man was knocked out easily at the first engagement. The second man was hit by just above his navel and collapsed. The third man hit by right on navel did not fall but slightly bent his body forward holding his body firmly and opening his arms in an encroaching shape. John dashed into his open arms and used his elbow to swiftly uppercut the man's chin to knock the man out. The packed audience was stilled and quieted. The audience was impressed.

The fourth man, the fifth man, finally the tenth man of the front line also knelt down before the front kick John exercised dexterously. John used only front kick on the first ten men. All the knocked-out judoists got back their consciousness in about five to ten seconds staggering to their feet by themselves.
The second ten-man group quickly lined up on the front line not to give a break to John. The spar continued. This time John used sidekick with less power because bone was involved. Once hit by the sidekick upon the side body, the body balance would be debilitated. As soon as the man's motor neuron was scrambled, John used his front fist for blowing the chin from right or left. Using this approach, the second ten-man group reeled and fell in. John's body condition looked getting fresher. His motion appeared getting more adroit. The action surprised the audience. The audience began to wonder a miraculous thing could happen: knockout of all the 100 judoists.

The third ten-man group was swiftly forwarded voluntarily because they knew they should not give any leeway for John to recuperate. The bout continued without a pause. The eager and fresher young athletes anxiously waited for their turn to seize their heroic opportunity to throw out John into the air. All they should do was to hold John's fast front-kick or sidekick with their two hands firmly. Once they would catch John's flying feet, then it would make their turn to demonstrate their mighty skill. This time John used

31

alternately left or right swing-kick to hit his counterpart's face. Already fixed mind-set of the third group met with an unexpected attacking approach. Their mind-set confused their nervous system to cause a notable neurosis. All of them fumbled their attempt to hold John's foot and were easily smitten unconscious. The audience grew increasingly elated and inflamed.

The fourth ten-man group quickly organized themselves with greater care, seriously considering creative ways to confront John's varied arsenal of attacks. The audience clenched their fists and took a quiet deep breath. The Judoists began to realize they faced a monster, not a lone vanguard. The fourth ten-man group gave up clenching the oncoming kick and rather stepped back quickly to avoid john's sharp attacking point first. Breaking the brunt of John's accurate, powerful kick would bring two immediate effects: John's labor in vain to cause him to feel atrophia; to let him exhaust double or triple or even more by continuous avoiding. The first man of the fourth group made a success to avoid John's first acute blow of sidekick. John quickly measured his counterpart's changed-tactics to prolong John's bout. John used a fake motion without an actual attack. All the Judoists of fourth group sprang up and down upon John's fake motion. John flew a real attack on the end motion of judoists' jumping-around to pin down his sharp attack on the counterpart's crucial weak-point. John easily whacked all of fourth group into a clear defeat.

The fifth group appeared most confident of any of the competitors so far. They implemented diversified approaches to avoid John's first hit by jumping up or downing their body or changing their position. In this manipulation, judoists moved round on the judo plate around John as for a delaying tactics to irritate and exhaust John. Acknowledging this group's different tactics, John pressurized each counterpart up to the hilt on the judo plate's periphery. Then John flew a

Article 3: Freshman's Icon

weak but crucial blow to cripple or stagger them. Without giving them any break, John used karate-chop of his open palm to hit the vital point for knocking them down. It looked now cat's playing with mouse. No judoist challenged John's attack face to face or tried to initiate any attack to John. John's stamina looked fresher than ever and his motion looked even sharper. His pose had been all the way firm and serious. The fifth group also experienced a humiliating beat-down. Now the audience felt some confidence that John might sweep the show.

The sixth group, however, abandoned all previous tactics, and instead rushed headlong at John in a kind of kamikaze move. The first, second, and third man of the sixth group were knocked down severely after ferocious charge upon John. Each judoist tried throwing its body against John in an attempt to knock him out of balance. John adeptly twisted his body to avoid a flying body with lightning speed. No matter how fast or dynamic motion the judoists cast, John's motion and judgment had been always outdoing the judoists. The matter hinged on the preserved strength and a faster motion. As long as the judoists could not motion faster than John, and as long as John could sustain the strength to exercise correctly, there was no chance for the judoists to throw out John. John's poise went imposing. This attitude simply radiated immeasurable energy and a clear, palpable fighting spirit to the audience. The audience reflected John's steady fighting spirit into the arena brightly.

The seventh group vigorously took on John's versatile attacks with alternating defense and offense, fake and real motion by using judo's typical "falling method." The seventh group dropped their bodies to the floor, rolled toward John to hook John's ankle with their foot, and tried to set a trap to trip John around toward the floor. John had to use a forceful front-kick or a dangerous tramp-kick on the shin of judoists' leg paved on the floor tightly. The applied front-kick or tramp-kick on

Super Constitution

the shin of the leg added an extra weight because the targeted body part had no space to move back. This situation gave no choice for John to avoid the possibility of cracking the bone. The first two men of the seventh group could not move their bodies after a grimly painful shock landed on the shin.

The umpires temporally stopped the bout to clear and examine the situation. They judged the bone had been cracked and asked one ambulance to take two guys to hospital. The two umpires briefly discussed the matter of judoists' manipulation of their legs by lying down on the judo plate. The umpires made a rule that the time of lying down on the floor more than five seconds should be considered as a "knocked out time." The new rule actually eliminated the judoist's manipulation of lying down on the floor. The seventh group collapsed quickly.

As soon as the seventh group collapsed, the general mood of the audience rode on a high spirit as if their wish to win the game took a big stride toward the finish line. The eighth, the ninth, and the tenth group lined up briskly and fell down without any magnitude. John's stature beamed a glow. He looked ready to tackle another 100. The audience rose on their feet. They went wild with hectic enthusiasm. John marked a local saga during his high school senior-year adding the above phenomenon on top of his preternatural talent of marvelous memory and powerful inferential faculty.

John's major obsession on the scholastic front had been pegged on the subject of electronic paradigm of audiovisual techniques. In addition to his absorption with electronics, his other major concern dwelled extensively on the weird story of Brenda Chen. Driven by these compelling preoccupations, John made a decision to come to Brown University.

The other phenomenal character and fascinating young genius James Leigh also came to Brown University just because of Brenda Chen. Seemingly, James Leigh came to the town of

Article 3: Freshman's Icon

Providence because he loved the seaport and its environment. But in real life, he was so much curious about the characterful sphinx of unknown depths of Brenda Chen. Ever since hearing of Brenda's arresting beauty, nymphomania and genius, his desire to meet her had gone from curiosity to fanatical desperation.

James Leigh displayed a stunning remark in the subject of physics. James especially entrapped himself in a theory of superconductivity, which represented one of the most sophisticated hi-tech in the human being's next generation for the super deliverance-technology. Along with the theory of superconductivity, James was crazy about the theoretical particles called "dark matter," which are thought to comprise almost all of the materials in the universe. (The astrophysical scientists in modern days have determined that the "dark matter or energy" makes up two-thirds of all materials in the universe.) The dark matter was believed to race right through ordinary matter of such as rock, soil, metal, water, and air without leaving a trace: penetrable into a few miles of solid rock at the speed of light without any trace.

James Leigh was born in 1992 in New York City to the immigrant parents. James's father and mother were educated in Korea up to the college work. Both of them had been recognized as brilliant students all the way through from elementary up to college. Both of them came to New York City at a different time to continue their study. But both of them dropped from the school to engage in the small business. Finally they met coincidentally and married and prospered in the wholesale business of general merchandise made in the Far East.

One day, a teacher of the elementary school James Leigh attended asked James's parent to come to his school. The teacher met James's father at her office.

Super Constitution

"Mr. Leigh, we found your son is a gifted child...very unusually talented. So we want to send him to a special school. We need your agreement."

"Well, it is surprising. My wife and I acknowledged our Jimmy's unusualness. But we, honestly, never thought he was that excellent genius. Of course, I agree with your recommendation to send my son to a special school."

James's father was so glad to hear from the teacher that his son James was an outstanding genius.

James Leigh's prominence actually started much earlier. But the parents only noticed their son's intelligence just grew up much earlier than other children.

James Leigh also developed a very unusual respiring organ for staying under water. From the early age of six or seven, James submerged under water and stayed extra long minutes holding his breath. The usual maximum length of time holding breath marked around five minutes. But James used to stay more than ten minutes. Later in high teen-ager, he endured even 20 minutes. His friends dubbed him "sea lion" because James moved so strongly and exceptionally fast under water without coming above water so long, indicating an extraordinary, inherent physical stamina in swimming.

He remarkably enjoyed physics. He became an odd ball because he often talked about black hole, dark matter, supernova, and superconductivity, which his peers would not understand.

John Smith and James Leigh never met each other until they came to Brown University as a freshman.

James Leigh's zeal on the matter of superconductivity and dark matter increasingly echoed his mind whenever his

Article 3: Freshman's Icon

thought came to those matters. Superconductivity would bring revolutionary change on human being's civilized lifestyle based on high-tech. Not only enormous waste of the modern electricity during transmitting the power through all types of wire would be eliminated, but also all type of transporting mechanism such as trains, cars, telephone systems including cellular phone would enhance its efficiency ten times, even 100 times. Entirely different concept of the transportation including aviation would be borne and would obsolete modern day's mobile capacity as a stone-aged one. The theory of the superconductivity had been confirmed by the modern science. The theory fascinated James Leigh's mind every day.

Also, along with the attractive theory of superconductivity through temperature-lowered substances, the theory of dark matter in the universe dazzled James's mind all the time. Scientists called the dark matter WIMPs (weakly interacting massive particles). Like the power of gravity, the mysterious dark matter, which pierces all of materials of living things and the densest metals in the universe without leaving any trace and makes up two-thirds of the universe, exists according to the modern astrophysicists. It would explain inconsistencies in the physical laws that govern the universe. One time, Einstein tried to formulate a single unified model that could combine all of natural forces and materials into one total theory. All the physicists, along with Einstein, considered the dark matter would provide that complete theory.

But James Leigh's interest was on a different angle. He developed a queer interest in the theory of the dark matter. He imagined he could devise some mysterious device, which would deliver some electromagnetic wave penetrable into miles of underground to certain target without leaving any trace.

James thought about finding out the exact functionality of the superconductivity and utilizing its functionality in a practical way on top of figuring out the moving behavior of the dark matter. He induced phenomenal natures into consistent natural laws: living things versus its cycles; every day's weather versus its unchangeable factor; solar system's orbital movement versus the existence of the universe; dynamism versus inertia. James felt confident of unveiling the secret of the nature's magic play in the subject of superconductivity and dark matter. Through finding the principles of the law of the dark matter, he figured, he would build a device to deliver any message or any power enough to destroy a concrete door like a hand grenade.

However, James concentrated his meditation on the co-relationship between the almost unlimited vast universe and the super-tiny genome "so called a single set of chromosomes" of a human body's cell. James's high school buddies used to swarm around him and threw simple questions about the universe to him and pretty often found funnier mysteries.

One time, one of James's buddies, Gordon Kennedy, pulled off a string of sticky questions on the black hole and super nova:

"James! So do the black holes really exist and what the hell is the super nova?"

"Well, the black holes exist. They are the densest stars in the universe of which gravity goes beyond our imagination. Even the light reflected from that star cannot escape from that star's gravity. Therefore we cannot see it. The black hole absorbs anything near to that star by its gigantic gravity. Because of its ever-increasing density, the gravity grows immensely."

James's disposition made him excited. His friends including Gordon also got excited. Gordon continued question:

Article 3: Freshman's Icon

"James! Then the black hole could absorb the whole universe, couldn't it?"

"No. Never! Before the black hole gets more gravity from the certain level, it would explode by itself because of its own pressure. That explosion, we call 'Super Nova,' finally release its reflective light by forming some stars or even some galaxy."

Another friend of his, Simon Cooper, intercepted.

"James, you used to say our universe is unlimited by its own limit. We cannot understand its real meaning of the unlimited skies of its own limit."

"Of course, you cannot understand the contradictory meaning. But I guess our universe, definitely, has its own limit. Seemingly our universe is unlimited. Because our modern scientists could see only the distance of 500 million light-years and only a couple of millions of galaxies, we never could figure out how far our universe stretches out beyond the distance of 500 million light-years. That's why we say, temporally right now, that our universe is unlimited. However, anything that exists physically has its own limit. Our universe exists physically. Therefore, by syllogism, our universe has its own limit."

James murmurously spewed his disgusting contradiction and dubiousness. But no matter how dubious or contradictory, James used to be fond of talking those silly talks with his buddies. Simon was always fond of that too. Also, Simon knew he played a sounding board to James's blurred connotation on the matter of the astrophysics. Simon continued a silly but interesting question.

"James, you say our solar system locates in the peripheral corner of our milky-way galaxy of which diameter fathoms

39

around sixty thousand light-years and distances around a couple of million light-years with its neighboring galaxies. So there are a couple of million galaxies distancing a couple of million light-years each other on the average in the space of about one billion light-years of diameter. Do you surely positively think that this vast area with trillions of stars moves according to a few natural laws and you can implement those laws to a certain device?"

Simon frowned upon James's interest in finding and implementing those natural laws. As usual, James smirked smugly on his interest and intuition into the secret natural laws that govern the movement of our immense universe, as human body creates offspring according to the basic several laws of its tiny gene the size of a trillionth of human body.

Keeping his smile, James, contently answered.

"Yes, of course, our universe moves around, kills some stars or galaxies, and creates them according to not a few laws but not too many laws either–maybe not more than five or six laws. Definitely, the superconductivity or dark matter is one of the countable basic laws governing the movement of our immense universe. The reason why I am mostly interested in the dark matter and superconductivity among the natural laws is that I think I can develop an unusual super means in transportation."

Gordon broke his silence and interrupted James's further talk.

"James, I think human being's modern technology on the transportation has reached its culmination. We only do refining and re-streamlining, and we cannot think of other means anything else on top of our present status."

Simon wandered about what Gordon's definition of the transportation was. Simon earnestly looked at James's smiling face, expecting that James would throw a positive funny theory into the sky.

"Well, Gordon is right, I agree. But my concept of the transportation, on the basis of a theory in the dark matter and superconductivity, is entirely different from the theory of the present status. My concept of the transportation has been focused on the means of an electromagnetic wave which enabled modern radio and a mobile telephone."

"Modern radio and a mobile telephone depend on radio frequency and radio transmitters. My electromagnetic wave riding on the theory of dark matter and superconductivity would not depend on any radio frequency and any transmitter or any computer-aided equipment to switch a call for mobile phone from one area to another enabling the present portable phone going on."

"My electromagnetic wave could travel anywhere in the sky, and underneath ground and water piercing through any material. Going through any material and going any direction without any transmitter or computer's switching equipment would provide super means to reach any part in this world. If we establish communicating capability and delivering means (delivering certain physical object) by using this electromagnetic wave, the present world on this earth is going to appear completely different from our modern world. That brings forth my excitement to make me so often smile smugly."

James, again, smirked pleasantly. Simon murmured with a vacant look.

"James, do you really think you can find the hidden law of the so called dark matter and apply it to reality?"

Super Constitution

"Of course, Simon, I feel confident. Everything around me inspires me straightway. Look at how the x-ray was found, how the transmitter was figured out, how the gravity was discovered and how the atom was analyzed. Quantum theory (the theory of energy state in atoms in the smallest quantity), the theory of relativity, our physical existence, our mental activity, the time and space of the universe, movement and inertia, the imagination and reality, every phenomenon, every incident, every law, and every intuition make me to perspire to aspire. I am sure that it is there. I am sure we are here in this world to find it, to use it, and to have fun finding it and using it."

Gordon and Simon became absent-minded. They felt they were intoxicated smoothly. They felt themselves getting high. Their conversation with James always induced their mind into a euphoric state. James used to pretty often please his friends by his specific interest in this odd classification of astrophysics with stunning statistics and logical reasoning power. His interest could appear as a hallucination, a laughing-stock, and a stupid subject to an ordinary mind. But to Gordon and Simon, it looked serious. James Leigh spent his high school days in a deluge of smiles with his lot of sounding boards. Now James Leigh walked onto the campus of Brown University to meet his icon Brenda Chen.

A significant moment in the lives of both John Smith and James Leigh will come when they will meet each other for the first time, as a freshman at Brown University.

Article 4

Reluctant Valedictorian

Brenda Chen heard about two oddball freshmen that had joined Brown University: the taekwondo-champ John Smith and the sea lion James Leigh.

Brenda felt, as a matter of fact, knew that the two boys were coming to her, not just to Brown University alone. She felt her libido rippled through her entire nervous system. Her imagination alone already tickled her tight string of her id. The campus-chitchat spilled all over the place about the new faces of the geniuses. John Smith and James Leigh over Brenda Chen created some unusual tension. The tension pleasantly spread among students. Already, the imaginary appearance of the triangle of characters cast some agitation, some rippling fantasy and spectacle.

Suspense showered everybody: students; professors; staff; John, James and Brenda. But each of them had a different suspense, of course. Every group or everybody perceived the oncoming triangle of characters onto the campus through their own spectrum. It portrayed, indeed, an eccentric imagination, which excited everyone. The imagination brought pleasure to everyone in different color. But no one even had a slightest idea on the oncoming giant wave that would hit the landscape of human culture, politics, and lifestyles on Earth.

Brenda Chen met the karate-champ (karateka: an expert in karate) John Smith on the campus one day soon. Brenda and John happened to know each other very well through the usual talk of the campus in circulation. The campus-paper, one time, put out a tabloid article of the taekwondo-champ and sea lion's joining Brown, including John and James's far outstanding physical and mental talent. The story vibrated everyone. The story forecast a big upshot in the field of molecular biology along with Brenda Chen, electromagnetic wave theory with John and astrophysics with James. While John was heading to an administrative office, he spotted a small group of students, circling around a very attractive young lady and exchanging some pensive talk—probably some academic subject. John noticed she must be Brenda. John approached the circle and Brenda noticed right away that the approaching boy must be John Smith.

Brenda broke her conversation with the circle and opened a casual dialogue with the smiling stranger:

"Are you John Smith?"

"Yes, I am. You must be Brenda Chen."

"Yes, I am. I am very glad to meet you, John."

"I am, too. I have been looking forward to seeing you. I have been hearing about you thunderously these days. It is certainly my great pleasure to meet you, Brenda."

All the students beamed. Everyone shook hands. Now, naturally everyone encircled around the two famous future authorities in the academics. The two beckoned one another. The glitter of their eyes sparkled in the air. They could read

Article 4: Reluctant Valedictorian

each other's mind. Their minds beat palatably. Onlookers of the circle noticed an accidental rendezvous of two giants. Nobody suggested anything. But one by one the onlookers dispersed, leaving the two alone. Brenda, suddenly, felt sentimental, as though she were having a reunion with a long separated kid brother.

Of course, John exulted. He was enraptured by a thrilling perception. Brenda rose from nowhere just to embrace him. She did not appear as a stranger at all. She did not come up to an imposing figure either. John came across his darling senior who valued him dearly. Brenda and John did not have to sweat to familiarize each other. They heard one another. They appreciated each other. Maybe, they even longed for an encounter sooner or later. While wandering under the trees for a while, Brenda aroused John with her bold offer.

"John, I'd like to invite you for dinner at my apartment. Do you mind?"

"No. It is my honor. When is it going to be?"

"How about tomorrow evening around eight?"

"Whoa! That fast?"

"Do you mind?"

"Absolutely, I don't. I prefer a fast pace rather than a slow one."

Brenda recited her apartment's address and phone number, and John scribbled them over in a corner of his brain. This way, the long awaited casual encounter John dreamed of came on casually sooner rather than later since he had learned Brenda's aloof outstanding character through the occasional campus-papers. Brenda's invitation word rang John's

Super Constitution

eardrum fantastically. Her words literally thundered through John's brain. The imagination alone created an outright ecstasy for a young vibrant genius. The magnetic attraction of Brenda's charming figure alone could intoxicate any man. On top of the outstanding physical beauty, her reputation as a super genius as well as a far-surpassing sexual pleasure-monger swept anything away in her way. John absolutely felt triumphant over Brenda's heedless overture.

Eight p.m. of the next day's evening came so slowly. John, however, enjoyed a ticking time of the long day and the long evening till eight p.m. amid a happy imagination on the melting crucible of her and him.

Brenda and John finished a simple but delectable dinner Brenda prepared. Their mood naturally mingled into a feeling of love for each other. Brenda's bold gesture set the scene. Their caress started. The caress sparkled their feeling. The sparkled feeling crescendoed exponentially. Of course, their hot fever paralyzed all the bright reasoning sense. Each other's sensory organs had been focussed on a sense of touch. The ecstatic sense of touch drove their feeling crazy to a compassionate spiritual state of self-annihilation.

Woman attracts man. Man does woman. The main source of attractiveness dwells on an appearance and a preconception. Both appearance and preconception play a devastating factor in rendering a charisma between man and woman. Even ordinary appearance alone, that vitalizes sensual stimulant between woman and man, triggers its opposite gender's libido if the appearance fits to stimulate a form of id residing in the unconscious: a certain appearance vibrates a certain id devastatingly. That is an ordinary reaction-formula between young man and woman. When the outstanding appearance comes on, it usually rocks one's id to its heels.

Article 4: Reluctant Valedictorian

Another great source of energy originates from charisma, which is formed by the accumulation of preconception on a certain achievement or on a talent. The preconception then forms a certain base or standard to judge or act upon. It dominates human brain's activity. It gives direction. It conducts a starting point. The preconception acts like a DNA. It has been written in the brain as an informative source. So the preconception works wonders like an education or brainwash, or a borne character that determines human behavior.

John's preconception about Brenda's extraordinary academic talent and her pleasure-giving super gift of her sexual drive sculptured an impressive charisma inside John's heart. John's psychic apparatus had been geared up to the mechanism of the sculptured charisma, which directed John's behavior. John absolutely favored Brenda. He absolutely became credulous on the matter of Brenda. Brenda's thrilling appearance and her towering charisma already mesmerized John's thinking mechanism. John's burning thirst had melted down John's vivacious spirit all the way to the biological limit unable to think anything else any more.

On top of this situation, Brenda's silky elastic muscle electrified John's whole nervous system. What's more was Brenda's vaginal structure, which fascinated and stunned every man. John could not help but only love Brenda. John repeated his husky word of "I love you" without end. John never experienced any strain of that thrill, and neither even imagined. John's muscle energy endured enormous exhaustion as proved by his local saga of the duel with 100 judoists during his high school days. John's athletic power and accuracy had showed up from his early age. The far extraordinary strength of his physical condition went beyond normal recognition. He also used to enjoy sexual activities in a too far surpassing degree. So far nobody matched him as far as John's knowledge concerned.

Super Constitution

Brenda and John stormed their scene continuously, maybe more than an hour, but both of them felt several hours because they lost a normal sense and drifted into a euphoric illusion. Both of them had been soaked in the sweat. The sweat covered all their bodies. When they finally finished the session, they looked like just stepping out of a shower.

Brenda had been exhausted first time in her sexual life. Brenda had completely satiated herself from her burning desire first time. Brenda appreciated John. Brenda had never recognized such a super athletic power. But still John had not physically exhausted. His physical strength still could go on for another session without any problem. However, John first time felt his limit in the sexual activity. First time, John felt his prostate had drained all the residual of his gland secrets, which used to signal extended desire for the action. John felt a complete drain of his action power. The action with Brenda totally cleaned even a drop of residue in John's tube. But fortunately Brenda had been knocked out. She could not ask anything any further.

Both of them arrived at dead calm. Their ever-brisk passion finally entered doldrums. John started to pick up his clothes. John left. Brenda fell asleep. The night gave them a tight sleep. In the early morning, Brenda woke up to a fresh new life. Brenda felt a light heart on her entire body buoyantly. All of a sudden, Brenda found a vivid yearning for John's stiffness all over again. She could not stand being without it. She picked up the phone. She asked John to come right away for another session of the last night's event.

"Brenda, please, I am still empty. I wonder if I even have a desire. I think I need another day at least to fill it up to activate it."

Article 4: Reluctant Valedictorian

John answered honestly. John still felt numb after a tight sleep. John felt great. But he felt sexually dormant yet on the doldrums. He, as yet, wandered around in complete satiation. John and Brenda acknowledged that John's pace ran one step behind Brenda in terms of a speed to fill it up. John felt sorry. Brenda was annoyed, herself.

One week darted away into an eternal past since Brenda and John's unforgettable event. They enjoyed their great encounter every other day. John felt up to the brim. Brenda always felt half the cup on a following day. They already confirmed that Brenda ran too fast and John caught up too slow. But both of them never felt sorry, even though both of them annoyed themselves in missing something between them.

Meanwhile, they found a great new face: James Leigh. James Leigh arrived at the campus from Los Angeles one week later than John Smith did. Again, Brenda encountered an accidental meeting with James in the corridor of the main administrative building at Brown. Brenda exerted an expertise at handling a date with her favorite boy. It signified their first meaningful meeting. Their mind visited each other endlessly. They missed each other already long enough. They greeted one another amidst hearty cheers. Their joy undulated forever. Of course, Brenda and James experienced the first date as an epochal history in their life. James's unusual respiratory function generated unprecedented pleasure that Brenda never experienced. The stamina of the body movement and the action power flailed Brenda down to the rock bottom. Nevertheless, James's breath ran smoothly forever.

And, here, again Brenda and James found Brenda's faster pace even though both of them lasted the climax of the session to the maximum extent. Brenda sensed the God's hand in the balance of troika. Brenda quickly came to the conclusion that Brenda needed John and James, and John and James needed

Super Constitution

Brenda for maintaining the balance of the unbalanced pace of Brenda.

Brenda never estimated that a seismic change of human life on Earth would go on in the balance of their troika's prodigious brainpower and enormous athletic strength. Right now, the only thing Brenda valued in the troika concerned the utopian circumstance that could entertain her exploding libido while satiating her intellectual isolation. Therefore now, she could talk about a deeper academic work, a delicately sentimentalized relationship, odd nuptial behavior, and a carefree casual chitchat or joke. So she could feel, all of a sudden, getting dressed to fit her body feeling and her sense of fashion, stepping out of her own familiar home, and mingling into the mainstream of her lifestyle. She felt great in the thought of the troika: John, James, and her.

Thus, Brenda formed a troika with John and James. She went through a new chapter of her life. The new chapter of her life gave her a vision of brand new territory for human beings. Her environment of her academic work, school, people, parent, all happenings and all surroundings approached her in an entirely different way. Naturally, her environment did not change. But that environment looked totally different now after the form of the troika. Her mentality's interpretation on her usual environment had been restyled after the troika. The life of the troika improvised Brenda with a fulfillment of ecstasy everyday.

Her libido's full satiation, her ever-pleasant expectation on her routine days, her carefree adaptation on her everyday events, as well as her soaring passion for John and James blazed up Brenda's sense with enthusiasm. Brenda's inner instinct maybe sparked upon encountering John and James. The super mentality had met its nemesis. The super outfit of their soul met its match. The super timing of the troika met its space. The troika's titanic match generated an igniting power to have

Article 4: Reluctant Valedictorian

the extraordinary desire and talent combust to a full extent. The troika's first year flew like an arrow in the air.

One day Brenda Chen summoned both John and James to her residence to discuss her valedictorian speech in the coming ceremony of her graduation.

"John and James, as both of you already heard from me, I have finished all the credits required to present my doctorate dissertation through the under and graduate courses in the last four full years. While I was preparing the dissertation on the human cell's hidden critical function that responds to specifically concocted electromagnetic wave, I have arrived at a conclusion. This specially structured, eccentric electromagnetic wave can not only cure diabetes's malfunction of a cell's receptiveness for the sugar but also, with a reverse shape of the wave, can kill human cells. This wave wreaks havoc on any internal organ which would result in death in a matter of three minutes, along with a severe pain."

Presently, scientists figured there could be billion, maybe trillion shapes of waves in the wave spectrum. A shortest wave has a length of 0.001 angstrom while a longest one has one million kilometers. Considering one kilometer has one million millimeters and one millimeter has one million angstroms, there exist more than one thousand trillion differences.

Brenda continued.

"I am going to publicize my theory on the valedictorian speech assigned to me. The reason I try to publicize my theory comes from that I'd like to constitute my own research institute. I am sure my theory will attract a national, maybe even worldwide attention that will bring enough fund-raising power for my research institute."

Super Constitution

John interrupted swiftly.

"Brenda, I am not sure what type of electromagnetic wave you are talking about. I think I am the guy who can claim anything that happens in the matter of electromagnetic wave. What on Earth is this specifically concocted wave? Do you know what it is? Did you find it accidentally or logically?"

"Well, simmer down, John. I know, John, you are the whiz kid in that area. Frankly speaking, I found it half-accidentally, half-logically. I was going to tell both of you sooner or later. But now I like to tell you that I know what the formula of the wave is. It will make a worldwide sensation."

"Wait a minute," James averred calmly.

"I think we are, all of a sudden, getting into a subject of a brand new sphere of human activity, beginning of a new world–maybe as great a change as from the stone age to a highly civilized world over night."

James took a very earnest disposition and continued his stately remark, with raising his hand in an unusual gesture.

"I would call Brenda's theory a 'killing power.' The certain cycle of the wave for the killing power could have been existed theoretically in the area of electromagnetic spectrum. But, virtually, the extracting process of the formula has been considered beyond human touch because the probability can only happen in a ratio of one out of thousand trillions. Time to time, I used to dream about that formula. But, practically, I have imagined it as the utter nonsense. However, Brenda here is talking about it as a reality."

Then, John confidently asserted his long-thought idea about that grave topic with a seriously looking face.

Article 4: Reluctant Valedictorian

"Brenda and James, both of you know that electromagnetism is my toy. I have been thinking long time only in my imaginary world about the maneuverability of the diverse electromagnetic wave: talking through the wave and watching people and scenes like TV through the wave anywhere in the world if I would be given delivering means. Now upon hearing Brenda's theory of killing power, I now can dauntlessly imagine that that delivering means can be possible by James's theory on the 'dark matter.' So called 'WIMPs' (weakly interacting massive particles), like the power of gravity, pierce all materials of living things and the densest metals in the universe without leaving any trace."

John continued.

"James, the other day, you mentioned about dark matter. You even mentioned about surpassing the speed of light: ten or a hundred or even a thousand times faster than the speed of light. James, do you remember you were fascinated in thinking about figuring out the speed of light and control of the speed of light in a mode of slower or faster gear? Now, I am thinking about what breed of power we can create with a combination of Brenda's killing power, James's delivering-means and my wizard communications (means of sending messages by wave). I feel I am too much excited. I would not know what else I could think about now."

For a moment, only silence flowed. Not a single word came out. Only their glittering eyes sparkled in the air. Everybody seemed roaming in a long period of thought in order to conjecture a reliable conclusion of the topic. Breaking the heavy silence, Brenda obtruded her opinion to the two guys.

"You guys go too sober, too grim, and too dejected. Theory stays in theory but not in practicality yet. It lives only in an imagination. It draws only a wild idea. I am trying to stimulate the scientific field. But, before I make any decision, I just feel in my bones that something weighs on my mind. That makes me request your advice."

Brenda felt something bothered her in publicizing her self-assumed theory. It could trigger a boondoggle or make a vociferous mischief-maker. She, however, felt, in a corner of her mind, that a great discovery itself gestured a monumental start. She had never experienced such an ambivalent straddle in making her decision.

James opened his mouth half-smiling and half-frowning.

"Brenda, I am very happy you brought the matter of your valedictorian speech. I strongly admonish you of your exposing any tinge of your theory of the killing power. I even advise you that you withdraw your role of delivering a valedictory. Give it to somebody else, and let's integrate our theories into one power without hinting anything to anybody. I believe we came across each other's deeply thinking area, which we have not sincerely cross-examined one another. Coincidentally, through Brenda's advice-seeking moment, each one's spearhead of the dormant idea has been surfaced as a portentous reality."

James took a momentous pause and continued his point.

"I used to vaguely think about contacting somebody for the practicality of my theory on the 'dark matter' with some help in the area of a specific technology of electromagnetic wave. I have always thought of John, but I haven't touched on the topic with you seriously yet. Thinking of Brenda's theory on the killing power, along with John and mine, I've now come up with an idea on how the three of us can make a great contribution to the world, to the people, to the modern civilization, and to the earth environment. In other words, we can help the world achieve a single sovereignty."

Article 4: Reluctant Valedictorian

"Presently, the world is wasting its energy, damaging people's freedom and welfare under divided situation of more than 200 sovereignties. If there would be only a single sovereignty on this earth, people could enjoy more prosperity, more freedom, and much more civilization. I am sure the three of us can organize a certain super power that directs the world into one sovereignty."

Brenda quickly realized what James was talking about. The torpid aggressiveness of her idiosyncratic character had been stimulated when the preying behavior underneath her calm composure was brought out onto the surface. Brenda commented on James's blatant obtrusiveness.

"James, you carry on so daring, analytical, and quick conclusion. I understand what you are talking about. It surely casts up a very interesting story. I agree with you. What about John?"

Brenda looked up at John who was sitting on the desk chair listening quietly to James and Brenda. John, firmly making his gentle poker face, questioned James:

"James, do you certainly think you can apply your theory of the dark matter in bringing actual means for delivering electromagnetic waves which pierce through any material without leaving any trace?"

"Yes, of course. I clearly understand, now, the colossal and dangerous consequences of the theory for me to be able to apply it to practicality."

John continued his quest:

"Then, James, do you indeed think you can mastermind a chart of operations to organize so called 'the direction of the super powers of the world'? It is going to be a hell of a complex strategic chart. If it fails, it is going to be a disaster for all of us."

James answered confidently.

"John, I see what you are talking about. John, you know I am such a complex maniac in the astrophysics. A chart of operations for carrying out the complex strategy in order to direct the super powers of the world is an easy manual to me."

John, still with the poker face, told Brenda with stiff-arm in favor of James.

"Brenda, I am absolutely glad you summoned us and revealed your dormant idea of your theory on your molecular-biological approach and your reluctant attitude on delivering your valedictory. As James indicated, if the focal point of the significance of our integrated theory were to be applied, I would also like to emphasize that any one of us should exercise extreme cautiousness not to touch upon even any near tint of our theory. Brenda, do you agree to that point?"

Brenda relaxed comfortably, pulled for a determined action, and epitomized an accorded chorus of the troika's innermost intuition offhand. Brenda declared decisively as well as incisively:

"Gentlemen, I am so delighted. My deeply seated anxiety has been cleared away from my way out of congested crossroad. Now I can put my mind on our focal point. I guess, first of all, we have to materialize our hidden theories, combine them, and situate it in the place to be operated without any flaw. Then we have to write a constitution for a sole sovereignty that will govern the world while extinguishing all other sovereignties."

Article 4: Reluctant Valedictorian

Smiling pleasantly, James offered several guidelines for their composite functions, in order to achieve their target.

"Well, you guys, I think we need some key guidelines for our activity and behavior from now on. First, we habituate our talking manner not to remark any related tone to our hidden technology and our desired sovereignty. Second, we have to customize our strategic points not to our wishful thinking but to its reality. Third, I guess, we have to promote our humility as a number one moral code. I think humility would provide with us the most powerful image not to provoke any doubtful hunches against us, and our humility would also bolster people's stances in favor of us."

"You are absolutely right, James." John put an accent to James's terse remark.

In this way, three geniuses finally came up with a way to catapult the upshot of their lone, bizarre theory. Ordinary people would laugh their theory as a ludicrous lack of intelligence. However, we will see in the later chapters that their laughable theory will not only give a birth to the giant and efficient single-sovereignty on this earth but also to a device for the simplest and cheapest "gravity-engine."

The gravity-engine uses the unlimited power source of gravity in the universe by reversing the principle and energy of gravity in the form of an electromagnetic wave of the dark matter. In other words, if the counterattraction of gravity would happen in the form of a wave of the dark matter through reverse superconductivity, that mechanism would activate the gravitational power in the reverse direction at an exact amount of the original innate energy.

If this mechanism of the generated reversed-direction were to be controlled by a perfect computation of the computer science, we could propel a flying object from a zero speed up to a speed of half million miles per hour in the outer reaches of space. A bullet flies 5,000 miles per hour in the air. Our modern rocket system pushes a flying object 50,000 miles an hour in the outer earth's atmospheric field.

James even used to think that the speed of light, which travels more than seven hundred million miles per hour, could be exponentially pushed to faster speed ten times, even 100 times better than its innate speed if we could utilize the theory of the expanding speed of our universe. A phenomenon of much faster speed than the speed of light right now occurs beyond 500 million light-years away from our solar system. But we cannot figure out how it happens right now.

Anyhow, Brenda, John, and James vaguely figured out the outline of their long thoughts of a unique power that could move an unmovable human motivation, and they agreed to apply that power to enhance human civilization into a miraculous rise.

It would revamp political philosophy, social behaviorism, religious ritual and belief, and economic paradigm on this earth into the most exciting moment human beings ever would have seen or even thought about. We will see the scenes from the next articles on about how the politicians will react to a nervous shock. We will examine how the social scientists will interpret the unpredictable social change. Also, we will observe how the theologians will justify an emerging new concept of their religion. And we will go sightseeing how the economists and businessmen will vehemently talk about "Utopia," based on intrinsic human nature.

Political power influences our daily lifestyle, maybe even our destiny. Political power can shake and energize social fabric, people's way of thought, and economic strength. People countlessly thought about erecting an empire to bring a state of Utopia to the world. But, without an overwhelming cutting

Article 4: Reluctant Valedictorian

edge of certain technology along with healthy political power, the dream will never come true. Dream stays as a listless dream until somebody talks loudly about its portentous result and a potent demagogue with clear vision agitates the people's torpid mind. The troika's mind agitated each other's mind with their unique technology and clear vision.

Article 5

Research Institute

In the year of 2011, Brown University's ceremony of graduation took place in balmy weather of May. Everyone buoyed its spirit. John and James upgraded their upholding mood. Brenda enjoyed the event in excitement too, of course. She extremely concerned herself with James's father who made an appointment, coming to celebrate the turning moment in her life's career.

James's father engaged in doing import-export business in southern California on the line of man-made "crystal ornament." At the time, James's father conducted thirty million dollars in sales a year and produced around five million dollars in net profit a year.

He became a prominent businessman in New York City area's Korean American community, holding a master degree in chemical engineering from Seoul National University. In 1975, upon graduation from his graduate school, he originally immigrated to New York City and naturalized engaging in trade business between Korea and America. Later, he moved

Article 5: Research Institute

to Los Angeles in 2002. But, in the beginning, he did not make as much progress as he had expected. However, he managed to make some fortune on the trade of general merchandise made in the Far East. Later, he bought a factory in China early 1990, which manufactured leaded crystal ornaments.

After half a decade's strenuous efforts put in technological research on optics of his optical glass product of leaded crystal ornament and crystal glass bead for jewelry industry, he significantly enhanced the quality and brilliance of his product. From here on, his fortune started to build in his favor.

Now, his ambition for higher achievement on moneymaking business rattled in the area of man-made fine jewels such as ruby, diamond, sapphire, emerald, opal, amber, hematite, garnet, peridot, pearl, and so on. His conclusion came to the idea of research institute for molecular biology because all natural jewels had been originally formed chemically along with biological matter. And he used to hear about the odd geniuses of Brown University through his son James: Brenda Chen and John Smith. He offered to establish a research institute with three million dollars for an annual budget available to Brenda through his son James. Brenda accepted. James's father never met Brenda. At the ceremony of Brown, they were going to meet as strangers.

Brenda was concerned about the first meeting with James's father. Also, John and James agreed to move to University of California in Los Angeles when Brenda would move over to California as soon as she would finish a dissertation for her Ph.D. degree.

Of course, Brenda had had many embarrassing difficulties to refuse tempting offers from many universities and institutes. The major reason Brenda accepted the offer from James's

Super Constitution

father arose from James's idea of the operation of the "Super Constitution."

James narrated the specific character of maneuvering technique of the ray's original point of the dark matter and the superconductivity. The ideal environment for managing the ray required warm weather and low humidity of clean air. James indicated Joshua tree National Park and Arizona desert as the most appropriate area for both technicality and security wise. John also reasoned out the security management and technical execution of various magnetic waves. The detailed explanations of this security and technical execution will automatically be revealed in the next article.

Finally, James's father appeared in the ceremonial court, attired in dark navy-blue suit with dark red-tone necktie. His medium-sized frame looked of rather small stature, and he seemed much younger than his age of 62. Bearing comfortable composure and gentle looking, he looked around for James. James easily found his father, and gestured his hand to his father. Upon finding his son, James's father grinned. James ushered his father through a congratulatory crowd towards Brenda, who was surrounded by a cluster of well-dressed congratulants.

James jostled through the small crowd and faced Brenda, introducing his farther.

"Brenda, this is my father."

"Oh! Mr. Leigh, how do you do? I am so glad to meet you."

"How are you? Brenda. It is truly my pleasure to meet you finally. I greatly appreciate your joining the research institute."

Article 5: Research Institute

"Oh! Mr. Leigh, I would like to introduce my academic advising professor, Mr. Krugman."

"Ah! You are the Mr. Leigh. How are you? I really wonder how on Earth you snatched this wonder woman!"

"How are you? Mr. Krugman. I heard a lot about you. My son, James often speaks of you. I am so glad to meet you, Mr. Krugman."

Brenda asked a friend standing nearby to take a picture and asked James's father and her advisor to take a pose along with her.

"Mr. Leigh, I am so glad for you to come here today. I badly wanted you meet Mr. Krugman."

"Brenda, please call me Mike."

Brenda approached toward Mr. Leigh's ear and whispered.

"May I call you Daddy, as James calls you?"

"Of course, it is my pleasure. That sounds even more palatable."

The small crowd wondered what conversation was going around between James's father and Brenda. In this way, Brenda's memorable ceremony of graduation started.

James's father Michael Leigh finally sat at the dining table in Brenda's apartment with John and James. Michael Leigh emphasized research projects as a spearhead of the education for propelling human prosperity. In other words, James's father Michael Leigh set forth his philosophy on setting up the research institute, slicing a lion's share from his growing yearly income of about five million dollars at the time.

Super Constitution

Michael Leigh sincerely voiced his opinion on his idea of establishing a research institute for his burgeoning business.

"A research institute signifies a refinement of the whole educational purpose. A research institute designates the nucleus of the whole school system. The research institute implies a great core in invention, discovery, improvement and change of human civilization and its lifestyle."

Michael, on an extensive scale, made a fluent introductory remark for intensive R&D, and continued on describing his philosophy for research and development in a long monologue as the following:

"What moves the human mind?"

"An attractive appearance may impress the human mind, but it cannot dominate or dictate an intelligent human mind. The human mind motivates simple in a sense. However, in other sense, the human mind moves by very incomprehensive enigma and complicated labyrinth. The human mind displays torrid barrens to the one who does not cultivate it, but to the one who instills nurture, it reveals magnificent vistas: fertile soil; colorful stark monolith; rainforest; diversified rich resources. When we file and polish the human mind, we can see brilliant jewels in there."

He went on:

"How are we going to find a productive mind and to harness it for human prosperity and harmony?"

"We have to continue to change and refine our social fabric for an ever better lifestyle. What does it make for the main driving force to change our society to an ever better paradigm? Of course, we can think of, for instance, a favorite historical

Article 5: Research Institute

momentum, natural resources, certain size of population, charismatic leadership, technology, discovery, and inventions."

Michael became more emphatic.

"The number one power to change our social lifestyles for the better, however, comes from the human mind, especially the educated one which thinks of betterment and the better-off. The educated mind brings practical efficiency to all fronts. The way of human thought plays the basic dynamism of the creative mind. The creative mind creates the eye of a typhoon of the driving force for touchstone. When the human mind motivates, it rekindles a momentum, resources and a leadership to its powerful jump-start. Education manufactures a creative motive in the human mind."

Michael continued his talk.

"Education sharpens a vision of the human mind. Education enriches information into the human mind. Education finally touches the human mind to rise up for a quality upsurge in every field: social organizations, technological development, economic upheaval and sound political ecology."

"In the long run, education shapes the human mind to lead a quality change. In creating quality upsurge, the creative human mind, as a prime powerful essence, far outclasses all other factors such as historical momentum, natural resources, leadership and technology. The people's mind, a leader's mind, a professional's one, and a scholar's one have to be first geared up to the determination for smart change. Without their smart determination, the opportunities and resources would sit or pass quiescently."

"No matter how good talent there glowed, no matter how many geniuses there gathered, no matter how powerful opportunities and resources there came, if any alert and educated human mind would not prevail in there, nothing outstanding could happen in human life. The determined human mind along with education only would build the main driving force in upgrading social fabric, economic conditions and political environment."

Still Michael proclaimed.

"In the matter of making money through businesses, the right insight and hard work represent every determinant for the success. Even bad luck cannot suffocate repeated trials at last. Some people say a success depends on a good luck. All success depends on the educational mind. If the mind were determined for a success and if that determined mind pursued education for the right insight and information along with incessant attempts, no failure would persist. The quality change would come. Therefore, education initiates the most important power in our life. And the research institute cultivates the most important core of the education."

Michael frankly stated his view of the research institute in his mind without any stammering mode of utterance.

Brenda broke a brief silence after Michael's long monologue.

"Daddy, your rhetoric sounds like my professor Krugman's way of talking. I truly agree with your idea. John, what do you think of our moving to the sunny southern California? So, we can work out our program along with our daddy's research institute. Isn't that an excellent idea?"

John gave her a big smile.

"Brenda, it sounds an excellent idea, a superb camouflage for our program too, and also we met a terrific sponsor like James's father who is, I earnestly think, our great congenial

Article 5: Research Institute

spiritual advisor.   Mr. Leigh, I greatly appreciate your understanding and joining our program."

Michael beamed and spoke while looking into John's eyes.

"John, I am very much delirious with joy at your positive attitude. I feel like having acquired a big son on a sudden without any charge. I'd like to consider you as my own son, James."

"Many thanks, Daddy."

Everybody in the room burst out laughing at John's terse word of "Many thanks, Daddy." Also, they all acknowledged that they never mentioned "Super Constitution": instead, they mentioned "program" as a cautious mannerism they were supposed to take even with their coterie alone.

Michael asked some basic explanation about a general concept of "electromagnetic wave" which is going to play a critical role in communication and a disturbing force to human body's cell structure. Putting aside the question of how to control the audiovisual communication with the desired target, Michael just wanted to set up some frame of reference to understand the extraordinary technological superiority which could dictate the "super powers of the world" to obey the "Super Constitution."

"Well, Daddy, the subject of electromagnetic wave portrays common stuff. But in terms of a disturbing force to human body's cell, it critically reveals a very unique character and very interesting subject, especially in connection with a theory that a certain disturbing force could knock down and kill human being by the specially concocted, ultra short wave form. This wave-form has never existed in the universe so far, but the impact of this short wave emerged as an awesome monster."

Super Constitution

"As you may know, Brenda prepares for that theory to be exposed. If it really happens as Brenda assures us, that wave's grave theme is going to set forth a spate of soaring enthusiasm. Herewith, I understand why you get an extraordinary interest in the subject of electromagnetic wave."

John seemed getting a bit excited and trying to find an appropriate plain language to explain the wave function.

"Primarily," John continued after a short pause.

"Electromagnetic radiation travels at the same velocity as light. But electromagnetic radiation has changeless character by the number of cycles of up and down, and by its wavelength between the cycles. And electromagnetic waves have many forms of its motion. As for the various returning motions after striking a surface, we call its phenomenon a reflection. The various changing degrees of direction while passing from one material into another, we call refraction. The various bending degrees of the waves that pass around obstacles in their pass, we describe as diffraction. The same cycle's various processing methods that combine and separate, we refer to as interference. Finally, the various appearances of the same waves, according to different directions, are called polarization."

John continued without a pause:

"In other words, electromagnetic wave shifts its appearance into immense variety according to specific environment without changing its original character of wavelength and the number of cycles of up and down. It sounds contradicting, Daddy. The electromagnetic wave creates magic kingdom. That magic kingdom has thousands of faces, and each face has its own function according to each appearance."

Article 5: Research Institute

Michael intercepted briefly.

"John, you are talking about Aladdin's magic lamp and ring with which he commands a jinn to embody his wish."

"Yes, Daddy, that story of Arabian Nights Entertainment overdraws every incident in hallucination. But I am talking about one real story on the phenomenon of existing universal law of electromagnetic wave form which lives with us forever."

"Well, John, it sounds to me, you talk like a spellbinder. Please go ahead telling me something of the physical aspects of the wave's core matters—the measurement of the target and the vibrating cycle's effect on human cells."

Michael was dying to hear John's speaking about the next topic. James and Brenda felt a pride at John's appropriate plain language and Michael's aroused interest.

"Daddy, as you may know, all electromagnetic waves transport energy from a source to a receiver, but unlike mechanical waves, the electromagnetic waves do not require a material medium. However, the electromagnetic waves cannot move forever, and also cannot pierce certain material either. It has limit on distance and against obstacles of materials. On this crucial drawback, I rely on James's theory of the dark matter, which has no limit on distance and no obstacles in transporting. Hereby, I'd like to just indicate a few physical characteristics of the waves and visualize its possible function of a disturbing force on human cells."

John then tried to bring some different types of waves in our real everyday life.

"In radio waves for the range of direct communication, for example, something like 100 miles distance requires 100 meters long wave. As another example, microwaves have a wavelength between one millimeter and thirty centimeters. Because of its short wavelength, it provides better precision of information than longer wavelength. Even much shorter length comes in an infrared wave, which measures shorter than visible light. The visible light's wavelength comes in between 7,000 angstroms to 4,000 angstroms. One million angstroms are equal to one millimeter. So, 5,000 angstroms mean one two-thousandth of one millimeter. Therefore, the shorter infrared wave that could penetrate more than visible light could be used for many types of practical applications, from physical therapy to detectors of military importance."

John continued.

"Let's look at another example, the x-ray. The wavelength exists from longest ten angstroms to shortest one-thousandth of one angstrom. Ten thousand angstroms measure one micron, and one thousand microns make one millimeter. An even shorter wave than the x-ray exists, called a gamma ray. It is not affected by a magnetic field which has very typical function that we can utilize for disturbing human cells."

"The shorter the wavelength happens, the more the frequencies of up and down cycles are rendered. The gamma ray and all extremely high-frequency electromagnetic waves, including x-rays, can be concocted by special equipment which cost about $5,000.00 to $100,000.00."

Michael was fascinated about the story of x-rays, which we could concoct with a fraction of his three million dollars' yearly budget for the research institute. Michael felt even greater than ever.

John got a little sanguine and further narrated some different angle of the electromagnetic wave.

Article 5: Research Institute

"In atomic and nuclear systems, radiation occurs during the transition from one quantum (the smallest unit of energy) state to another. The relatively high frequencies (which means shorter wavelength) of x-ray and gamma radiation are likely to change the internal structure of atoms and molecules."

John, now, tried to get to the point of how we get our message to cross over to a certain person through the character of the electromagnetic wave form, and tried to describe some character of atoms, which would help more clearly understand about the project (the Super Constitution).

"Basically, atoms constitute the fundamental building blocks from which each molecule is constructed, and each molecule forms the smallest unit of a pure compound that retains its own characteristic properties. Even though we find only a hundred atoms in the world, the atoms combine into tens of millions of different molecules. Modern day chemists have added new brands of molecules, at a rate of more than 100,000 molecules per year. So it is a big task for modern chemistry to determine the arrangement of atoms in molecules and to explain the molecule's bonding force and characteristics. Each molecule has its own typical weight and characteristics. Therefore, molecular weight ranges into the millions of differences as well as millions of characteristics. For example, hydrogen is so light: about seventy times lighter molecule than the DNA."

Michael solemnly intercepted.

"John, it seems to me you are crossing over the border of physics and entering into the territory of molecular biology."

"Yes, I am, Daddy!"

John Smith made a pause in his dry scientific talk and emphasized, with a pleasant smile, his logic about the uncanny knack of the theory of the wave function and molecular characteristics. The mysterious wonder of the relationship between the typical electromagnetic wave and the typical molecular function in human cell really titillated a tingling sensation over everybody in the room.

"Daddy, I am going to relay my baton to Brenda upon a few more words in the territory of molecular biology."

"Well, disregarding how small a unit it is and how many varieties there are, each kind has its own characteristics. Molecular biology means handling indefinite numbers of characteristics and relationships of tens of millions of probability in each cell, each tissue, and each organ. Of course, there exist billions of trillions of cases and instances. But when we desire a certain case or a certain instance to be traced or explained, in other words, to try to invent something for something, it is not that complex a matter if we combine our unique theories that only super calculation can explain the cause and effect. With this, I would like to ask Brenda to take over my baton with regard to the molecular structure of our body's cell: a type of disturbing wave pertinent to human cells."

Brenda hugged John and kissed him on the cheek as praise for John's simple style of narration on the subject. Brenda smiled a big smile looking at Michael and James. Brenda's beaming face produced a more friendly air and pleased everyone with a pleasant confidence. Brenda always transpired some sort of inexplicable delight to her surroundings. Brenda's eyes seemed to emit brilliant inspiration over the subject she was going to talk. John and James felt great on Brenda's confident posture. Michael also felt even some enigmatic on Brenda's dignified beaming.

"Gentlemen, I am so glad to join this meeting, I feel so proud of Daddy's determined interest in our project (Super

Article 5: Research Institute

Constitution). I am so proud of our daddy's urbane manner in science."

Actually, Brenda's sensation stirred up with a joy of getting together with John and James along with Michael's enthusiastic support. Brenda couldn't be happier at that moment. Brenda tried as simple a narration on the cell as she can possibly manage.

"Human cell's diameter is about twenty microns (one micron: one-thousandth of one millimeter), and each human being is composed of ten trillion cells. (One trillion means one million times one million: if we count the numbers of ten trillion by the second, it will take us a time of more than three hundred seventeen thousand years.) Each cell has many catalysts, membranes, and only one nucleus, which contains DNA that measures six microns in diameter and yet contains 1.8 meters of DNA. If we could enlarge one nucleus of a human cell one million times, the nucleus would contain 1,125 miles long DNA at 6 meters in diameter."

"The cell catalysts are special collections of molecules which contain hydrogen, oxygen, nitrogen and carbon consisting of millions of atoms linked together in specific arrays. (Molecule: the smallest physical unit of an element or compound, consisting of one or more same atoms in an element and two or more different atoms in a compound; element: one of a class of substances that cannot be separated into simpler substances by chemical means; compound: a pure substance composed of two or more elements whose composition is constant.) Through many cycles of cell growth and division, each cell can create millions of duplicate cells, in the process converting large amounts of inanimate matter into biologically active molecules. Cooperative assemblies of similar cells form tissues and a cooperation between tissues result to form organs–the functional units of an organism."

Super Constitution

Brenda and Michael looked at each other and smiled at one another. Michael expressed his peculiar thoughts about the cell.

"Brenda, it is funny. I am listening to you and you are talking to me. You are composed of trillions of cells and so am I. Cell is talking to cell, and cell is listening to cell. Of course, I guess you feel wonder, and I feel wonder too. It seems to me we are all marvelous biological machines, aren't we?"

"You are right, Daddy. I am exactly thinking about the same thing you are thinking now. It is really wonderful thinking cells. Well, Daddy, let me talk about the cell further."

Brenda now felt even greater.

"Cells, as a self replicating network of catalytic molecules, drive biosynthesis to form a life with the help of energy (food) and information (DNA). The DNA contained in a nucleus of the cell is composed of millions of molecular bases, which hold the genetic information. The segment of a DNA undergoes rearrangements upon stimulation by an invading particle, resulting in a great variety of antibodies."

Michael responded especially to Brenda's mention about cell structure's reaction to certain stimulation with a more heightened enthusiasm. Michael asked.

"Brenda, do you mean that the function of human cell can be changed by a certain external wave?"

Brenda answered quickly and went further on in the subject of the cell biology.

"Daddy, the answer is yes and no. Structures of a cell can be affected or disturbed by a certain type of the wave. But no wave form can change innate structures of a cell. Chemical

Article 5: Research Institute

processes in biology are controlled by the function of complex molecular aggregates in order to fit together in certain place. In other words, brand new chemical process can be borne by a new molecule or complex molecular aggregates. This brand new process can be brought about by not only a chemical property but also by some motion of energy such as an electromagnetic wave. That new process or a different type of wave can affect the innate chemical bonds of a cell, either to activate the original function of a certain organ or to destruct its original function."

Brenda, after taking a deep breath, continued talking.

"Sometimes, rather subtle structural differences even in identical molecules determine whether its difference is going to be toxic or harmless, explosive or inert, effective or inactive as a trigger. We call this phenomenon as isomerism. That means the relationship of two or more compounds of same kind numbers of atoms but of different atomic arrangement in structure could produce a different effect. In other words, even the same molecules function different way according to a different order of atomic arrangement in the structure."

Michael understood what Brenda was trying to bring to the point.

"Brenda, do you mean that you have some theoretical conclusion that some form of ultra short cycle of wave disturbs human cells critically?"

Brenda, smiling confidently and comfortably, concluded.

"These days, increasingly, scientists armed with blueprints of our genes, can identify the individual molecules that make us susceptible to a particular disease or some form of motion (electromagnetic wave). With that information—and some high-speed silicon-age machinery (computer technology)—we can build new molecules that home in on our targets to function or destruct the cell. So, if a specifically concocted electromagnetic wave, suddenly, vibrates some molecular bases in the cell of the tissue of lung or heart, any man suffers pain and dysfunction of that lung or heart, resulting in death in a matter of three minutes."

Michael Leigh had a deep breath and a grave looking after listening to Brenda's assurance in the theory of "killing power" she found in the cell structure and yet did not revealed her finding to any other source. Michael opened his mouth after a brief, heavy silence.

"Brenda, John, and James, all of you understand how serious, immeasurable magnitude of your commitment to "the project (Super Constitution)" incurs! Don't you?"

"Of course!" the troika answered in chorus.

"Well, Brenda, John, and James, I also cast my destiny along with yours. Let's stage a careful planning, and implement it in uncanny accuracy."

In this way, the actual giant step had finally taken place for the Super Constitution.

Any super technology could not exist outstandingly by itself alone, nor could it be developed exclusively separated from its surroundings. One unique or outstanding technology is related to its vicinity, and is based on the development of its homogeneity: nothing like a mutation.

However, certain quantity changes or alters the original character of quality. For instance, a small number of materials or individual existence carries its original character all the way. But when substantial numbers of materials or individual existences accumulate beyond a certain point, its quality

Article 5: Research Institute

changes, its character changes, its consequences could create entirely different dimension.

On this point, the troika definitely took an advantage of the day's deluge of information, knowledge, and heterogeneous technology scattered all around the world independently. The troika's unprecedented advantages originated from their extraordinarily powerful memory, their intimate multiple combination, and their soaring creative power. On top of the above individual talents and coincidental combination, the timing of modern historical development had hit the bull's eye.

Article 6

Confrontation

May 2014, three years after Brenda's graduation and the move out to California of the troika of Brenda, John, and James, and just 2 years before "D" day, the countdown for the smooth operation of their combined theories began. James's means of delivery, which implemented his theory of the dark matter's super conductivity, John's specific ultra short wave-I and -II, and Brenda's killing energy through an electromagnetic waveform had been accurately assembled.

During the last three years, John had established his specific, ultra, short wave-I and -II. The wave I dealt with the radar beacon on DNA, which pinpointed any human's DNA and instantly located its whereabouts anywhere in the world by a precision length of the distance. The wave II dealt with communicating method in both video and audio anywhere in the world.

Over a period of three years from 2011 to 2014, Michael's business jumped five folds out of the findings that Brenda's Research Institute brought about in the field of optic material. The new optic material enhanced the degree of brilliance of leaded crystal glass from 1.6 to 2.4 for its index of refraction, which is similar to top quality diamond by applying a new

Article 6: Confrontation

bonding material composed of newly processed molecular chemicals: the index of refraction for regular glass: 1.4; the one of ordinary leaded crystal glass: 1.6.

Michael's business yielded almost twenty million dollars' net profit yearly before taxes. Compared with five million dollars in 2011, the twenty million dollars in 2014 changed the façade of his wealth and financial power. Michael offered ten million dollars a yearly budget to Brenda's Research Institute from the year of 2015, which covertly included John's special instruments to figure out his wave-I and -II, and James's equipment to fathom the behavior of his theory of the "dark matter and superconductivity." Actually, John and James had completed the test of children's gadget-like prototype. Also, Brenda's disturbing formula on the human cell's structure had been pinpointed.

Of course, Brenda's prime target of her research had openly and publicly been focused on the formula of controlling molecular function for diabetes and cancer. As for the extreme security measures, the special room was built like bank's walk-in volt with an installation of pewter panels all around the wall and ceiling to prevent the penetration of any eavesdropping electronic wave. Also, only the troika had keys and code numbers for access.

Seemingly, John had been concentrated on the study of intelligent semiconductor device (electronic circuit element). And James's subject always had been a study of the phenomena of supernova, which could be the big bang of a black hole: a general astronomy rather than a specific astrophysics–a branch of astronomy that studies the physical properties and the interaction between matter and radiation in the interstellar space.

Super Constitution

Because of the troika's cover story, people around the troika never imagined that they could be involved in any part of the "Super Constitution."

The powerful backbone of the "Super Constitution," stemmed from an unprecedented and extraordinary upshot in the unexpected technological edge and incredible combination of the troika's farfetched theories. Only a super genius job with the serendipity of the troika's emerging time frame made it possible. Therefore, nobody could imagine, at the current pace of popular science in the modern world, that the modern technology could concoct the super technology enough to create the "Super Constitution."

John invented a new form of electromagnetic wave which could pinpoint any human's DNA, store the individual's DNA fingerprint into a computer's memory drive, and immediately find the person's exact location by sending out his wave I. The wave I identified the DNA like a fingerprint through its radar beacon by the speed of light around the world. The wave I could penetrate any material without leaving any trace according to the delivering means of the dark matter. When the wave I was activated with the information of certain DNA fingerprint, a computer screen immediately showed up its location. The wave I went anywhere in the world, underneath ground and water and into space along with the delivering means of the dark matter. The wave I not only traveled back and force, but also carried the wave of disturbing force into human cells.

John's wave II established audiovisual techniques in order to conduct communications with the spot the wave I located. So, the troika could conduct business with any person in the world without revealing the troika's identity. John's wave-I and -II traveled back and forth in a form of the behavior of the dark matter's superconductivity. That was why the ordinary

Article 6: Confrontation

satellite's electromagnetic wave could not trace the John's wave-I and -II.

Nevertheless, John's wave-I and -II would need a setup of a hookup to seal off the wave's origin and destination in case of ordinary science's discovery of the dark matter's behavior of delivering means. If ordinary science would come to find out the dark matter's behavior, their first contact would be the hookup.

Therefore, the hookup would have to be located at a lone place in a substantially far away area from the troika's living quarters while it shouldn't be too far from the troika's reach. They came up with the idea of using the area of Joshua tree National Park in the southeastern part of California located on the northern side of Route 10 near the town of Palm Tree.

Joshua tree National Park has no thick forest, no deep valleys and steep hills. The Park is composed of a lot of unusual boulders, which entertain and inspire the visitors' curiosity with a rather wonder. It gives visitors an exotic feeling like they've just entered an alien land. Bizarre boulders are indiscriminately scattered all around among sparse Joshua trees, which have thick and short trunk with long twisted branches and scanty leaves.

Joshua tree National Park presented the ideal place for the troika to plant their hookup. While they set up a camp in the area they favored, the troika installed a small relaying device for their communication composed of an antennary stem and a honeycomb-like button on a branch of one of the Joshua trees.

Their hookup looked like a part of the Joshua tree. Nobody could notice it. John tightly braced a node of the hookup as a part of the tree, which would stay and stand there even though the tree would fall by a storm. Joshua tree would never fall by any form of storm because the tree was stocky, solid, and so stabilized.

Everything was ready for action. The troika looked for a case for trial. The case came along as follows:

The modern scientific age symbolizes a fast track of the high-tech, which provides an easy access to sophisticated, dangerous mass destruction or mass killing. If a lone scientist or a singular, evil genius sickened by some strike of schizophrenia or severe pathological symptoms, that somebody could launch treacherous actions by igniting a suitcase with nuclear bomb or diffusing biochemical weapons. The evil mind or crazy science-nerd can easily trigger the most harmful weapons in hiding.

The terrorist attacks on September 11, 2001, on prosperous and free America, were only a peanut compared with this catastrophe on October 12, 2015: a nuclear bomb set off in Rome (Roma). A person in hiding claimed this. The crazy somebody declared, through the Wall Street Journal and the New York Times, that he had planted similar suitcases of nuclear bombs in Moscow, Beijing, and Washington, D.C. He demanded unconditional surrender of the U.S., Russia, and China to his request. If any country would not follow his request, he would detonate the other nuclear bombs.

The demands were these:

Wipe out all arsenals of nuclear, biological, and chemical arms, and reduce the present size of defense power of the United States, Russia, and China. Also, to carry out the above demands, the three nations should furnish a "special institute" with funds. The amount of the funds would be composed of 1% of each country's annual budget. The representatives from Germany, France, India, Japan, and South Korea would organize this special institute. These five nations should

Article 6: Confrontation

establish direct responsibility to organize and oversee the special institute's personnel and operation.

These demands dropped a shocking bombshell on the world, especially to the targeted three nations and their capitals of Washington, D.C., Moscow, and Beijing. Most people all over the world were amazed except the people of the directly stricken areas of Washington, D.C., Moscow, Beijing, and Rome. People literally wondered. People were truly bemused. How are the world's super powers going to handle these demands? Are the demands really going to be able to proceed? The development of the demands became a big global agenda, a giant social topic, a pain in the neck to some people, and a spectacular show to others across the world.

The three nations' presidents and national security teams teemed with meetings and meetings. Finally, the subject had been focused on "how to meet the demand." The intimidating somebody in a fog flatly denied any possible negotiation. He set up his own schedule to organize the "special institute." Furthermore, he already designated the financial sources and amounts of dollars. Accordingly, there was no choice of talking or discussion at all. To avoid another nuclear bombs' blast off, they had to start the process as the intimidating somebody demanded.

In fact, the three super powers did want a reduction of the over-killing arsenals. But they could not manage to have their own hair cut by themselves; furthermore, the intimidating somebody had not presented any master plan for how to cut and decommission all of those dangerous facilities and materials. Therefore, they had a plenty of time and occasions to communicate with that somebody; and so to speak, the three nations' security teams figured that they could manage to trace the intimidating somebody's whereabouts during the processing time and communications that would inevitably take place. They had all types of secret gadgets they were playing around with tracing the source of communication.

So, the "special institute" began to be organized. The enormous fund started to flow smoothly. The special institute was borne. The operating personnel had been selected in 6 months as demanded. Nevertheless, when the special institute commenced various hearings on the matter of general process and know-how of managing dangerous materials, hundreds of ideas blossomed. Confusion on the method of managing the reduction of the hazardous weapons and materials had surfaced. Strong, clear-cut leadership mattered. No one knew who it should be. Nobody presented an outstanding solution. The special institute darted into chaos even before it installed some ad hoc committee or sub committees.

Authenticating any agenda requires expertise and time consuming. Building a sophisticated weapon system necessitates an intricate maze of weaving in and out of top technologies. Disassembling those cannot be done by the will power alone. So, the special institute stalled even before taking off. The three super powers tried amicably to open dialogue with the man in hiding to process his demands.

Furthermore, the man in hiding had, by then, realized that the modernized eavesdropping facilities could pinpoint his whereabouts if he continued communicating over a length of time. He felt his power to dictate falling away, repeatedly hesitated, and ducked from the act of communication.

The more time went on, the more confused situation developed. His bold action of nuclear bombing in Rome and the decisive demands on organizing the special institute, stunned people's minds. The super powers reeled in the beginning. But the one-man show without proper communicating tools crippled his power to dictate further. He lost his spirit to move forward. The super powers tried to

Article 6: Confrontation

appease the man. The super powers suggested the man for reducing over-killing arsenals in the appropriate pace by super powers themselves in the announcement through various media. The super powers asked him where he planted the suitcases of nuclear bombs. The man at large gave in and disappeared forever from the public. In this way, one crazy man's incident rocketed into the sky and dropped as a stick.

This unbelievable confrontation shocked the world. This crazy confrontation paved a way for the troika's confrontation with the super powers in terms of seriousness of the "Super Constitution." The troika's equipments to dictate the super powers were all set. Now the troika needed guidelines to confront the world: the content of the "Super Constitution." The troika made a decision, along with Michel Leigh's advice, on drafting the "Super Constitution" as in the simplest way as possible. The troika came up with the following terms:

1, the Purpose of the Constitution

2, the Contents of the Constitution

1, the Purpose of the Constitution:

Why do we live on this earth? Where are we from? And where are we heading? We do not know why we live on this earth and where we are from. But, we do know where we are heading. As a human being, and the lord of all creations, we want to live in freedom, and we want to live in happiness. Freedom from poverty, disease, corruption, crime and imposition: freedom of residence, movements, enjoyment, and choice. Definitely the above freedom would provide happy life with an overwhelming majority of people on this earth. How to interpret happiness or how to define what the happy things are, is everyone's liberty. Nobody should force anyone how to interpret or how to define personal happiness. Nobody should be governed, or controlled.

Super Constitution

No organization, no institute, and no format should frame anyone's freedom and happiness as long as that freedom and happiness are being pursued in her or his limit and choice. As long as that freedom and happiness would not disturb anybody physically or mentally, that freedom and happiness shouldn't be disturbed. Physical harms are clear and distinct. But mental harms sometimes are not black and white. This portion of judging mental harms has to be cleared by norms and laws. Regarding these norms and laws, a part of the contents of the Super Constitution would set up a general guideline.

The absolute principles and orders, which this Super Constitution aims at, come from the point of view that human wants to live in maximum freedom and the utmost happiness along with minimum regulation. The regulation exists for maximizing an individual's freedom and happiness. All the norms and laws should be formed, regulated, simplified and understood for an individual's freedom and happiness. The purpose of the Super Constitution derives from how humans want to live. The absolute majority of people suffer from the confinement of our society by the pressure of chauvinism, dogma, empty ethics, and geopolitics.

Therefore, we have to verify if we have a distinct reason to declare that the content of the Super Constitution serves the purpose. The purpose has to indicate the direction. The purpose should clarify meaningfulness. The purpose must gather consensus. The purpose equals the whole contents. The whole contents must satisfy the purpose. Accordingly, the purpose is to be set clearly, simply, and firmly.

The purpose of the Super Constitution has existed throughout human history. From the beginning of human history, the pursuit of freedom and happiness began, continued, but continued without the perennial ultimate. Criminals and corruptions continued to rampage through. Tyrants paraded

Article 6: Confrontation

one after another. Diseases persisted and spread mercilessly. Tragic starvation and impecunious predicament tenaciously prevailed throughout human history.

Human intelligence, historically by far, had concluded that disappointments, sadness, hard times, pains and bad luck accompanied human life. We had to be prepared. We even had to welcome earlier coming because we were supposed to go through and endure those hardships. They said we were destined. Those difficult situations set in human life could mean a touchstone of human ability. Actually, those evil stuffs reinforced true grit. Being a great man required going through all sort of afflictions. Maybe it was true. Maybe it was a necessary evil in the old days of much less civilization. When uncivilized circumstances encroached upon human society, rather like the process of natural selection, maybe, such evils were justified.

But now in modern days, we don't have to go through and endure any hardship of injustice, any difficulty of wrong process, and any sacrifice of bad environment. We are no longer destined to suffer from such evils. We are not borne to lead a hard life but we are borne to enjoy our life. Just because of geopolitics and wrong moral frames and imposing factors, innocent people suffer, a wrong situation fetters honest people, and a few greedy interest groups justify the vested power of their control and confine people's freedom at their discretion.

Modern day's science and technology could improvise people on this earth with enough supplies for comfortable living, but because of those geopolitical dogma and hypocritical practices of conventional politics, economics, ethics and beliefs, the balanced distribution of goods and the freedom to enjoy our life have been severely disturbed. In order to get rid of those innate huddles of the present social fabric of this earth, we definitely need a "single global sovereignty," demolishing all others. We, hereby, pronounce the birth of the "Super

Super Constitution

Constitution" to achieve the above purpose and set up its application as follows:

2, the Contents of the Constitution:

Paragraph 1: Global Executive
Paragraph 2: Global Court
Paragraph 3: Global Legislature

Paragraph 1-1: Global Presidency:
The global president represents the global executive body, and has the right to appoint and dismiss the chiefs of the following executive branches of the global government: 1, the chief of the political affairs; 2, the chief of the economic matters; 3, the chief of the intelligence network; 4, the chief of the armed forces; 5, the chief of the world's social services.

Paragraph 1-2: Global Political Affairs:
The job of the world's political affairs concerns on all major political subjects of all national governments' critical and controversial issues.

Paragraph 1-3: Global Economic Matters:
The job of the world economy handles all strains of economic and financial issues to affect the global economy, including the lowest possible taxation and unilateral currency.

Paragraph 1-4: Global Intelligence Network:
The global institute of the world's intelligence network manages the job of information gatherings without any restriction with president's warrant in order to find out any breed of major fraudulent actions, processes, and sources.

Paragraph 1-5: Global Military Power:
The world's armed forces department will be consisted of army, navy, Air Force, marine, and Coast Guard. The armed department acts as a stabilizing force against any violent mob

Article 6: Confrontation

or any illegal organization's violence in the world. The armed department would supervise a special commission to decommission all classifications of WMD.

Paragraph 1-6: Sociological Behavior:
The global social service department is going to oversee all nations' social welfare work, watch and audit the fair practices of all sorts of social developments and behaviors, including the administration of food, drug, environment, and the basic standard of general ethics and beliefs.

Paragraph 1-7: Election of President:
The global president will be elected from the global congress of combined upper and lower house. However, the writer of the "Super Constitution" will nominate the first global president with a four-year term.

Paragraph 1-8: Global Language:
There must be a single, official global language. All the nations in the world must use local language together with the global language on all official announcements and papers. But after five years, no local language is going to be allowed for any official purpose.

Paragraph 1-9: Size of Government:
All the governments in the world must scale down the size of government to 10% of the present scale. Also, the global government would make the smallest government as far as possible. The smallest, yet the most efficient government should be pursued.

Paragraph 1-10: Term of President:
The global president can have three-consecutive terms, and each term is four years.

Paragraph 2-1: Supreme Court:

Super Constitution

The global Supreme Court will be composed of five supreme judges in addition to one chairperson-judge. The majority will make the decision. In case of a tie of three to three, the chairperson will make the decision. The global president will nominate five supreme judges and a chairperson, and the nomination must be endorsed by the world legislature.

Paragraph 2-2: Human Resources:
The global Supreme Court will organize an administrative office to study and develop human resources for qualified lawyers and general management for the legal affairs.

Paragraph 2-3: Attorney General:
The Supreme Court will appoint an attorney general with the consent of the global legislature. The attorney general appoints all the prosecuting attorneys with the endorsement of the Supreme Court. The Supreme Court can dismiss the attorney general without anyone's consent. The attorney general handles all investigative activities with a right to dismiss any attorney and staff.

Paragraph 2-4: Legal Writings:
The global Supreme Court has to write all the detailed interpretations and explanations of all statutes. All the laws must be simplified as far as possible in order to eliminate complicated and redundant litigation. The global courts will manage most of legal disputes.

Paragraph 2-5: Appointment of Judges:
The global Supreme Court appoints three managing-judges in each nation with the agreement of Global Congress. The global Supreme Court will audit about 450 members of the managing judges with a right to dismiss. The three managing-judges in each nation will establish field judges in each nation who are going to work with each nation's prosecutors.

Paragraph 2-6: Strict Application of Law:

Article 6: Confrontation

The global courts will use the least leniency and the harshest punishment to the criminals in order to make the world safe, and to make sure that honest, creative, and hard working people get the appropriate reward.

Paragraph 2-7: Field Judges:
The field judges will issue warrant to prosecutors. The field judges select jurors from the experts or professionals in the field. Jurors must be paid according to the high standard of professionals. The field court is going to be composed of three judges. There will be only one appeals court.

Paragraph 2-8: Law School:
Court judges, prosecutors, and solicitors must have a certificate of master degree of law, and judges must have minimum three years of experience as a prosecutor or a solicitor.

Paragraph 2-9: Independency:
The global court must not be influenced by any organization or opinion. The global court has complete authority to make judgments, independent of any institute.

Paragraph 2-10: Term:
The Supreme Judge's serving term is a lifetime.

Paragraph 3-1: Global Legislature:
The global legislature will make laws and check the global court and presidency. This legislature will be composed of an upper house (about 300 members) and lower house (about 650 members). The presidents of the world nations and the chairpersons of national legislatures will constitute the upper house. The representatives elected from every nation's local constituencies will form the lower house. Every nation will have two to eight constituencies according to one unit for every ten million in population.

Super Constitution

Paragraph 3-2: Research Institute:
The global legislature will form a research institute for setting up the soundest policies and laws to fulfill the spirit of the Super Constitution. It should organize an appropriate number of committees and sub committees to let the committees work for research projects.

Paragraph 3-3: Investigative:
The global legislature will establish its own corps of investigative bodies, such as independent prosecutors, auditing accountants, and special task forces to check injustices or wrongdoings by government officials.

Paragraph 3-4: Qualification:
The members of the lower house of the global legislature must have a national certificate of such as Ph.D., lawyer, medical doctor, CPA, college professor, scientist, successful businessman, theologian, and national or global medal-holder. They should have not only professional knowledge in their field but also have a reputation of upright behavior.

Paragraph 3-5: Job Performance:
The global legislature's lawmakers will enjoy a prerogative to meet high-ranking court or executive officials and ask questions. The high-ranking government officials have legal obligation to meet the member, and to answer immediately and concretely.

Paragraph 3-6: Inquiry & Hearing:
The global legislature's committee or sub committee may conduct their own inquiry and hearing on the official works of the global court and executive branches at any time, in advance notice, besides formal ones.

Paragraph 3-7: Opinion Research:
The global legislature has the right and obligation to stage a special opinion-research on all fields.

Article 6: Confrontation

Paragraph 3-8: Election of Chairperson:
The Super Constitution writer will nominate the first chairpersons of the upper house and the lower house. The term will be four years. From the second term on, each house will elect chairpersons. The first chairperson will organize an elect process for each house's chairpersons.

Paragraph 3-9: Impeachment:
The global legislature may mobilize the power of impeachment of the global Supreme Court and the executive President, with a majority of two-thirds of two houses.

Paragraph 3-10: Limited Terms:
The global representatives of the lower house could serve three-consecutive terms with each four years. The Super Constitution writer will nominate the founding representatives.

Article 7

Killing Power

John's special instrument of wave-I and -II can exert whopping power in terms of politics and weapons systems. (The wave I in p. 80 identified human DNA like a fingerprint through its radar beacon by the delivering means of dark matter; and the wave II in p. 80 established audiovisual facilities to communicate with the spot the wave I locates.) The formation of instrument itself resulted in the combination of the pinnacle of electromagnetic technology and the wonder of the universe's magnificent astrophysical law.

Brenda's finding of the specific wave that disturbed human cells to die in a matter of three minutes added awesome consequences to human history and civilization along with John's wave-I and -II. We would call Brenda's cell-disturbing wave "killing power."

When a person dies, she or he no longer exists. She will not even know that she once was born. She will not recognize anything in the universe. She cannot function anything for the life or living thing. She will not remember any detestation, any favorite, any enemy, and any friend: nothing exists to a dead

Article 7: Killing Power

man. So, killing power means nothing to a dead person. However, killing power means something supreme to the alive, to the bereaved, and to the moving human world. In this juncture, the killing power matters. The killing power exhibits supreme power over the human mind's determination. The killing power is the number one source to make a final decision on human affairs. No one can exchange anything for the dead if that death does not mean anything else.

Brenda's killing power armed with John's communicating capability and James's delivering means loomed in the living human world as a stark existence. What's more, that killing power was not known publicly. That killing power had been known superficially to the offices of the presidents of China, Russia, and the U.S. in the early summer of 2016, under the name of Miss Ohara from the star Ohara, twenty-one light-years away from the earth.

As we read the conversation between the Chinese president and Miss Ohara (p. 1&2), the killing power had been introduced to begin the enactment of the Super Constitution. But, as usual, with any historical moment or movement of human life, human's historical reality had been always marked with a great deal of mass sacrifice: bloodshed, economic disaster, and a lot of suffering and distraction. Sometimes it was monumental, sometimes a boondoggle. No matter how powerful the movement embarked on, the bigger the movement, the stronger the resistance it confronted. The enactment of the Super Constitution could create the biggest historical implementation of the human world affair.

The three-biggest world powers the U.S., Russia and China, are no joke. Their size of land, population, asset, capability, and military organization goes beyond ordinary people's imagination. They could do almost anything if they were united. The introduction of the killing power from Miss Ohara pushed them into a united front, naturally and automatically.

Super Constitution

The killing power must have displayed its awesome mystery of the inexplicable technology. The troika tried minimization of the suffering, time consuming, mind boggling, and antagonism.

The three chiefs of the world's super powers conferred with two or three nations through a hot line. Each nation's president held busy, long conferences with their national security advisors, sometimes including the president's chief of staff, defense minister, and intelligence chief. Each nation agreed to cover up this incident in top secret, limiting to only the smallest inner circle. President's interpreters and secretaries understood the magnitude of the incident.

June 7, 2016,
Miss Ohara's second vocal appearance for the communication came along after three days of the first one (page 1).

This time, Miss Ohara told the three presidents of how to organize the special commission to decommission all the weapons systems of nuclear, biological, and chemical arms of each country, as well as all other nations' weapons of mass destruction. In addition to this order, Miss Ohara issued the commencement of the Super Constitution, for the global political institute under a single sovereignty.

Miss Ohara ordered the three presidents to finance the commission to decommission all the weapons systems of mass destruction, exactly in the same way as the man in hiding did on October 12, 2015, when the man in a fog blasted a suitcase with nuclear bomb in Rome (p. 82): using 1 % of each country's annual budget, and with the commission's members from Germany, France, India, Japan, and South Korea.

Regarding the commencement of the Supper Constitution for the global political institute under a single sovereignty, Miss Ohara gave two-month time to finish the organization, and

Article 7: Killing Power

gave a two-week deadline to announce the joint statement for the public hearing on the Super Constitution.

Three nations kept themselves busy and tense with so much talking. Three nations agreed to organize the commission to decommission all the weapons systems of mass destruction, and to set up the global political institute the way the troika presented under the form of constitution.

Three nations figured that they had nothing to lose. They had realized how difficult and time consuming to draw an agreement for arms reduction. The world had seen too many standoffs and dead locks, too often. But people all over the world were amused and shocked again to see three superpowers had united, all of a sudden. And three nations issued a joint communiqué to form a global political institute according to the Super Constitution in two-month time.

The three nations' joint statement on June 20, 2016, rocked the earth. The undulating giant wave agitated brainstorming across the globe. Everybody woke up from the deep sleep and found their world changing entirely in a rapid advance. Nobody could believe it. Everyone wondered what was happening. Millions of speculations on social norms, economic situations, and people's lifestyles had literally amassed for parade.

However, this unprecedented, historical big-change would undergo a tremendous amount of huddles to jump over. Human beings accumulated and organized historical data of human life. The bigger the change loomed, the brighter brain it required. Also, the innate human nature is not so simple as to be directed in one way. Leaders of the three nations would not simply play a robot, just taking an order and executing it. Human curiosity and willpower to dominate the world never disappear. The leaders would vigorously figure out the source of this unbelievable technology of the killing power. And also the three nations' presidents, sooner or later, had to explain about the killing power coming from the star Ohara to the legislature and people, in order to get Miss Ohara's order going on.

The troika sat together at their vaulted room for conference among them after the shocking statement went worldwide. John opened his mouth first.

"Right now, the current status of the modern scientific technology would take substantial time to figure out the specific electromagnetic waves we are using for communication and locating the person wanted by identifying DNA. But, sooner or later, the three nations' task forces for dealing with our demand would find out the origin of the waves that we planted in Joshua tree National Park. At the moment, we send out the wave to Washington, D.C., Beijing, and Moscow from the same place in Joshua tree National Park. Of course, it will take quite a time for them to figure out the shape and frequency of the wave, and to fathom the distance between the point they receive the wave and the point the wave originated, through trigonometry."

Brenda turned her face toward James at the word of trigonometry, seemingly raising a question about the math. matter. James's eyes blinked at meeting Brenda's gaze. James smiled a little, and then talked.

"Well, actually, I have been already thinking about the matter John mentioned a little while ago. I am sure that the current science can figure out the originating spot of the wave in a matter of more or less than a year, by measuring the angles of the waves Beijing and Moscow have received through the sine and cosine figures of trigonometry."

James stared blankly into the air in a little bit, and then continued.

Article 7: Killing Power

"I think we have two choices. One is having three antenna-locations. We now have only one at Joshua tree National Park. Let's say, we install another one at Phoenix, for example, for Beijing only, and the other one at San Francisco, for Moscow. If we use three locations separately, they will never locate our originated spot because our wave travels piercing through the underground without leaving any other base to calculate a trigonometric function. But we need to check these places time to time.

"Or for the other one, we can use one of hundreds of satellites circling the earth right now by using a reflective mechanism. If we use the reflective mechanism of the surface of the satellite, they will figure out that the wave they receive is coming from the earth. However, nobody could think it feasible for anybody to go up to the satellite and to check the incoming direction of the wave from the earth."

Brenda asserted her opinion when James paused.

"James, I think we'd better use the satellite surface rather than three locations. Anyway, soon, they will notice or imagine the wave we send now is being originated from the earth. As long as they could not guess the originated area, we don't have to worry. What do you think, James?"

"Well, I agree to your idea."

James looked up at John's face, expressing some questioning of John's idea. John responded.

"I also think we'd better use the satellite. Of course, I have to make some computer switchboard to calculate the right spot on the surface of the satellite for matching the angle and to adjust the present antenna's rendering wave-form. It won't be too much a hassle."

Super Constitution

"All right, gentlemen! Let's fix the mechanism later. We are going to have a heavy volume of communications soon."

Brenda felt confidence in conducting the business of the Super Constitution at full scale.

Meanwhile the presidential offices of China, Russia, and the U.S. kept themselves vociferous in preparation for organizing the commission to decommission weapons systems of mass destruction and the global political institute under a single supreme sovereignty. Even though the commission of decommissioning would be composed of five nations as Miss Ohara indicated, the three powers had to toil over assisting the formation of the commission as a mandatory duty. The three powers and the five nations had to set up the formal channel for financial flow and enforcing-power unit, which the commission would use as for executing the decommissioning job.

Also, the three power's top officials brainstormed themselves to be perfect in implementing the global political institute, for the sake of their nations' national interest and for that of the other nations of the world as well.

While the three powers were perspiring over good results from the new venture, naturally, they put themselves to extraordinarily hard work in investigating the source and technology of the killing power. The U.S. President's National Security Advisor Steve Johnson made more frequent visits to the Oval Office everyday. The fierce debate went on almost all day long among the inner circle: Defense Secretary Charles Manatt, Intelligence Czar Malcom Stark, Chief of Presidential Staff Edmund Murduck, Chairman of the joint Chiefs of Staff Clark Powell, and National Security Advisor Steve Johnson. The debate continued everyday.

Article 7: Killing Power

One day, the intelligence czar Malcom Stark suggested to the President the "Special Secret Task Force": the SSTF (special secret task force) should be organized under the National Security advisor's authority to report to President directly everyday. The members of the SSTF would come from scientists, spymasters, special military commandoes, and business talents. The main job would be organizing anything for searching all the pertinent technologies related to the killing power, and conducting guerilla war to locate the source of operating the killing power. They guessed the killing power was not from extra-terrestrials but from the earth, probably one of advanced nations such as Russia, China, Japan, India, France, Germany, South Korea, or some other nation.

The U.S. President's National Security Advisor Mr. Steve Johnson finished organizing the clandestine SSTF and made a report to President, talking to the President in the Oval Office.

"Mr. President, I have talked with a lot of scientists about the killing power. The technology of the killing power alone involves lots of experts, at least a half dozen specialists in the fields of biology, neuron science, and wave theory. Regarding how they send the electromagnetic wave of audio and video along with the wave of killing power, our scientists have not figured it out yet. The killing power which disturbs human cells by the wave is still in the area of theory, not in the practical phase."

The President took a deep breath. He sighed a little. Then he asked.

"Can our people find out exactly where the wave had been originated?"

"No sir. Not yet!"

Super Constitution

"How come our advanced modern technology cannot find out the origin of the wave?"

Steve Johnson seriously paused for a little while, and then earnestly answered in a poker face.

"Sir, we have located the direction where it is coming from, but it is not easy job to fathom the wave's distance from the origin. They say that they have to trace the wave by our specific radar beacon. Because the wave is coming from under the ground, we cannot trace it, so we have to only imagine where the wave is being entered. From the entering point, they have to catch up with the incoming wave, and trace it to find the origin out."

The President asked.

"Then how soon can they trace it to find out?"

"Well, Mr. President, they said it would take time, may be half or one year because they have to install a special mechanism to check the wave's direction and wave's passing time by nanotechnology. Presently, they consider the wave's origin lies in the west of our country."

The president dropped his head a little, thinking about something. Then he straightened his head, looking at Steve's eyes.

"Don't you guess the origin of the wave exists in the Far East, may be, such as in Japan or South Korea?"

While the inner circle of the U.S. President was suspecting the Far East area, the same inner circles of China and Russia were exchanging their strong suspicions of the U.S. because their scientists made a report that the origin of the wave laid in the east of their countries.

Article 7: Killing Power

No matter how rich the nation is, no matter how powerfully sophisticated military strength the nation has, or no matter how much talented pool of scientists the nation contains, if the nation were simply exposed to the unknown killing power from nowhere, the nation would have to listen to the source of the killing power: the nation has to follow the direction as the source of the killing power tells. When the owner of the killing power, who can exercise it at her will and time without any appearance from nowhere with her mysterious remote control, tells the nation to pay taxes, to organize institutes, and to administer a work, the nation has to do it. Now, here, the owner of the killing power, fortunately, orders not evil things but blessed ones, like God would do.

If we raised an intelligent dog as a lovely pet, how would we treat it? If the pet dog behaves very loyal to the owner, if the dog does listen to the owner very well, we love the dog. The dog does not care if the owner deserts him or treats him badly. No matter what the owner does against the dog's welfare, the pet dog never bites, never snarls or runs away. The ordinary character of healthy human would never abuse his pet dog. In terms of human imagination, the pet dog does not have any similar thinking mechanism that humans practice. The pet dog will never doubt on his owner's behavior.

But humans have a logical thinking power, which analyses history and measures future development of human affairs. The human mind understands his environment and the power he has to deal. He thinks about the power that can conquer the other power he has to deal.

While the nations and the leaders were listening to the overwhelming power, they put themselves into a cantankerous position of catching up with the unknown killing power.

Super Constitution

In the level of intelligent thinking mechanism, human brainwork functions so much different from the pet dog: there is no ghost in human thinking mechanism. Human beings will never give up their strenuous and conspicuous effort to find out the source of the killing power, even though they know they are under surveillance from the source of that killing power.

Primitive man found fire, which has enormous power in the living world. Primitive man found weapons such as throwing stones, arrows, knives, sword, spears, and explosives. And then development continued to go on to the modern age to invent steam engine, railroad, automobile, airplane, and computer. Now, man is talking about intelligent semiconductor and copying human beings themselves. Furthermore, man is talking about human extinction because the never-ending advance of technology may be able to manufacture humans themselves and control living things and their affairs sooner or later. In this stage, the killing power can be one of many toys.

However, right now, Miss Ohara's killing power was the only one super-weapon man recognized.

In our written human history, we can see endless wars to kill each other to tell somebody's will to dominate human affairs. We see through history that somebody dominated some part of geopolitics and some length of time with limited, some superiority in killing power.

So far, as the human history indicates, there has never been the supreme and most comprehensive killing power to exert the power to set up a ruling order for worldwide decision-making. That makes the one reason there exists no single, super sovereignty on Earth. Instead, various sovereignties snarled and compromised each other under the name of their own national sovereignty. Here, for instance, Japanese people have

Article 7: Killing Power

to pay ten times higher prices for the rice than the U.S. while the American citizen has to pay twenty times higher wages than China. Of course, each country or each society has its own specific infrastructure so much different. However, because of each nation's holy and mystique sovereignty, the people of the world suffer, and the peace of the world has been sacrificed. Correctly enhancing civilization of human beings has been dragged and delayed.

To rule human society, we need a ruling power. The ruling power comes ultimately from the killing power. But so far, the killing power to rule has had a limit geographically in the category of nationality, under the name of sovereignty, and a social barrier of language and religion. In older days, which did not have transportation and communications of these days, and during tens of thousand years, human races and languages had been framed individually. But even 2,400 years ago, Plato wrote up in the "Republic" for Utopia. Now, in modern days, Plato's idea could be materialized if we could utilize the killing power established by the troika of Brenda, John, and James.

There are so many killing powers: knives, guns, poison, even raw muscle power in the manner of simple murder, organized crimes, special commandoes, terrorism, wars, and court order. Whatever it is, if that killing power has some difficulty to exercise as is happening now, it is going to be a limited power.

During Second World War, German U-boats (submarines) sank about 1,500 American merchant ships while the U.S.'s destroyers and attack planes destroyed about 1,500 German U-boats. So many killing powers were mobilized. Those kinds of killing powers stood awesome but not much usable to have an effective control on decision-making for the most effective world politics.

Super Constitution

Miss Ohara's killing power operated very simple to exercise its power and stay in dark, and left no trace at all. If this killing power could continue its status as it was without revealing its colors as the troika prepared, it could produce the power to create a world politics, and Utopia of the earth.

Politics determines economy. Economy directs the human mind. The human mind sets forth politics. This circle has no end. This circle moves by its own gravity and inertia. The mobile element of this gravity occurs from the killing power. When a guy realizes he gathered an enough killing power to tell his will to his neighbor, he invades into his neighbor to tell his will.

400 years ago, a Japanese samurai named "Hideyoshi" unified Japan after many struggles and wars, and then invaded Korea with 150,000 men in well trained army along with 1,000 sturdy battle ships. Hideyoshi's army landed at a southern most Korean port without any resistance because Korea never expected and never prepared for this. The Japanese army advanced up to the northern part of Korea at full gallop. The united force of China and Korea finally stopped the Japanese advance. The war went on for seven years. During the seven years of war, of course, hundreds of thousands of soldiers and civilians were slaughtered. It was a historic massacre and historically cruel killing.

Hideyoshi never expected the Korean people's uprising. Also he never expected that there was an unknown Korean admiral who expected Japan's invasion, and prepared for naval war with 100 poor battle ships. Korean admiral's name was Lee Soon Shin. He led Korean navy to stop Japanese fleet's advance for Japanese army's logistics. General Lee Soon Shin won twenty-three battles out of twenty-three engagements, destroying half the Japanese fleet. More than one-third of Japanese soldiers were killed in the water by the Korean naval force.

Article 7: Killing Power

Hitler killed Jewish people during Second World War: the systematic mass slaughter of European Jews in Nazi concentration camps: Holocaust. In this way, the greedy human mind produces political motive to tell something to somebody. That something sums up economic gain. That economic reward moves the human mind to move on. That movement results in killing power. By far, no one has yet created a super killing power to control the world politics.

Through written human history, we again and again see that many wars, dictators, criminals commit killing without considering consequences or with a short vision on people's resilience in their resistance. Too many talented people who had too much more bravery than their symmetric intelligence, tended to get an opportunity to exercise political decision-making to satisfy their greed. They always thought they had enough killing power to dominate. They only tried to conquer the world. They only wanted to impose their doctrine. Sometimes it worked. Sometimes it lasted long enough creating prosperous dynasties and empires.

In the old days' infrastructure of human society, no effective ruling regime could be possible. In these days, the modernized infrastructure and some unique killing power, amid a balanced power struggle of the world, can definitely function to set up a right ruling machinery under one "Super Constitution" if the justice stands behind the ruling force. But who is going to make the final decision whether the ruling power stems from pure justice? In this circumstance, the troika and the advisor Michael Leigh happened to debate.

In the vaulted ample room, Michael Leigh, Brenda, John, and James took their seats. There were one sofa and three arm-chairs. Mr. Leigh opened the session:

Super Constitution

"Brenda, John, and James, I am so glad. We finally begin our project. As I usually talked about the justice on every decision we make, we have to clear our own understanding before we act."

John, looking at everybody's faces, joined in the talk,

"Of course, Dad, we don't have any bias. We don't have any interest in anything else except one thing. The only thing we are interested in is the smooth going of our project."

Brenda intercepted.

"Dad is right, John is right. But we have to think about the consequences and the ripple effect of the decision we make on the going of our project. There are going to be many unexpected questions we'll have to answer, time to time, on time."

Michael continued.

"Absolutely, we are not going to be involved. Actually we cannot get involved in any actual going or happening in the project. We can only issue a peremptory command on going or not going. Sometimes we have to conduct a lot of talks and long conversation. As much as possible, we must collect all of their questions, and answer them after we have discussed them in full length."

John added.

"In case somebody tries to approach our secret technology, even though we have already warned them, we have to take a decisive and fast action. I mean we have to get rid of her or him immediately by sending the killing wave to him or her to let them know we are conducting serious business. So no one would try to approach us in any manner,"

Article 7: Killing Power

Brenda asked James whether he had any point to talk. And James, smiling, answered.

"I don't see any mistakes or dubious minds on the going of our project. I am sure we are holding the rudder firm to keep everything in the category of the spirit of justice. We are trying our best not to use the killing wave. But as John has already assured, if the case becomes inevitable, we have to activate it decisively."

The troika and Michael Leigh did not get involved in actual management of the processes in the globalization of the Super Constitution. That alone could provide substantial objectivity with their judgment. And their whole interests in the globalization with the Super Constitution came from a naïve concept of their technology's contribution to the simple justice. Clear vision without any greedy mind can bring justice.

Article 8

Delivering Means

Delivery means result. Delivery makes things happen and possible. Success comes through all types of a right delivery. All sorts of desirable physical movements depend on the right method of logistics. Without a right delivery, a promise ends up empty. Our life goes on through delivery physically and mentally.

If there would have been no right delivering means for desirable effect, even that awesome killing power, no matter how powerful it was, would have been like a tiger in a cage. So far, there was no incident the killing power invoked. The clear-cut vocal appearances to three presidents of three powers two times, without any trace alone, produced a deep impression on the authority.

July 1, 2016,
Brenda delivered the third vocal appearance, which had been filtered through a special device. The special commission

Article 8: Delivering Means

composed of Germany, France, India, Japan, and South Korea made a list of following questions to present to Miss Ohara: What decision-making process should the special commission adopt? What percentage of the WMD should they eliminate? Where should they dump the dangerous materials incurred by the decommissioning?

The three powers' security teams set up eavesdrop-gear facilities to catch the incoming wave's direction and the character of the voice. The conversation between Miss Ohara and the spokesman went on almost 30 minutes. Miss Ohara gave fully understandable instructions: the Secretary General of the commission would carry on the decisions made by the committee in its majority; and each nation would take a turn every two months for chairmanship. The reduction of the WMD should be down to ten warheads of each country of Russia and the U.S. The dumping area should be located in each country by the majority decision of each country's legislature. The official name of the above commission would be the "WMD Commission."

Not only three powers' security team, but also many worldwide scientists focused their curious attention on the electronic wave form Miss Ohara used and the existence of a cell-disturbing wave to cause death. How on Earth could somebody deliver her or his voice without a trace? How could they manage the listening device through the radar beacon? The three nations' security team made a strenuous effort to figure it out. No one could think of any clue.

When any technology has not been yet formalized theoretically or practically, no human intelligence can imagine the paradigm of the technology. Therefore, only random speculations and foggy puzzles danced wildly. Every class of sophisticated and up-to-date modern-gadgets was mobilized to catch up with any clues of Miss Ohara's voice. But only darkness and labyrinthine enigmas permeated everybody's brain.

The U.S. President's National Security Advisor Steve Johnson made a phone call to Intelligence Czar Malcom Stark.

"Malcom, I feel I am a blind man climbing Sequoia mountaintop alone. Do you have any idea where we should try to start?"

"I have no idea at all either, Steve. I only see dire darkness. Let's wait for further development of encounters with Miss Ohara. The commission of the WMD and the global political institute are not a bad idea at all. Maybe Miss Ohara is listening to every conversation we are conducting. Steve, we'd better carefully try to do our best in following Miss Ohars's instruction, and not to disturb her. So far, her instructions look good for the global order."

Steve casually responded to Malcom's careful approach,

"Of course, Malcom, everything looks all right. But also, we have to try to find who Miss Ohara truly is, and what her real technology is. Our SSTF is at a quite alarmingly good speed for locating the origin of the wave of audiovisual facilities Miss Ohara is using, and analyzing her voice."

"The origin of the wave does not go beyond the Pacific Ocean, probably from the West Coast of our continent. The character of her voice has been filtered through a micron size of polypropylene net: her age is about 30. We don't have a technology to tell the race by the voice analysis yet. However, we will progress to the point that we can guess who is indeed behind Miss Ohara."

Steve got pretty much excited at the words of "behind Miss Ohara," and asked Malcom what he thought of the SSTF's

Article 8: Delivering Means

advances. And Malcom slowly started to open his mouth after a little pause with a slight sigh.

"Steve I am worrying about your sharp curiosity about Miss Ohara. Frankly speaking, we are in complete darkness about Miss Ohara, and what's more, she has gargantuan mystery, which we should not touch any part of it until she shows certain frame. Actually your SSTF plays a dangerous game. I advised, the other day, with Mr. President that we'd better wait because a lot of talented people could be hurt."

Every major important conversation in three nations' presidential and National Security offices had been automatically monitored most of the days by the troika's vault room facilities. Brenda, John, and James checked the recordings: Brenda for China, John for the U.S., and James for Russia; Brenda's second language was Chinese, John's German, James's Russian.

The troika edited each nation's top dialogues over the period of Ohara's second and third vocal-appearances. They summarized their monitoring records and they discussed that they had to get rid of several people, to expedite the procedure of organizing the commission and the global political institute, and to stop three nations' further investigation into the existence of the troika's technology.

July 1, 2016 (page 110), after Ohara's third appearance for the set of the special commission's concrete job, the representatives of the three superpowers of the U.S., Russia, and China gathered together at the U.N. building. They discussed setting up a public hearing on the matter of the Super Constitution set by the troika.

The three U.N. ambassadors of the U.S., Russia, and China had notified the Security Council and Secretary General Mr. Conjie Tumba, about the public hearing in the General

Super Constitution

Assembly Hall on the Super Constitution for the global political institute set by the troika. Only authorized persons from all over the world could enter the Hall and take their designated seats: only two officials from each country of the world, professors related to the study of constitution invited by the three nations, and media moguls also designated by the three nations. Other people interested in, had to watch live TV broadcast, set at 8 p.m. Eastern time on July 19, 2016.

New York City policemen in plain clothes with hidden id, U.S. MPs, several units of Coast Guard, a score of army Apache attack helicopters, ambulances, and fire engine corps filled the U.N. building area. Authorities had closed off civilian traffics on 1st avenue from 42nd street to 49th street, and even East River highway from 34th street to 57th street. Literally, the area of the U.N. building had been fortified as an isolated castle. The area looked like the busy 8th Army Headquarters, wringing out an emergent battle tactics.

"Ladies and gentlemen, my name is Glen Marshall, ambassador of the United States of America, one of three chairs of tonight's event for the public hearing on the Super Constitution. As you may know about Miss Ohara's special instructions on this Super Constitution, I am honored to announce the opening of the public hearing for the draft of the Super Constitution, according to the order issued by Miss Ohara."

The General Assembly Hall echoed with deafening silence for a moment. With the largest audience ever recorded in history through the worldwide TV media, people of the world were glued to TV screen. Mr. Glen Marshall continued after a brief silence.

"Ladies and gentlemen, Mr. Georgio Pravonsky, ambassador of the Republic of Russia, is going to announce the procedure for tonight's hearing. Thank you."

Article 8: Delivering Means

U.S. ambassador Mr. Glen Marshall turned the podium over to Russian ambassador Mr. Georgio Pravonsky. Three ambassadors had a seat at the top of the Hall. Right below the top headcounter, ten panelists took their seats. Special ten representatives from five nations' commission of Germany, France, India, Japan, and South Korea took the front headcounter of the Hall. And the U.N. Secretary General and his entourage took seats at the front side of the Hall's right wing, and the U.N. security task forces took seats at the front side of the Hall's left wing. The Hall's atmosphere appeared heavy and serious.

Russian ambassador Mr. Georgio Pravonsky stood up from his seat at the top headcounter. He took the podium, looked around the Hall, and opened his mouth by sincere appearances.

"Good evening, ladies and gentlemen! I am honored to be here tonight. My name is Georgio Pravonsky from Russia. I sincerely wish that tonight's event will definitely usher our world into the greatest moment of world peace and individual happiness. The history of human life had been stained with blood, killing, and corruption. In fact, humans have constantly suffered from the absence of super world order. The suffering has been so sticky, yet still it is going on, and it looks like it's going to go on forever."

"Here, we have happened to confront an absolute order from Miss Ohara to adopt this Super Constitution for the earth. According to Miss Ohara's quote, the earth is the only planet of living things beside the star Ohara, twenty-one light-years away from our solar system, in the earth's neighborhood within 1,000 light-years."

Georgio Provonsky, the Russia's U.N. ambassador, continued.

Super Constitution

"Ladies and gentlemen, no matter if we like it or not, we have been given an absolute order to take on the Super Constitution. Fortunately, it looks great. If we find something through this hearing, we would like to suggest any modifications or additions to Miss Ohara before promulgation. Ladies and gentlemen, I would like to unveil the simple procedures of tonight's hearing as follows: First, the ten panelists will introduce her or his point on the Super Constitution in only fifteen minutes. Second, we are going to have an intermission after five panelists' delivery. Third, every nation's suggestion would be accepted through the U.N. Secretary General's office. Fourth, the conductor of procedures Chinese ambassador Mr. Yaobang Chang will briefly introduce each panelist. Ladies and gentlemen, I would like to give the podium to Mr. Yaobang Chang. Thank you very much!"

Mr. Georgio Pravonsky spoke fluent English. He had been educated in Yale University for eight years, with Ph.D. degree in economics. The American economic scholars had considered him as a future icon for the Russia's economic modernization.

Chinese ambassador Mr. Yaobang Chang was a Harvard graduate in law. At one time, he served as a top interpreter for former China's President Jermin Chang. Yaobang Chang stood up from his seat, walked toward the lectern to deliver the procedure, and settled his position for performing his job.

"Ladies and gentlemen, my name is Yaobang Chang. According to the instructions given by Miss Ohara, we don't intend to criticize the Super Constitution at all. Tonight's total purpose is to let the world get to know what the Super Constitution is. Therefore, if there are any wrong introductions or messages, I am going to stop the speaker right away. However, I encourage these panelists to make constructive suggestions for any amendments or additions to the

Article 8: Delivering Means

constitution. I would like to introduce to you Mr. Jacques Chevron from France, a very famous sovereignty professor from Sorbonne University. Mr. Jacques Chevron, please go ahead."

First panelist Mr. Chevron delivered his message.

"Thank you for Mr. Glen Marshal's opening statement, and thank you for Mr.Georgio Pravonsky's remark about the spirit of the Super Constitution, and I fully understand Mr. Yaobang Chang's assertion explaining the purpose and vision of the Super Constitution. Ladies and gentlemen! I am honored and thrilled to speak about something on this Super Constitution. I think the draft of the Super Constitution stands for simplicity, easy understanding, and yet so much integrity."

Mr. Chevron from France praised and admired the spirit and ruling power of the Super Constitution to finally bring a fantastic world order to this beautiful earth. If this Super Constitution worked as it intended, the real and desirable super human society could be formed first time in the human history. Mr. Chevron quoted many religious incidents of the human history, and received standing ovation from the audience.

Mr. Yaobang Chang introduced the second panelist from Germany Mr. Reinhard Schmidt.

"My dear fellow people, I am honored to be here tonight. Economically, we, as civilized, modern people, have been wasting too much on too many fronts of our life because so many nations strive in an excessive competition, restrict and duplicate unnecessaries, cover up failures, dictate and tax cruelly. Please look at every government's spending binge, using people's money on boondoggle in the manner of most inefficiency with the least quality of service. Every government recedes into the shell of sovereignty and shouts for patriotism and national interest."

Mr. Schmidt presented many cases of all nations' egoistic compromise by disregarding world people's true interest. Mr. Schmidt indicated the Super Constitution's terse but comprehensive approach to the world's ruling power. He also received standing ovation at the end of his quiet speech.

Mr. Yaobang Chang seriously introduced the third panelist from Korea Mr. Nam Kook Gah: a puzzled representative from South Korea because South Korea was not one of G8 nations, neither considered as one of the world's noticeable powers yet, but nominated as one of five nations in Miss Ohara's announcement. Mr. Nam Kook Gah was one of the most prominent constitution lawyers in South Korea.

"Good evening, my fellow citizens! My name is Nam Kook Gah, which means some southern country's price. So far, humans have paid too high price for our happiness because unstabilized politics, uneven economic course, unequal society, and intolerable religion. Every nation has its custom duties, visas, and citizenships in order to regulate people's movement and transportation of their goods under the name of sovereignty."

"We have to demolish the high wall of each nation's borders for people's freedom. This Super Constitution is trying to provide people with true political power to live happy life. I love this constitution because it loves people. I am sure every one of you understands what this constitution says."

Audiences gave earnest standing ovation at this moment. Mr. Gah went through the list of political predicaments in history. At the end of his speech, he received another standing ovation.

Article 8: Delivering Means

Now, Mr. Yaobang Chang eagerly brought in the fourth panelist from Japan Mr. Hiroshi Takashimaya. Mr. Hiroshi Takashimaya graduated from Princeton law School, and an outstanding law professor in Japan.

"Good evening, everybody, I am very much pleased to speak as one of panelists today. I insist that legal words or sentences must narrate things or incidents in brevity. The true value of the law stands for succinctness. For human communication, language has been developed along with the law."

"Right now, so many sovereignties exist in the world, just as too many languages exist. During hundreds of thousand years of human prehistory, the law must have been occurred together with language. In the old days, transporting means were in a terrible shape. Nature's wall was too high and too tough to cross over. So, hundreds of sovereignties and languages had sprung out. But nowadays, the earth means a different environment to humans. The Pacific and Atlantic oceans are only big rivers to cross. We need new order, new law, new constitution, and a new language that facilitate our modern life. I seriously welcome the Super Constitution. I welcome its brevity. With this Super Constitution, we don't have to worry about so called corrupted politicians and inefficient bureaucrats."

Mr. Takashimaya emphasized the need of one-world language, along with sincerely presenting several cases to activate the spirit of the Super Constitution. He also received an ardent standing ovation from the audience.

Not only the people in the Hall, but also the worldwide TV watchers felt deeply excited on the possibility for the world to be able to create a real paradise on this earth, using that unbelievable Super Constitution. People in the Hall and those glued to TV enjoyed the great momentum developed by the hearings. They thirstily waited for the next panelist to speak out.

Yaobang Chang appeared again in the front of the podium with ever more confident dignity. He proudly announced Miss Indira Gandhi II from India as the fifth panelist. People in the Hall gave a roaring standing ovation as soon as she started walking toward the podium even before they heard anything from her.

Miss Indira Gandhi stood in the front of the podium and made a little and short smile, and opened her mouth.

"My deer friend, how are you, tonight! I am so honored to have your standing ovation even before my speech! Ladies and gentlemen! We, as humans, have come a long way to finally have this wonderful supreme law to unite our world under a single sovereignty. Of course, we will enjoy one military power on this earth. The military power must be used for the world's new order, for the people's welfare, and by the people's will. I am thrilled at the vision that neither dictator nor cunning politician could exploit the governing power under the shield of security forces because the Super Constitution and the unknown killing power had been motivated for the people."

Miss Indira Gandhi enumerated a variety of beautiful points of the only one military-power's unique existence in this world. The people all over the world glued to TV had been fascinated by the imagination of the ever-giant military strength that was going to be friendly to the people of the world. Once again, a roaring standing ovation fulfilled the Hall at the end of her speech.

Yaobang Chang vigorously added the sixth panelist after a fifteen-minute interlude. The second French man Mr. Nicolas

Article 8: Delivering Means

Sartre appeared at the refreshed podium with a pleasing posture.

Mr. Nicolas Sartre was noted as the number one national debater in the field of spiritual justice concerning human society's basic legal affairs, which were committed to and concerned with human society's general fairness. He frequently questioned, "What is justice?" and "What is fairness?" Mr. Sartre started his usual debating manner with a confident stance.

"How are you? My fellow people! It is my pleasure to address my point of view on the side of spiritual justice of this Super Constitution. Socially and economically, humans are political animal, constantly searching for comparable behavior along with its surrounding people. Interest groups are formed. Associations are organized. Cronies develop. Friendship goes. We often see unfair behavior appears: such as nepotism; sweet heart deal, corruption, and foul play. Historically, we suffer from inequality on acquiring an opportunity for social or economic development. We suffer from unfair judgment on creativity and competition. The poor stays poor. The rich gets advantage. The power holders cross the river by boat while other disadvantaged people swim. We must provide a fair opportunity for the distribution of wealth with the creative and honest people. The creative, honest, and hard working people should prosper. Double-crossers, crooks, and thieves must be punished accordingly."

Mr. Sartre presented many ideas for boosting fair opportunities for the creative and honest people while preventing unfair practices, cheating, and infringement upon intellectual property. Mr. Sartre emphasized heavy penalties for crime and the need of separating criminals from ordinary society. The people gave an enthusiastic standing ovation at Mr. Sartre's emphasis on the serious criminal treatment of criminals.

Super Constitution

The Hearing Procedure Director Yaobang Chang introduced the 7th panelist from Germany: Mr. Henning Kant.

Mr. Kant walked toward the podium. The people in the U.N. General Assembly Hall and the people who were watching TV in the world now felt comfortable with what was going on. The scene that people were so much interested in and excited at really entertained the audience. The scene now looked familiar, and they were expecting what type of the next pleasant speech was going to go on.

"Good evening, ladies and gentlemen, I am very much pleased to see your relaxed pose tonight. I am convinced this Super Constitution shall pave an excellent super highway for our euphoric educational frame of reference. The educational matter should be a joyful journey, warranted by ironclad regulations for entering a school according to the children's born intelligence and their achievement. For example, children should take a test to show their natural ability and their earned achievement at their 6th, 9TH, and 12th grade respectively. According to their achieved academic record, they will enter the art school, vocational school, ordinary school, and a special school for the gifted children. A prominent scholar's son and daughter could go to a vocational school, and an illiterate parents' child could go to a special school."

"Education should not cost the student any money. Success and happiness do not necessarily come from only higher and better school. It is coming from the most appropriate education that would eradicate any varieties of scandals, irrationalities, disappointments, and agonies. A fair procedure will bring peace of mind, social stability, and a happy educational time for human lifestyles. The best institute must be invented. This Super Constitution clearly intends for the world's best educational framework to create the maximum

Article 8: Delivering Means

equality and fairness according to a student's talents and achievements."

Mr. Kant also listed several clear examples of how many irrational and infuriating incidents had infested our daily life just because of the wrong practice and noxious bias on the education. Upon finishing his speech, Mr. Kant also received an enthusiastic response from the people in the Hall.

Yaobang Chang presented the 8th panelist from Korea, Dr. Sonny Jinho Bahng, who was educated in Los Angeles from the age of six. He had a Ph.D. degree in law and had taught the constitutional law at UCLA for more than ten years, and at the moment was teaching at Seoul National University.

"My fellow citizens, good evening, my name is Sonny Bahng. I'd like to bring your attention to the matter of public enterprise and public administration under the auspices of the Super Constitution."

Dr. Bahng was of short stature, but well built around shoulders and neck, and gave a bold impression.

"Ladies and gentlemen, there are many public enterprises the heavy size of 800-pound gorillas, which have no boss, and there are so many public administration offices, which neglect efficient services to the people. All of them are developed with people's money for the sake of people. But their management and services are getting lousier. Their negligence suffocates the service spirit. They usurp public funds. They abuse so much of the public's valuable assets. Actually, the administrators there don't care. However, the size, importance, and power of influence are too big to leave them alone. Those are people's property. People have a downright authority to pick a right and smart manager. We need a smart organization to screen right aspirants at least 3 or 4, and we have to let concerned people decide who the most appropriate administrator is. We must set up a method for exclusion from political appointees or cronies."

Dr. Bahng told his stories about the representative misuse of public enterprises and public administrative offices, which produced a roar of laughter from the audience. Dr Bahng also retired in a thunderous applause from the Hall.

Yaobang Chang appeared again, smiling, and he brought up Mr. Yoshimi Hideyoshi from Japan as the 9th panelist.

Mr Hideyoshi received Ph.D. degree in economics from Princeton University. He had been involved in the field of higher education for public law, steered by the mind-set of fair distribution of wealth. He always insisted on the fair redistribution of wealth for a robust economic growth.

"My dear fellow citizens, how are you today? Frankly speaking, I love capitalism. I appreciate capitalism because it is the only way to develop our prosperity, considering egoistic human nature. However, socialism must be applied for the humanitarian purpose. We must exercise socialism to reshuffle the niches of social opportunities. Rich man's offspring starts much earlier for the finish line, with much more efficient tools. The race is unfairly set from the beginning. Lot of creative young men can never achieve a target with empty hands. They can never take off in empty hands."

"Ladies and gentlemen, here, we have very useful resources and leverage: the tax reform. Nowadays, we use the taxation mostly only for public service, welfare work, health care, defense expense, and governmental administration. The taxation is not being used for the prosperity of creative people. Public services—welfare work, health care, and public administration—must be overhauled by getting rid of special interest groups. Public enterprises must be run by profit-oriented minds to produce a substantial yielding. And we

Article 8: Delivering Means

could strike off the gargantuan expenses of the defense. Now with those incomes, we could accumulate huge fund along with the usual current income from taxation. This huge fund could be used for the loans to create necessary small businesses for the people who have no capital but creative mind, experience, and good ideas. We could set up an examining institute. In this socialistic redistribution, we could spread the capitalistic prosperity all over the world."

People were so much excited on this "incentive taxation" introduced by Mr. Hideyoshi. Standing ovation went roaring on. People all over the world in the front of TV were just amused. People felt a tectonic shift of their emotion.

Yaobang Chang, being sanguine, proudly named the 10th panelist. Everyone felt missed at the last panelist. Everybody wanted more items to be mentioned: Surely, there were more than ten topics. But this occasion was just introducing the face of the Super Constitution to the world.

Dr. Sanjay Chandra from India took the podium amid a vigorous mood of the General Assembly Hall of the U.N., of which emotional state never existed before. It was now almost in a feasting atmosphere.

"How are you this evening? Ladies and gentlemen! I am the last person to talk about the great side of the Super Constitution's intention. It is too bad for us to have only ten commentators today. But I am sure we will see, sooner or later, undulating spillover-effects the Super Constitution is going to generate, wave after wave. I would like to bring your attention to creating absolute free trade on our earth with only a 1% duty because we need the right statistics to record what merchandise moves from where to where with how much quantity and dollar amount in a certain period."

Super Constitution

"There are going to be no restricted items, except some specific ones. Most major natural resources should be controlled by the appropriate public enterprises. Supplies and demands are going to be geared up to the market economy with a minimum amount of regulations from the world government. Not only natural resources but also most of public enterprises should be coordinated by the world's economic concerns. Except natural resources and public enterprises, all other economic activities should be steered by the dynamism of the general marketplace under free trade environment."

The people were truly excited by the idea of the worldwide free trade. The people imagined the world in free movement: not only commodity but also free residence: a real freedom for humans. Dr. Chandra also itemized various cases that would save a colossal financial power, which could energize other extra human affairs. Dr. Chandra stepped off the podium amidst thunderous clapping and cheering.

Article 9

Communicating Capability

Communicating capability, along with the killing power and delivering means, definitely plays one of three major elements to carry on the Super Constitution.

"Communicate" means to give or interchange thoughts, feelings, knowledge, information or the like by writing or speaking, etc. There are many words concerned on the act or process of communication: signal, signify, denote, connote, express, suggest, indicate, illustrate, explicit, implicit, gesture, posture, smile, frown. The synonym for communication has more than forty words such as tell, impart, divulge, get through, etc.

A human being is the lord of all creations because humans can communicate with each other. No communication: no civilization. The capability of communication is the end part of human intelligence. Through the capability of communication, the human history was born, and the human intelligence achieved the modern culture, civilization, and technology.

Super Constitution

When we communicate with each other, we know one another, existence by existence, and what we are by what they are. But, sometimes we communicate without knowing the other communicating party; we communicate ourselves with an imagination or inspiration. In religion, we communicate with our God.

In the matter of this Super Constitution, one party knew the other party completely. However, the party who received an order did not know the party who issued the order at all. The receiving party only knew that the issuing party had some monstrous and mysterious technology, which existed beyond a thick fog and caused utter bewilderment to the scientists and politicians.

The U.N. public hearing of the Super Constitution as a P.R. activity to the worldwide people went on in good shape. Now, the troika got together again in the vault room to discuss the procedure of decommissioning the WMD (weapons of mass destruction: nuclear bombs, biological germs, chemical warfare, and the like). The troika concluded their schedules as the following.

Brenda led the conversation.

"I think, John and James, we'd better give the Special Commission a concrete schedule of decommissioning the WMD, and also we'd better set up a clear-cut, realistic procedure for materializing the Global Government according to the Super Constitution."

"Right, I am sure we have to issue authentic orders by the number of official promulgations," John said, relaying Brenda's initiative, and John presented as the following.

"We have to formalize an official channel for our resolute communication with the right party."

Article 9: Communicating Capability

"Absolutely," Brenda agreed, emphatically. John continued.

"I have been thinking about an organized communicating channel; I think we have to tell them that they have to designate an official spokesperson for the Special Commission and for organizing the global government."

James gave the following suggestion.

"Let's tell them they name one spokesperson and one deputy, and one general manger for the office of communication that is going to receive our orders, exchange talk, and contact us."

"That is a good idea."

John immediately adopted James's proposal.

Brenda went on to make her fourth appearance.

July 20, 2016, the next day, Miss Ohara appeared on the major TV channels at 8 p.m., New York time for her fourth appearance (her 3rd vocal appearance of July 1, 2016 at p. 110): her first actual, visual appearance. This time she appeared not only with her voice, but also with her figure from head to foot. However, her figure and face showed a completely different phenotype: a tall blonde with blue eyes. Needless to say, she had disguised to give a different impression to those who were stubbornly tracing her identity.

It was big news to the world. Miss Ohara from the star Ohara, twenty-one light-years away from the earth, appeared about the same as a Caucasian. Her English intonation resembled the "New England accent" of the northeastern part of the United States.

Super Constitution

People all over the world were excited by this incident. With a pleasant smile, she issued an order to form a communication office, and to select three key personnel, as Miss Ohara's first promulgation. It had a defined schedule, to form the office of communication within two weeks.

On August 5, 2016, with only voice for her fifth appearance, Brenda appeared in the Office of Communication with the second promulgation (p. 96: for the order Miss Ohara gave two-month time to finish the organization of Global Government: the commencement of the Super Constitution, on June 7, 2016). According to the first promulgation (p. 129: July 20, 2016), China, Russia, and the U.S. quickly organized the Office of Communication at the U.N. building: Russia's U.N. ambassador Georgio Provonsky as the spokes person, U.S. ambassador Glen Marshall as the deputy, and Chinese ambassador Yaobang Chang as the general manager.

Three ambassadors got together at Georgio's office to discuss the order of the second promulgation that was the official execution for the order issued by Miss Ohara on June 7. 2016.

August 15, 2016: the day for the announcement of the execution of the second promulgation, which was issued to the three powers of the U.S., Russia, and China on August 5, 2016, through the Office of Communication.

The second promulgation (given on August 5, 2016) demanded that three powers' presidents to present one candidate for global president, another one for global chief justice, and third one for global congressional chairperson from each nation, totaling to nine candidates who must speak English fluently. The candidates must have high scholastic record. The nine candidates, for three of each position would be introduced at another public hearing for the Super Constitution at the General Assembly Hall of the U.N. on August 15, 2016. If Miss Ohara could not find a qualified

Article 9: Communicating Capability

person, she would nominate other persons. That was the promulgation number two.

For the first four years of the Global Government, the troika had made a decision that the troika would be involved in electing major figures such as global Supreme Court judges, congressional members, and the global president and his major cabinet members. The troika made a decision to sanction the selection, appointment, and basic principle to choose.

The troika prepared for the great sanction for the top job of the world to be announced at the second public hearing for the Super Constitution at the U.N. General Assembly Hall set on 8 p.m. August 15, 2016.

The date of August 15 would be an epoch-making event of the human history. It would be the date of human rebirth. The news spread all over the world. People were much too excited. The powerful nations' major politicians became nervous. The mass media incited wild speculations. The top brass and bureaucrats underwent brainstorming. Professionals felt prideful. Crony capitalists trembled with trepidation. Dictators tried to bury their head in the sand. The second promulgation once again agitated the earth.

Three ambassadors from Russia, China, and the U.S. took a seat at the conference table in the room of Russia's Georgio Provonsky. Georgio opened his mouth with a grim face.

"During the last several days I exchanged a lot of serious talks with my country's president about picking candidates for the global president, chief justice, and congressional chairperson. My country's president decided to nominate me for the global president, my country's present chief justice for the global chief justice, and my country's present congressional chairperson as a candidate for the global congressional chairperson."

Super Constitution

China's Yaobang and the U.S.'s Marshall startled and opened their eyes wide. They were actually appalled at three nations' coincidence in making exact same choices. The three nations looked like forming a united front. These three persons of the communicating office recognized an arising trouble spot. This was an expression that three nations would consider the global government as a liaison office.

The three ambassadors felt their approach in a pinch. They sensed they would sit sandwiched in the middle of the three powers and Miss Ohara. The three ambassadors perceived that any suspicious tones emanating from the three nations would irritate Miss Ohara. Irritating Ohara could trigger the killing power. Once the killing power would set in motion, hard feeling would result.

Instead of peace of mind, fear would permeate. It would make the job of communication toilsome. Harsh communicating job meant having a feud with ongoing affairs. The communication on the affairs could exert considerable leverage over the power struggle and their conflicting interests. These ambassadors concluded that they should do their best to convey Miss Ohara's orders and three nations' intentions clearly in black and white by authenticating the chronology and topics

By the way, the troika of Brenda, John, and James did homework in order to pick up the right persons for the top jobs of the global government by contacting experts in management for human resources since the early part of June 2016. The troika gave them stern warnings to keep confidential on their contact. The troika, since the early part of June 2016, had steadily collected live, valuable information on the human resources in the field of economics, politics, sociology, religion, science, auditing, management, statistics, and law practice.

Article 9: Communicating Capability

The troika made a special organization: the HR-apparatus composed of prominent HR-experts. The troika contacted each member of HR-apparatus regularly for the process of selection. The troika organized HR-members in a group for court affairs, congressional affairs, and executive affairs. The troika did let them present a shadow cabinet, the congressional leaders, and the judges for the Supreme Court with a one-page resume for each candidate. For Congress, the troika ordered to present only sub-committee chairpersons and other key research and management members only totaling to ninety-six; the Supreme Court for eight, including one attorney general and one legal administrator; and nine members for the executive branch.

The troika did not believe that three powers would simply follow Ohara's order. The troika figured the three powers had humongous bureaucracy. Miss Ohara's orders would easily reach the political institute through the Office of Communication. But the overlapping bureaucratic membranes of the passively obedient, immobility-minded bureaucrats would stall the process of carrying out the order. The troika discussed the matter of bureaucracy with Michael Leigh the other day. They concluded, after long hours of discussion, that they would have to employ a cruel crushing force to break up the ordinary concepts of the human mind in order to create the new world order by the Super Constitution.

The crushing force the troika was going to employ meant mass killing to demonstrate the determination of the Super Constitution to the political institutes. The global government meant business: not a joke, not a decoration; no threat but relentless action; no compromises but notifications only; and no delay but instant follow-throughs. All the personnel involved in the process along with politicians, bureaucrats, and technocrats should respond instantly to the orders from the global government. Otherwise, they would face a snap judgment to be executed without a court of appeal. The global government meant the absolute authority to issue thoroughgoing orders.

The new world order would consolidate the permanent frame for each nation to create Utopia. The global government would not allow any resignation of any responsible personnel, any subterfuge, any excuse or substitute. The whole world would go through the throes of revolution until a certain length of time for the new order's settlement. The above guideline was the troika's conclusion. This troika's conclusion would kick off upon the 2nd hearing of August 15, 2016, for the Super Constitution at the U.N. General Assembly Hall to present the candidates for the top global governments' offices, according to the second promulgation (p. 130).

August 15, 2016, approached fast. There was only about a week left. People were so much curious about the candidates. After all, who would be nominated for the top job of the global governments? Mass media began to dance wildly in their speculations. People began to talk in whispers. The speculation in the media and from mouth to mouth spilled all over the place. The topic stretched out thousands of miles without any means of transportation. People's inquisitive sense on this topic tortuously soared to the sky. Who would be the global president? Who would be the global justice? Who would be the global congressional leaders? How would they manage the world's powerful nations? How would they organize the new world order? How would they control the gargantuan military powers? How would they lullaby people in the world?

One day, a person on the street walking with her friend asked her a question.

"Jenny, what do you think about August 15th?"

Article 9: Communicating Capability

"Well, I think it'll be very interesting to see if it's a big joke on the big shots."

"Do you really think the hearing is going to be a big joke?"

"Yes, I do, Mary."

"But Jenny, I think it is a great idea to put the world under one constitution."

"Of course, it is a great wonder. But how could it be done? The human mind is so complicated. Human destiny is unpredictable. Humans are much too egoistic, greedy, timid, and sneaky."

"Jenny, you see only the bad side. Of course, we have a negative side in the human life. But, we have geniuses, engineering minds, consciences, and honest and hard working people. I am sure August 15 will be a turning point for humans on the positive side."

"Well, Mary, I hope you're right. But frankly speaking, I worry about Miss Ohara's fault or mistake or bad happening in the mysterious technology."

"Jenny, I worry too."

Elsewhere, one guy talked to his buddy while sipping whisky at his neighbor's bar.

"Tom, what do you think about August 15?"

"I am sure a great, marvelous thing is going to happen. I'd like to experience a complete change of the world order."

"Maybe, a change could go. But Tom, I don't think Utopia can happen as Miss Ohara wants."

Super Constitution

"Bob, I think Utopia can happen. Human beings are political animals. Politics resembles an organism. Politics composes, after all, a group of interdependent people sharing same purpose or idea for life processes. Animals stand for living things, which fear of death the most. Animals know most clearly what the death remarks. Animals have the most sensitive instinct on their death. Therefore, Miss Ohara's absolute technology to annihilate any living thing anytime, anywhere, would dispatch her order at full gallop."

"Tom, your syllogism sounds likely. However, carrying a theory into practice is not that simple. Unexpected hurdles come into life all the time. History weaves in and out. Uncontrollable curves carve out human fate. Tom, I really hope Miss Ohara's new order could speed up like a plumped sail boat."

"I know what bothers your mind."

"Tom, let's drink just one punch more. It is none of our business. Anyway, we are onlookers."

"Of course, Bob, we are not the player, not the sided spectator either. However, I can't help but be really concerned."

"Tom, you're right. I am definitely concerned too."

Communication plays delicate matter. If the thing that one guy would understand were the same as the one that the other guy would understand, the communication would go easy. But if that were not the same, the relevant parties would sweat it out: perspiration, drudgery, upset, anxiety, distraction, and any hard nut to crack. If a person who comprehends what the reality and its significance are, he emerges as a plausible leader to shoot any trouble. A problem transpires when people misunderstand happenings to their interest. The human mind

Article 9: Communicating Capability

tends to stick with their interest not to see the reality of their environment. The one who seizes the reality better can conduct better communication.

When overwhelming capability bears out its awesome mightiness, it can calm down any protest or any opposition from any conflicting interest group. Only overwhelming capability can persuade them from their differences. Balanced powers could hardly settle the differences. However, the troika figured that comprehending the environment and its reality must have preceded issuing orders or commanding something to be done. That was where the troika drew a conclusion to activate a special force of human resources and to pile up data of human resources before the second hearing.

August 15, 2016, the U.N. General Assembly Hall once again attracted the world's most intensive attention up to the hilt. The whole world was glued to TV. The event fascinated observers. Everyone on Earth flattered each one in watching this odd phenomenon. Most people thought this queer standout featured a deluge of illusions or hallucinations. People imagined that nothing else in their life could entertain their fantasies or pipedreams as likely as this event. The giant stature of the world superpowers looked like a puppy's wagging tail. Up to now, the big powers did not have anything to lose, and did not hurt their prestige either.

With the second hearing of the Super Constitution, the world nations would not feel any knock-off effect just because of a word of the global government; the global government had not opened its package. But they sensed the power of the global government would tower above any governing forces on Earth. It would overshadow many historical affairs as mentioned on the first hearing of the Super Constitution by ten panelists: rattling political institute, sweeping official world language, only one military power, simplified and deeply downsized tax reform, fresh social reorganization, people's

Super Constitution

extraordinarily new general concept, entirely creative welfare work, revolutionized plausible business practice, dramatically inspiring educational issues, and so on.

The spokesperson for the Office of Communication of the U.N. Georgio Provonsky appeared on major TV networks at 8 p.m. Eastern time, grimaced with the instructive papers from his country of Russia.

"Good evening, my fellow world people, according to Miss Ohara's promulgation number two, my country's president instructed me to present myself as a candidate for the global president, the present Russia's chief justice as the global justice, and the present Russia's congressional leader as the global congressional chairman. Thank you everyone!"

Russia's Provonsky announced tersely and returned to his seat. The audience of the world felt a downcast against their elated expectations. People of the world went through dumbfound and stood aghast at the same announcement followed on by the U.S. and China's ambassadors. The U.N. General Assembly Hall and the whole world paused in dead silence. Everyone felt a chill running through one's spine. The first head-on collision between the three powers and the most mysterious Miss Ohara sparked thunderously without any noise. The audience of the world imagined that a tornado had cut a swath of destruction through the U.N. hearing. The Super Constitution momentarily looked like committing a misstep.

The three powers showed off their gargantuan bureaucratic monster. Until now, Miss Ohara's appearances advanced with an irresistible force. The consequence of Miss Ohara's fifth appearance, which ordered to prepare candidates for the global government's top positions, met, all of a sudden, a dizzy canyon to cross. At this surprising challenge, color drained from the audience's face. The audiences of the world turned pale at the three powers' bold and rude gesture. That was a

Article 9: Communicating Capability

simple and quiet dare to test the will power of Miss Ohara. The spectators of the world momentarily experienced a tense moment on what sort of a terrible upshot would overflow at the U.N. General Assembly Hall.

The Office of Communication of the U.N. had finished their announcement of presenting nine candidates for the global government's top positions without any sincere consideration in about ten minutes. That brief announcement in no substance indicated that the three powers did not care about the global government's birth, influence, and its future. The concept of centralized governing power of the global government could not materialize in the three powers' hands because that meant a great power shift from the three powers to the one-super global government. The three powers did not like to lose their present status quo.

It signified a natural movement. It symbolized an intrinsic psychological credo. It divulged an indigenous, implicit action of the three powers' innate interest. Nobody wanted to lose its gripping paw on the present perquisite.

The three powers preferred a tug of war among them to succumbing to any superior force in the world. That was why they could not present the real, smart characters to muster the world's complicated affairs and to run the world. They would rather take a snail's pace to attack the current affair's problems than take on the posed challenges and problems that needed to be solved immediately. It was not in their interest to rectify the wrongs and lose their power.

After all, nobody could ask a cat to protect the fish in the fish bowl. In order to mobilize the Super Constitution, the global government needed a great deal of gifted people in many fields. Miss Ohara had to take action. Miss Ohara did a lot of homework to place a right talent on the position in case the three powers would not go cooperative. At the pinnacle of the intensive tension in the U.N. General Assembly Hall, Miss Ohara appeared with her full posture in front of the world through major TV channels. This marked the second actual in-person appearance.

"My fellow citizens of Earth, I am glad to come here tonight to deliver the name of the president of the global government and the schedule of the inauguration of the global government. I had expedited a special 'Human Resources Task Forces' with HR (human resources) experts, behind the closed doors in a substantial length of time. I hoped the three powers would cooperate positively. But I had to prepare for the case that the three powers could not provide a reasonable pool of talented people, as I wanted."

"I am going to give the list of ninety-six congressional leaders I selected with HR Task Forces along with eight Supreme Court members including one attorney general and one legal administrator, and 8 executive members for the global government's president. Also, I am going to give the inauguration schedule to the global president. My fellow citizens! The name of the president is Mr. George Kirkman. My dear Mr. George Kirkman, please stand up."

Miss Ohara, at the troika's special meeting the other day, made a decision for the spokesperson of the Office of Communication of the U.N. Georgio Provonsky, to send out unusual invitation cards to George Kirkman together with ninety-six future world congressional leaders, eight legal professionals, and nine cabinet members (including three special presidential aids of spokes person, budget director, and chief of staff): thirty subcommittee chairpersons in addition of thirty subcommittee secretary generals and another thirty subcommittee research generals of the future congress, and four vice chairpersons and two chairpersons of the world congress; five Supreme Court judges on top of one chief justice and one attorney general and one legal administrator.

Article 9: Communicating Capability

Those 113 special guests including George Kirkman were sitting among VIP's section of the General Assembly Hall. George Kirkman slowly stood up. He was a young man in his mid-thirties. He turned around 360 degrees to greet all audiences, lifting his two arms high and smiling a big smile.

People of the U.N. General Assembly Hall looked frozen for a moment and kept themselves quiet. People were stunned—there was no clapping, no whispering either, and the air was so quiet for a while until Miss Ohara continued upon George Kirkman's sitting down.

"My fellows, the earth citizens, I am glad to see all of those world government's 113 key fellows attended here. I would like to order all of those 113 key people to start organizing the global governments from the next week, according to the guidelines of the Super Constitution. My fellow earth citizens! I formally announce the start of the global governments. Thank you!"

The three powers lost their prestigious authority to be involved in the formulating process of the world's global governments by placing their bureaucratic advantage and their awesome interests prior to people's interests. Under only one Super Constitution, many nations' countless chauvinists, a great deal of interest groups, idle big shots, and hypocritical patriots would suffer from losing excessively profiteering privilege, which had exploited hard working people and extraordinarily procreative talents.

High tax, custom duties, bottomless waste of public fund, run-away negligence on the public expenses, and any of profiteering prerogatives of public offices should be eliminated. The global government under the Super Constitution was the only way to rectify the monstrous mess caused by thousands of years of chaotic human history. Virtually, the world had had no order.

The communication between the three powers and the troika had been opened but did not go through for the intended target. Now, the communication between the global governments and the troika had opened to make results.

Especially, U-Penn.'s (University of Pennsylvania State) gifted young professor George Kirkman emerged as a gem the troika found through the HR (Human Resources) Task Forces. George Kirkman, 36, born in 1980 in Austin, Texas, one of outstanding geniuses in the world, had skipped over four years during his junior and senior years of high school, in college and in graduate courses, one year each.

He got Ph.D. degree at U-Penn in mathematical economics on the subject of "hypothetical marginal effect of various social dynamisms of current economic affairs" induced by algebra. The above thesis had been written in ten pages, without any quotations, and only with narrated mathematical consequences by using algebraic function (example: ax plus bx plus c). The examining professors had to get help from a mathematic professor to understand the logic. The examining professors praised the thesis as the best ever in the current economics because of its strikingly clear logic in the relationships among economic affairs influencing each other.

The troika was impressed by not only George Kirkman's outstanding scholastic point, but also his hidden ambitions expressed in his unpublished book. The book talked about a modern version of Plato's "Republic," one of classic books written by the Greek philosopher Plato, 2,400 years ago. George Kirkman's idea identified with the troika's one. The only difference between the troika and Kirkman's book was that it did not present any of the technology the troika invented.

Article 9: Communicating Capability

George Kirkman wrote about a single world government that could carry out the job which would stop war, starvation, exploitation, public squander by reducing the present consumption of natural resources in half and increasing the present world's economic growth rate in triple. George Kirkman understood the troika's idea by reading the Super Constitution.The troika understood George Kirkman by reading Kirkman's modern version of Plato's "Republic." The communication between the troika and George Kirkman would be done easily.

The troika sent a message to George Kirkman. The message asked when Kirkman would like to have the inauguration. Kirkman answered right back: Kirkman would like to have the ceremony on August 25 in very simple manner and immediately assume organizing for a new world order.

The Russian army's Security Commander, brigadier one-star general Andrei Milovanov would run the intelligence ministry of the Global Government. He spoke fluent English. He graduated from Russian Military Academy with straight "A." He loved engaging himself to organize information-gathering institutes and analyze all major incidents and happenings. He was a born spy.

For the position of military minister in the Global Government, George Kirkman acknowledged Dr. Wang Yen-Jee, the Chinese Central Military Committee's strategic advisor to committee chairman. Wang Yen-Jee was a Harvard graduate majored in political science. He studied political science but he pursued an interest in military power and its organization all the time. His memory-power exerted an extraordinary capacity to contain five thousand people's names for several months after reading it two times, and learning by heart.

Super Constitution

For the minister of politics, the troika recommended Japanese historian Dr. Toro Yono, who taught world history at University of Tokyo. Dr. Toro Yono was a famous professor as well as a prominent history author. The current world's academic circle considered Dr. Toro Yono as one of giant figures in the field of contemporary philosophy. Dr. Yono's vision on the current world's historic direction moved every reader of his books.

For the minister of economics, the troika recommended Dr. Jay Kim who received Ph.D. degree from Stanford University: another outstanding economic professor teaching at Florida University. Originally, Dr. Kim studied physics. But Dr. Kim became ambitious in the current world affairs. In the field of the world's economic affairs, he especially emphasized mathematical concepts in dealing the current world's economic problems.

The most controversial and forward-moving sociologist in Germany Dr. Wolfgang Thierse, taught at University of Bonne. He was favored by George Kirkman, and was picked up for the post of ministry of sociology for the Global Government.

The above five ministers of the ministries of intelligence, military, politics, economics, and sociology, along with the chief of presidential staff, the director of presidential budget office, and the President's spokesperson, came to a total of eight key members for the President's cabinet. The official cabinet was formed and announced through major media instantly.

The first Inauguration Day of the Global President was set and announced to be August 25, 2016, with temporary offices arranged at the U.N. building.

Article 10

Beijing's Government

August 15, 2016,

Miss Ohara's sixth and 2nd visual appearance in front of the world through the major TV channels, in order to designate key people for running the Global Governments, had finally actuated the Super Constitution to rectify the existing lukewarm world order. The presently weak world order actually drifted in the doldrums because the balanced powers in the world had watched each other in a high tension. The big powers could exert an enormous influence. But no one had a crushing force to dominate the decision-making process.

Now, George Kirkman, young, charismatic, conspicuously talented, and energetically ambitious, came suddenly forward to the world from obscurity, armed with Miss Ohara's blessings. George Kirkman communicated with Miss Ohara long hours, regarding what to do first in politics and with military power management, along with brand new electronic equipments fabricated by John Smith and James Leigh. The new audiovisual gadgetry had been derived from the device the troika set up for communications with any person in the world.

The new, small, portable audiovisual gadgetry, in terms of function, resembled the device installed in the "Vault Room" of the troika's safe house. The portable new gadgetry consisted of two equipments, and had limited capacity in distance without a killing wave. One of the equipments had a thousand-mile radius fixed in a certain place while the other had a fifty-mile radius to communicate and watch in detail, which could be installed in an automobile. Both of them had to be hooked up to the main device, which had a control panel able to put those equipments into action. George Kirkman, intelligence minister Andrei Milovanov, and politics minister Dr. Toro Yono had been informed about these equipments.

They were dazzled. They felt they acquired millions in army manpower to expedite their governing ability. Now they felt they had a divine authority to materialize their idea. George Kirkman could install these equipments of gadgetry anywhere in the world to exert communicating capabilities with anybody he wanted, at anytime.

Intelligence Minister Andrei Milovanov could eavesdrop on anybody anywhere within a thousand-mile radius and could check anyplace anytime on the spot with a fifty-mile mobile equipment, the same as if he could look around his own garden or living room without exposing him to anybody else. Andrei Milovanov could provide with the Global Government any perfect information on anyone's whereabouts, their conversation, their attire, their facial expression, and any of their belongings.

George Kirkman talked to Dr. Toro Yono, the Minister of Politics.

Article 10: Beijing's Government

"Dr. Yono, I exchanged a lot of talks with Miss Ohara about the basic political framework we are going to set up."

"What type of framework is it?"

Kirkman explained to Dr. Yono as the following:

"Well, this is a very exciting idea, and a very challenging approach. Miss Ohara wants each nation to have a population from a minimum of twenty millions to a maximum of eighty millions. That means we have to divide big countries and to unify some of the small countries. Dr. Yono, could you draw the detailed blue print and discuss with me before we talk to Miss Ohara?"

"Sure, no problem, it is my pleasure. I used to dream of that idea pretty often."

The Politics Minister Dr. Toro Yono used to dream about the ideal form of the most efficient administrative unit of nation of the world, almost the same as the county of the U.S. state government: dividing, for example, India and China into twenty nations, and the U.S. and Russia into six nations. Japan would be divided into 2 nations, and the nations of Guatelama, Honduras, El Salvador, Nicaragua, Costa Rica, and Panama would be united into one nation.

The new world map of divided and unified nations would create a new political nucleus, which would direct the social growth and function in generating the new social value. Each nation would function as a neural network for the world's order, peace, and prosperity by coordinating under the Global Government's power. For the basic frame of the reference in the world politics, the above classification of division and unification must have been done as soon as possible. Kirkman named this program as "Yono Plan." Dr. Toro Yono squeezed out his extraordinarily gifted talent day and night in order to instantaneously draw up a magnificent master plan able to impress people of all walks of life, according to his long thought idea without any hesitation.

Kirkman, after long hours of discussion with Dr. Toro Yono on the detailed "Yono Plan" in his blue print, agreed with Dr. Yono on the detailed blue print. He sent the blue print to Miss Ohara through the Office of Communication of the Global Government's presidency according to a channel set up with the troika's "Vault Room."

The troika sat together with Michael Leigh to evaluate the "Yono Plan."

Brenda Chen initiated the conversation.

"Gentlemen, I guess the 'Yono Plan' sounds fascinating. I am sure it is going to shake the whole world. It is going to create a brand new, mega-weighted concept in the human mind for the first time since its written history. I am so delighted by the imagination about materializing the 'Yono Plan.' "

"I agree."

John Smith joined in the conversation.

"I think we are going to see a parade of the most wonderful and most beautiful surprises sooner or later. I think the Yono Plan is only an appetizer, and splendid main dishes are going to appear such as the world's single military organization, one economic unit, coexistence of various religions, multicultural correlation of the world and the practice of one-world language. I am really thrilled of thinking those things."

James Leigh followed, bearing a pleasant smile on his face.

Article 10: Beijing's Government

"You guys want too much, too fast. Those things look beautiful. They are not going to be done easily. Limited intelligent grip of average guys, a stupid inertia of mind set, egoistic and sticky interest of headlong and headstrong majority people, bureaucratic knots and mob psychology would pitch a camp on the way. How are you guys going to sweep away those monstrous lumps?"

"James, you are right. Every coin has another side. We have to always think of and prepare for something to deal the negative side along with the positive side. James, do you have any idea about liquidating the negative side?"

Brenda asked a question to James with a serious posture.

James talked in a decisive manner.

"In liquidating the negative side, first, you have to understand its nature and scale. Second, you have to prepare an overwhelming power to crush it and establish a perfect schedule to sweep it out. The nature of the negative side has no reason to be persuaded. Argument is never going to work. No generosity should be applied. So we have to exercise a super strict order. We have already talked about 'crushing force' several times, in order for the people involved to acknowledge the downright upshot of their negligence. Of course, we must try our best to minimize the killing. But then again, we must make our determination visible, final and absolute."

Michael Leigh advised.

"I guess we should analyze the cruel reality of the negative side all the time. Also, George Kirkman and his cabinet should brainstorm too. Nevertheless, we have to take a careful watch on the effect of an overflow in the process of the plan. Something unexpected could be tossed in. Otherwise, I am sure the Yono Plan will be a wonderful appetizer in our program."

Brenda concluded their evaluation of the Yono Plan.

"We conclude the Yono Plan has been firmly based on wisdom. George Kirkman and his cabinet members should carry on the wisdom through over all unlit rough roads, chaotic tunnels, useless by-paths and many obstacles. But we are sure we will prevail. I am going to give the go-signal to Kirkman."

George Kirkman announced the detail of the Yono Plan to the world through his Communication Office without any delay. The Yono Plan shook the world, shocked the super powers such as the U.S., Russia, and China. It, literally, shattered the iron shell of Chinese awesome Politburo, which was composed of nine supreme political decision-makers in a form of oligarchy. China's Politburo dictated Chinese governing capacity by setting up national agenda, directions, and procedures.

Now, China's preeminent "Invincible Armada" of the Politburo faced a moment of imminent perishing. China must be divided into twenty nations, according to the new map drawn by the Yono Plan. Each nation of the world must proceed to elect its own governments as soon as possible according to the decree of the Yono Plan.

Hot potatoes were thrown into the hands of China's Politburo, and the nine members stood on a hot tin roof. The Politburo members conducted heated debates. The Government of Beijing was virtually placed into a boiling pot. The President of Beijing's Government must present his follow-up blue print for organizing twenty nations' executive branches in one month until the end of September.

Article 10: Beijing's Government

Inside the closed door of Politburo Office in the conferencing, hot debates had boiled up one after another for long hours. Among a number of countless arguments, one Politburo member continued his argument.

"Comrades, the unbelievable has happened. It seems to me we don't have any power, any choice, but to succumb to the orders from the Global Government."

At this display of heated desperation, another Politburo member quietly argued as the following:

"The killing wave has not tested yet. We have not seen the horrible destructive power of the killing wave. Besides us, there are Russia, the U.S., India, and many other formidable countries that oppose the Global Government. Just think about it: the Global Government has only a handful of players while their opposing powers are a bagful. We also have to consider the image of Miss Ohara: Miss Ohara, I guess, cannot, and will not dare to exhibit a cruel bloodshed to the world. Our country has three thousand years of written history, the most integrated race and culture, and the most distinguished national territory. If our country were divided into twenty nations, a bewailing fate would wrap us forever. We have to fight, resist, and at least try to compromise something."

Another Politburo member, C also argued strongly.

"My fellow members, if we unite to resist in spite of facing death, we will save our great country. If we just seek survival under an intimidation, we will perish. If we dare to risk our life, we will survive. We would better die rather than we would witness our country's sinking. I am willing to sacrifice my personal life to preserve our country's integrity.

Politburo member D stood up firmly, with a grave look on his face.

Super Constitution

"My beloved comrades, I am desperately determined to do my holy duty to protect my country. What is our job here? It is so clear. We must demonstrate and instill our intrepid loyalty to our country and people. I would die a hero's death rather than would live as a laughing stock of the world. We have a big country: a great deal of populations, economic strength, military power, and the most important spiritual culture, which resonates in the flood-tide nationalism. I am sure we have to withstand."

Another Politburo member E obtained the floor for his voice.

"Great comrades, do you really realize how great we are, how strong we are, and how gallantly our people support our nation? The consequence of our surrender is as clear as black and white. Our yield to the killing wave only indicates we are cowards and moronic schizophrenias, and merely proves we are wise guys or turncoats."

He impressively gazed around his listening colleagues.

"We are giants. We have to understand ourselves. We must recognize our grand conception and mentality. We should not be scared of death. We have lived a good life so far. Instead of having a dreadful and despicable life, we would better disappear from the ugly scene. My fellow comrades! Let's stand up for our dignity."

The debate and deliberation continued in favor of rising up against the order of the Global Government to divide the China into twenty nations.

Politburo member F emphasized as the following:

"During last three thousand years of written history of China, our country has suffered from internecine wars continuously exchanging the division and unification periodically. But our

Article 10: Beijing's Government

country's unique native culture has bonded our existence, and created resilient Chinese philosophy, which depicts a logical depth of the human nature and has inherited respectful moral values to the human society. The specific civilization of China has been developed and carved into a tractable trace. China played a guide to the world history. Now, cutting China apart into twenty pieces will rescind China from history. The global Government's order to divide China will engrave an inerasable stigma on China's history which is about to happen during the age of our steering term."

Two additional members argued for fighting against the division. All of the Politburo members, one by one, opened each one's heart tersely. Except for the first and last member, seven members expressed their negative opinion on the division of China. All of their negative opinions focused on a fighting spirit and preserving China's integrity. The last member's speech, nevertheless, hit the bull's eye in this inexorable moment.

"My fellow comrades, I agree with all of your points of view. However, we have to face the cruel reality. All of us know politics has hinged on a physical power but not on metaphysics at all. We have an indisputable history and an undeniable culture. China has established fine moral values, deep philosophy, historical achievements, and honored heritage. People traditionally enjoyed courageous patriotism and national pride. China's integrity as a unit of a national entity overwhelmingly outweighs any attempts to erase its great scene from the world stage. Dividing China will only magnify a terrible shame. It is going to surely reflect the greatest mistake in the human history."

He paused for a moment, and then continued.

"Unfortunately, we are in facing the biggest tsunami wave of an invisible technological power and the uncompromising globalization-demand. Fundamentally, we cannot fight against an invisible nemesis with our eyes blinded. What's more, the Global Government's globalization-demand rides on the crest of the people's favor. And the demand looks winning the people's mind in every case, with each passing day."

The last Politburo member's abysmal tone but clearly visional conclusion swept the floor of the heavily weighted office into a silent desolation. The hot debate and utterance for fighting spirit, all of a sudden, stood on the edge of a cliff. However, the first Politburo member, who spoke about accepting Global Government's order without resistance, broke a bleak silence of the Politburo member's conference-room.

"My fellow comrades, there might be a way for us to work through this. I would like to present a compromise to the Global Government."

The chairman gave a right to the Politburo member A to speak out for his idea of "compromise."

"Thank you, Mr. Chairman, and all esteemed members here today!"

He cleared his throat, and began speaking, nervously at first but slowly gaining confidence with the momentum of his speech.

"Well, first, my idea is this. According to some promulgation, the Global Government has a special temporary agenda and procedure for fulfilling the aims of the Super Constitution in setting up the Global Governments during the first term. In other words, instead of having a general election by the people for the executive members and legislative bodies of the Global Governments, Miss Ohara is going to appoint, through a special apparatus, the job of executives and legislatives for the start-up of the new world organizations. So, all of these bring me to my idea: we should ask the Global Government to

Article 10: Beijing's Government

appoint the slate our Politburo submits for organizing twenty nations, so that we can manipulate them and continue to keep China's current mainframe for its integrity and philosophy."

The highly tense mood of the Politburo's conference-room had been changed from the rigidity to the ductility. When a desperate mind accepts death as an unavoidable reality, it will take any path that leads to a way out as an excuse. If the Global Government agreed with the Chinese Politburo's slated appointment, then it would save face for the Politburo while reducing workload of the Global Government. It will not only make the Global Government less work but also will furnish the Global Government with a justification to substitute for a wrong appointment in case the slated appointments prove improper.

This idea of compromise looked feasible. After receiving communications on the matter, George Kirkman found he shared the same view with Minister of Politics Dr. Toro Yono on the matter.

The idea of the compromise on the slated accommodation soon made its way to the troika's table. Brenda initiated the conversation.

"Gentlemen, what do you think about this offer on the slate-idea of the Chinese politics?"

As usual, John clearly asserted his idea.

"The slate means collective leadership. It is a close game with a leadership of the Politburo. It could create a coterie or a band of cluster to form a united front. If they form and organize a gang to achieve one entity, dividing China into twenty nations could become a mere scrap of paper. I'd like to hear something on this slate-matter from James. James usually point one side with the other side together to be able to make a comfortable decision."

Brenda looked at James, and asked a question. James, with a sober countenance, replied to Brenda.

"Basically, I agree with John. The slated practice comes and goes, to dictate or monopolize a decision-making power for a certain sector's homogeneous interest. Of course, it is a form of coterie. But it has a weak composition as an entity. Even though the appointment comes as a whole at one time, the individual head of twenty nations is going to be one distinct entity. The individual entity of twenty nations already forms an essential and independent part of the whole China. The Global Government's political order can exert an absolute power to disperse the informal collective gatherings of twenty nations. The individual entity moves like a liquid while the authority of our Super Constitution acts like a solid form. The solid form can forge a form of liquid flow of an individual entity onto a fragment. It resembles a universal physical law. Once China divided, that denotes the end of one China."

James's interpretation of the cohesive power in the slated appointment cleared away some doubtful consideration on the process disbanding China's one political entity. Each unit of twenty nations of China would develop its own governing power and style for its own region's interest. Once each unit begins making deals with the Global Government, each unit will no longer consult the others for the whole of the twenty nations, which do not exist as one unit. The concept of twenty nations as one entity carries only vague name; but it has no substance of military power, diplomatic authority, and communicating capability.

Meanwhile, Beijing's central government maintained the governing body while preparing the slated appointment-list. Hundreds of thousands of government officials and military

Article 10: Beijing's Government

staffs of Beijing's government felt void, lethargic, weightless, and chaotic. High-ranking official's imposing and demanding look turned its color from an awesome sight to a drab scene. Their condescending posture and authentic power reputations went withered by the announcement of the central government's breakup.

India, Russia, U.S.A., and all other nation's capitals on Earth suffered a shock at the loss of central government. But Beijing's government felt the weight of shocking wave most heavily as it had exercised the most immense central power in the greatest effectiveness with the most desirable results. Beijing's government felt the storm of upheaval from the changes of global power most severely.

The nature of human political power has been described by the history again and again through endless wars, revolutions, violent demonstrations, legal battles, diplomatic wrangles, and election campaigns. The political power looks like Aladdin's jinn. Whatever the possessor demands to be done, will be done. Beijing's government could not help but listen to Miss Ohara's promulgation and the Global Government's orders.

Beijing's central government maintained the communicating institutes, presidential office and military organizations as they were, until a further instruction from the Global Government. All the former China's local governments would be separated into twenty nations according to the Yono Plan. The China's president broadcasted the list of slate formed by former China's central Politburo members through "CCTV" (central China's television station). All of a sudden, twenty nations in the old China went on for its daily business without Beijing's government but with the new Global Government. Still, the armada of the old China's huge military organizations would have to idly stand by until receiving the orders on what to do from the Global Government.

Super Constitution

Since Beijing's government had been ordered to dissolve all the central governmental organizations except the communication institutes, presidential office and military organizations, all the central government's offices executed a voluntary windup without any disbanding ceremony. Without the central government, each government of the twenty nations of the old China received their president appointed by the slated list. Each government of the twenty nations must organize a legislative body and the court of law with the brand new president who made a descent through a high-handed personnel administration.

Also each nation had to adopt the appropriate mode of operation for the trade of import and export, the appropriate administration for the migration of people, and the appropriate diplomacy. Beijing's government, virtually, had been suspended from action, emptied its function, kept silent, and formed into a complete inertia: a social phenomenon of a political demise.

The Yono Plan organizer Toro Yono, Minister of Politics of the Global Government, sat down across the rectangular conference table facing George Kirkman, exchanged a serious political talk with Kirkman.

"President Kirkman, the vacuum status of Beijing's government has created some big chaos, which every walk of life never imagined. It truly sounds a spectacular bang, which resonates all over the world. I cannot figure it out how long the ripple effect is going to make that hair-raising trip."

"Well, Dr. Yono, I guess you have to work out the economic mode with Minister of Economics Dr. Jay Kim (p. 144). To begin with, the political frame you set up must now be filled by an ideal economic mode. Otherwise, the frame will easily crumble."

Article 10: Beijing's Government

"I understand what you mean. I think economy plays the content to make politics alive. A good political frame forms a handsome and strong shell. The economic life is going to settle its ideal flesh in that shell. I have to rush things with Dr. Kim."

The next day, Toro Yono discussed things with Dr Kim at his office. Toro Yono initiated the conversation.

"Dr. Kim, I think we have to give some clear guidelines to the twenty nations of former China for economic activities on the matter of trade, customs, and migrations."

"Dr. Yono, you are right. I have a general idea of the blue print on the matter of trade, customs, and migration. My plan would sweep all the garbage of the old regulations in the world trade. The old regulations, which had been made only according to the interest of each nation's national niche, contradict each other and block a smooth natural flow of economic activities of the world people. People suffered from the burden, which had been produced by those regulations. People pay too much unnecessary taxes which in turn pushes economic costs higher to cause to retard economic growth and to harm people's welfare."

"Well, Dr. Kim, I am very much interested in your plan's detail. When are you going to have the plan printed?"

"Dr. Yono, basically, I am going to have a preliminary rough plan. I have to take care of urgent occurrences followed by your new political map of the Yono Plan. The change of Beijing's government brewed a first incident in a mega size, which irritates the most significant stir in history. We face the most monstrous tackle in our project. It surely challenges our determination. But I have a piece of cake to handle that transition."

Super Constitution

Toro Yono, having glistening eyes upon hearing Dr. Jay Kim's confident hint, admired Jay Kim's rough plan, which was yet to be unfolded.

"Dr. Kim, what is the outline of your preliminary rough plan to handle the transitional bubble of Beijing's government?"

"The preliminary rough plan is simple. Each of the twenty nations should take the guidelines or standards or regulations of former China. Until the Global Government's decrees come to their table, they have to follow the old rule as a temporary measurement. I am going to prepare a general direction for that temporary measurement which has to be moderated here and there. However, I am going to set up a brand new concrete plan sooner or later."

Toro Yono took a deep breath, and thanking Jay Kim on his quick answers, mentioned about his downright feeling on the impact of the absence of Beijing's government.

"Dr. Kim, the sheer impact of the nihilism of Beijing's central government   banged my ear much heavier than my imagination. Your confidence relieved my stress   from the mud. I wish your plan strikes the bull's eye sooner or later."

"Don't worry, Dr. Yono, my plan will play havoc with all of those worries and those rubbishy regulations."

Toro Yono worried about some negative consequences of the disappearance of Beijing's government. But Jay did not worry at all. In fact, Jay Kim, riding on a buoyant political upgrade of the global politics, kicked off his ambitious global economic plan which would reduce the world's economic cost to half while booming the world's economic activities double to relieve poverty from the world.

Article 10: Beijing's Government

Jay, along with a strong sensation on the global rise of people's genuine welfare state, felt a thrilling academic victory over the dumb bureaucratic authority. The tardy mentality of bureaucracy had killed an efficient process of procreative academic advance because of the bureaucrat's hardened selfish-interest.

The paradigm of the Global Government's restructuring of the political framework and economic policy would guide the world to a new civilization. To Jay Kim, the transformation of Beijing's government into twenty nations meant fresh hope for the rise of people's interest.

Therefore, Jay could not have any doubt on the rise of the Global Government. Jay would not have any worry on Miss Ohara's intention. Jay had a confidence in Miss Ohara's mystic technology, Miss Ohara's iron management of the technology's secrecy, and her genius in dealing consequences.

Since Jay's early college days in validating some of mathematically logical economic formula, which transcends Fisher's monetary theory or Rostow's idea on strategic economic development for the developing countries, or Adam Smith's the "wealth of nations," his pipe dream as a mathematical genius in the human social affairs met its momentum through troika's mystic technology and George Kirkman's global team.

The dramatic emergence of the Global Government and the Global Government's hand pick of Jay Kim as the Minister of Economics helped increase the level of Jay's serotonin. (A potent chemical that functions as a neuron transmitter, is localized in distinct regions of the brain, and changes mental states by its concentration: an increase of the serotonin level enhances creative ideas; and an increase happens when a brain feels ecstasy or success.) Jay's academic theory supported by the troika and Global Government indeed gave a pungent wit to Jay. Jay's morale soared into the sky to be able to see the earth as a ball.

Now, from the next page on, we are going to see what's happening in Moscow and Washington, D.C. in the globalizing process.

Article 11

Citadel of Moscow

According to Miss Ohara's 2nd personal appearance (p. 140), the global President, 36 years old, George Kirkman's first job with Dr. Toro Yono was a handling of China's division into 20 nations. Now, his 2nd job with Dr. Yono was a handling of Russia's political reshuffle and the WMD (weapons of mass destruction).

At page ninety-six (Article Seven: Killing Power), on Miss Ohara's 2nd vocal appearance of June 7, 2016, Miss Ohara ordered three world powers to organize a "special commission to decommission all the weapons systems of nuclear, biological, and chemical arms" along with the issuance of the commencement of the "Super Constitution."

At page 110 (Article Eight: Delivering Means), on Miss Ohara's 3rd vocal appearance of July 1, 2016, Brenda delivered some instructions about the special commission's organization and its job as the following: the five member nations would be Germany, France, India, Japan, and South

Super Constitution

Korea; decommissioning all the WMD except ten nuclear war heads with ten pieces of launching equipments in Russia and the U.S. respectively; and the official name of the special commission: the WMD Commission.

Over the phone, George Kirkman, President of the Global Government, talked to the President of Russia.

"Mr. President, how are you? This is George Kirkman from my office in the U.N. building. I am sending our Minister of Politics Dr. Toro Yono and Military Minister Dr. Wang Yen Jee, to discuss the matter of decommissioning your country's WMD the next week. I wish you could produce a constructive and creative historical landmark. The world is watching your all-embracing initiative. Please accept my congratulations for the great result in advance."

The Russian President, being out of temper on George Kirkman's almost insulting challenge, felt an imminent temperamental outburst; however, he exercised a temperate response.

"Yes, thank you Mr. President Kirkman. I would try my best to draw up a nice result for decommissioning the WMD."

"Thank you Mr. President Brodsky. I wish you good luck."

George Kirkman ended the phone-talk calmly and decisively, figuring that the Russian President took on struggling against a stress for the sake of Russia's safety and interests. The Russian people saw the simple change of big China in broad daylight. George Kirkman was aware of that Dr. Yono and Wang carried a bundle of policies of monstrous demand, which Russian politicians would severely agonize themselves.

Russia stands out in the world as the world's largest country (8,749, 500 square miles covering one-sixth of the total land

Article 11: Citadel of Moscow

surface of the earth; however, since Russia's falloff in 1991, the size of land had been reduced to 76% of the former Russia to 6,592,800 spuare miles; still, the largest country in the world). Russia boasts the world's greatest hydroelectric resources: more than 120,000 rivers. Even though the Russian language represents official one, more than 100 ethno linguistic groups use its own language as a co-official. Russia's wealth of natural mineral resources count as the world's largest: its coal, petroleum, and natural gas reserves demand among the largest in the world. Still depending on western imports for its food requirement, Russian agriculture's development has become highly mechanized on a large scale, producing one of the largest volumes of potatoes, sugar beets, wheat, barley, oats, corn, and rye.

The Politburo of the communist party used to pioneer the real seat of political power before its collapse during 1990s. Since the Vladimir Lenin's Bolsheviks defeated Russian Czar 1920, forming the Union of Soviet Socialist Republics, through Joseph Stalin and Nikita Khrushchev, Russia used to hurl the awesome nemesis to the free world. It commands more than 20,000 nuclear warheads in its vast land (the U.S. commands about 10,000 nuclear warheads), including the most formidable armed forces of an army, Air Force, navy, air defense, and intelligence network of KGB.

The Moscow "Kremlin Palace" originally built in 1156, which had continued its enlargements and reconstructions from the 16th century, has been used for the executive branch of the government of Russia especially in regard to its foreign affairs. The Kremlin has been considered by the people of the world as a black hole of secret political affairs. The executive branch of Russia conducted monstrous job of the biggest business on the most complicated human affairs on the earth: not by a democratic way but by dictatorship and secret police state.

Super Constitution

On the above serious circumstances, all sorts of anxieties dominate the job: dread, nightmare, and phobia could threaten the jobholder's mind day and night. They needed an absolute power to grasp what was going on. The Kremlin, the executive branch's palace became a synonym for world-class secret headquarters. However, actually, the modern paramount reputation on the Kremlin has come along with the existence and activity of the KGB.

The acronym of KGB stands for "Committee for State Security" in Russian. Organized in 1954, reaching back to the "Cheka" created in 1917 by the Bolshevik for combating counterrevolution and sabotage, the KGB is the largest secret police and ever-enigmatic espionage in the world. Its organization is comprised of 17 entities with a number of chief directorates concerned on such matters as counter intelligence, foreign espionage, and internal security. For an example, one of the chief directorates, the Border Guards Chief Directorate controls the KGB's 300,000 troops with armor, artillery, and naval vessels. The KGB's professional competence is widely respected and whose power and influence press enormously. The KGB conducts the most extensive espionage-operations in the world, sometimes using "covers" such as Soviet trade organizations, the Soviet news agency "Tass" as well as the diplomatic covers. The KGB is known to have infiltrated every major Western intelligence services.

On October 2, 2016, Dr. Yono and Wang and their entourage arrived at Moscow international airport in the early afternoon. The weather was chilly and sunny as usual in the fall season of Moscow. The official protocol called for the Global Government's ministers as the level of a nation's president. In real life, there are about more than 200 nations' presidents versus only eight cabinet members in the Global Government. Not only a number of positions, but quality of power, caliber of talent, weight of responsibility, impact of influence and spill-over effect of leadership are poles asunder.

Article 11: Citadel of Moscow

The creativity, integrity, and vision of the Global Government's cabinet members play the most critical role in steering the current world affairs. In addition, the cabinet members could exercise an omnipotent authority in dealing the world's prominent affairs through the spirit of the Super Constitution and Miss Ohara's delegation of power.

These two geniuses Dr. Yono and Dr. Wang are actually academic and deskbound nobodies. Just because extraordinary authority to conduct the supreme global job was vested in these two guys on the matter of world politics and military concerns, they looked like a 600-pound gorilla to the world's national presidents, especially to the powerful governing members of Russia. Russian President Fyodor Brodsky, under heavy pressure from the wave of China's division into 20 nations, received the Yono and Wang party at the Kremlin palace amidst intricate feelings and the mood of anxiety, melancholy, and pessimism in the late morning, on October 3, 2016.

The Russian President Brodsky welcomed the Yono and Wang party with a pleasant gesture and expression on the floor of majestic reception hall of the Kremlin.

"Welcome, Dr. Yono and Dr. Wang! It is my honor to meet you. I have been hearing about the Yono Plan. It has indeed made a lightning quick change. Frankly speaking, I envy the job you have achieved in your marvelous profession. Now, I am under a circumstance to look forward to hearing from you on the matter of dividing Russia into six nations and decommissioning the WMD of the world."

President Brodsky spoke very fluent English. Dr. Wang responded while smiling.

"Mr. President Brodsky, it is my pleasure to meet you in this historic palace. I heard you received Ph.D. degree in politics in America. I am excited to hear your excellent English. I feel I am meeting one of my old senior classmates. Mr. President, please feel free to be optimistic of me. I know what your circumstance is, and I think I know what you want. I am not here to give you a stress, but actually I am here to help you."

President Brodsky was startled by Dr. Wang's straightforward manner of talking without any hesitation. Anyway, President Brodsky felt somewhat relieved of stress upon hearing Dr. Wang's concern on his state of mind-boggling uncertainty.

In regards to the decommissioning job of the WMD in addition to dividing Russia into six nations, Russian supreme key leaders had endless meetings and conferences, brainstorming for the best ideas and solutions. Not only a political restructure and a new economic environment, but also the subjects of gargantuan military institutes, the titanic KGB network, and other heaping-up crucial matters, had knocked them out to exhaustion. They badly needed a strong and fresh rescue team.

Not only Russia, but also the U.S., Iran, and North Korea, as well as a lot of other big powers and famous dictators worked hard with a great deal of trouble, struggling and wriggling in agony as they tried to save at least some of their preexisting perquisites. They truly scrambled quietly, clutching at a straw. They would not spare even a last spurt-effort. Since China's sudden mutation, every nation's chiefdoms lost their commanding sense. They stood dumbfounded. Virtually, their nervous systems went numb.

China's example went great for the Global Government's favor. All of the authentic powerful stature of giant Goliath became pitiful, dwarf-sized trifling toys. People used to consider the world, especially the world's political power balance or power struggle as a labyrinthine puzzle or as an invincible wizard. But now to the people of the world, the world looked like an enjoyable ballgame on the ground played

Article 11: Citadel of Moscow

by professional players. People no longer had to be frightened away over wild, ferocious, 400-pound cats, but would enjoy patting 10-pound, cute cubs. The power shift in human affairs by any means could change the situation of command as easy as pie.

Dr. Yen-Jee Wang, together with Dr. Toro Yono, read and understood the hidden reality of President Brodsky's stressful, mind-boggling status over the matters of Russian division, the destiny of Russian military future, the spectacular, full scope of the KGB network. Dr. Wang and Yono assessed their efforts of how to capitalize on the highest quality of raw materials of Russia's abysmal human and natural resources. The great lump of concerns majestically loomed on the horizon. The stake weighed too heavy. Handling the WMD deal came to the surface as only an entering job of the front door. Dr. Wang's agenda, above all things, focused on the spot for the liquidation of the WMD. That would bring a wedging point. That would bring a substantial leverage to open a highway toward an effective prelude to world politics, one-world military organization, one-world economic determinism (admiring resources, productive capacity, technologies, and distribution of wealth), and one-world language.

However, the boiling anxiety of President Brodsky's mind-set rattled his capacity to make a deal with Dr. Wang and Dr. Yono. Reading well Mr. Brodsky's mind-set, Dr Wang presented his agenda for the WMD to the Russian President at the conference table

"Mr. President, as our President George Kirkman, I assume, indicated over the phone with you, I would like to explain to you about the plan the Global Government has set for the liquidation of the WMD."

"What about the matter of the division of Russia, the Russian military machines, and the KGB network?"

Super Constitution

"Mr. President, those things are going to be addressed by Dr. Yono right after your full understanding the general process of dismantling the WMD. Upon the basis of your understanding the procedure of dismantling the WMD, I am sure, your mind-set will settle down into better ductility. Mr. President, I hope that you will get out of the straight jacket of pressing stress from the Russian frame. The hard shell of your Russian frame, you don't have to shoulder anymore. The older Russian chapter is a history. If you would drag yourself through a past history, you could not create a new history. The door of the old history has been already locked. The door of the new history has been already opened. Mr. President, please be my guest. I want a friendship with you."

Upon Dr. Wang's pleasant gesture, President Brodsky wondered why this guy Dr. Wang was approaching him with a sunshine policy instead of with a heavy hand or a high hand even though they have a dominant crushing force. Russian leaders had heard about a cruel crushing force behind the charming Miss Ohara's attractive and sexy appearance. Russian leaders expected Dr. Wang and Yono party would lay an overwhelmingly charismatic impression on the table. But their attitude appeared too humble. Their talking manner sounded too soft. Their overture behaved too gentle.

President Brodsky even sensed some sort of lull in a storm. Extremely condensed and powerful sudden change in even the most fluidal air could create tornadoes or typhoons. The overnight change of the colossal Russia's mighty complex of the most sophisticated politics, most significant military institutes, most intricate network of the KGB, and most composite interlocking of its social fabric could breed a seed of a whirlwind. George Kirkman's Cabinet might reap the whirlwind.

George Kirkman, the Global President, Dr. Yen-Jee Wang, the Global Military Minister, and Dr. Toro Yono, the Global

Article 11: Citadel of Moscow

Minister of Politics, represented outstanding, world-class geniuses and equipped themselves with shrewd integrity for the current world affairs.

They were well aware of the dominant crushing force of the troika's technology. They knew how to use the force in cracking down on local governments. Nevertheless, they also fully understood a basic trait of the human mind in terms of "acknowledgement": the acknowledgement on quality, performance, ability, environment, reality and so on. Especially, intelligent, experienced, and educated people form acknowledgement-sensitive behavior. It is even much easier to handle those people rather than dumb greedy character. We can trust their capacity, consistency, and wits. The best policy to move witty people originates from the acknowledgement.

Acknowledgement grows very well through humility and generosity. The global cabinet members also understood that they need a pool of human resources in every field. They had to cultivate the motivation to move mass human resources across the world, in all walks of life. Of course, the global cabinet had a monstrous scare tactics behind them. But they knew the scare tactics must be used as a last resort.

Dismantling the WMD required a good management of technological expertise, political and financial support from relevant super powers of such as G8 countries or the like. The WMD commission which was composed of Germany, France, India, Japan, and South Korea had already advanced in the area of financial arrangement, and finished organization of sub committees of nuclear arms, biological germs, chemical warfare, inspection, demolition, dumping, and HR (human resources) totaling to seven subcommittees.

Dr. Wang's job for dismantling the WMD of the world mainly consisted of securing Russian President Brodsky's positive follow-up cooperation for the sake of acquiring Russian experts in the WMD as for Dr. Wang's special aid on top of obtaining the portfolio of total Russian WMD. Getting the portfolio and Russian experts in the WMD from President Brodsky's cooperation, denoted half the total job of dismantling the WMD of the world. Naturally, Russian President wanted quid pro quos for his full cooperation.

Russian President Brodsky valued three agenda: the subject of the division of Russia, its military machines, and the KGB– the most overpowering concerns.   In fact, to the Russian leaders, dismantling the Russian WMD did not set forth any crucial damage. But they figured they could extract something salvageable from the shake-up of Russia into the new world order. However, to the Global Government, to the Minister of Politics Dr. Yono and the Minister of Military Dr. Wang, the agenda of the WMD signified the most urgent homework because getting rid of the WMD could drag by endlessly. The job of getting rid of WMD would entail time consuming effort and dangerous involvements from the start to the end.

The steady accumulation of the WMD throughout more than half dozen decades had formed a menacing presence. It did not mean a simple cleaning job. It resembled a job of a bomb-defusing squad. Any mistake of the sophisticated technology could produce a disaster like the U.S.'s three-island nuclear generator or a breakdown of Russia's Chernobyl nuclear power plant. The poisons of chemical weapons raised a very serious challenge in dealing scientific knowledge and technology for its complicated dissecting process. Also the biological weapons contained terribly scary disease-producing germs or viruses which human being couldn't see and could spread without human's notice. With those WMD, we just could not simply throw everything away or dump them out.

Making a decision on dismantling and actual processing job did not matter too much conflicting. The real hazard on getting rid of the WMD had double-edged danger. The one indicated

Article 11: Citadel of Moscow

the possibility of creating endless dangers on the earth by mistake or mismanagement. The other one pointed out the unexpected consequences of damaged impression of the Global Government's reputation in case of dragging by or unfortunate accidents. Fully realizing the perilous minefields ahead on the process of getting rid of the WMD, Kirkman's cabinet members established one secret plan appealing to "Machiavellianism."

Kirkman, Yono, and Wang had concluded their conversation about the dismantling job before Yono and Wang's arrival at Moscow. They implanted two tactics in their mind. One plan was to frankly brief Russian leaders about the potential dangers and time consuming dragging of the dismantling job. The Global Government genuinely sought Russian leaders' positive cooperation for the completion of the job. The other tactic implanted in their mind dwelled on using a Machiavellianism: a political secret promise on the de facto federal system of 6 nations of Russia; so the Russia's political cohesion could temporally continue by its head nation.

The Global Government figured that they could reason to the world as a model case. The Global Government figured they could change anytime according to the situation later after solidifying dismantlement of the WMD. Often, people describe power struggles or manipulation as a Machiavellianism. It used to work as one of natural phenomena. Dr. Wang informed President Brodsky of a special promise approved by Miss Ohara for the "Russian de facto federal system" after briefing him on the dismantling process of the WMD.

Upon Dr. Wang's sincere remark in a secret political promise of de facto Russian federation, President Brodsky felt more or less sentimental, rather than thought-out functional calculus: compassionate rather than cognitive: inclination toward emotion. Emotion effected much stronger than cold calculation in pushing a target of human affairs. President Brodsky immediately responded.

"Dr. Wang, I appreciate your sincere consideration on our concern for the Russian political framework. Taking Russia as a model case for a bigger unit of national entity, I would keep that plan in silence until an official announcement would be issued from the Global Government."

"Thank you! Mr. President. I am going to discuss the matter of an official announcement with President George Kirkman. And, I am going to inform you about the major developments of the discussion."

In this way, the Yono and Wang party seemed to achieve their intention on the Russian front: satisfying the present Russian leadership on the matter of political restructure and drawing up Russia's full cooperation on the matter of dismantling the WMD.

However, the Russian military brass and top KGB directorates had raised some doubt about Miss Ohara's current address in its origin. They wondered about if Miss Ohara actually disguised a piece of work of the U.S. Therefore, the Russian military and KGB had steadily tried to trace Miss Ohara's footsteps. Unfortunately, they could not locate any clue yet to convince themselves whether Miss Ohara was a disguised product of the U.S. or not. It could generate a crucial blow to the Russian brass and KGB members if Miss Ohara played a puppet of the U.S. The Russian military and KGB had worked so hard with every trouble and puzzle. One of the Russian high-ranking military officers emphasized at one of the meetings that at least they had to understand Miss Ohara's real intention before they would stage a full-scale campaign to dismantle the WMD.

Article 11: Citadel of Moscow

Dr. Wang's first step on the Russian front was concerned about politicians. The second step focused on the Russian technocrats of the WMD: the pertinent military brass and KGB directorates. Without the technocrats' ardent participation, the dismantling program could face a wall. To bring the technocrats in line, moral justification alone could not produce enough. The crushing force would not pitch a panacea either. The straightforward and direct appeal from Miss Ohara would kill the suspicious minds in order to encourage their compassionate motives and to nourish their thinking mechanism to its favorable attitude. Dr. Wang talked over on the subject with President Brodsky.

"Mr. President, I'd like to have Miss Ohara appear in front of your top professional group of the WMD to give a pep talk. Your group of the WMD has deep-rooted suspicions of Miss Ohara's neutrality in the global new order. How do you like the idea?"

"Excellent! Dr. Wang. I could bring those suspicious WMD experts over here tomorrow morning. Could you make an arrangement?"

"Of course, I could make it. I had a word from President Kirkman before I left the U.N. building."

The KGB and the Russian military machine's symmetrical counter part of the U.S.'s 16 intelligence agents tried to trace Miss Ohara's whereabouts, decipher Miss Ohara's electro magnetic waves, and fathom Miss Ohara's wave origin. They thought they touched upon a very sensitive nerve in the waveform and its origin. Sometimes, they were even scared about being killed by Miss Ohara's killing wave because they thought they approached close enough to locate the true face of Miss Ohara. But they failed time and again.

Super Constitution

When they experienced they were not interfered on their active search, they became bolder and bolder in investigating Miss Ohara's wave origin. The more advancement they made, the more darkness they got into. They got more puzzles. They fell into deeper crevices. Now they could meet Miss Ohara face to face even though it was on wireless through the scaffolding-screen with her direct voice. They were excited. The occasion itself engendered a pride and joy to them. The event truly agitated their enigmatic curiosity.

The citadel of Moscow boiled, burnt, glowed, fevered, and even fantasized its own image with Miss Ohara's direct appearance. A group of top Russian technocrats who had gone through a large variety of trials and sweating efforts to locate Miss Ohara's origin fantasized themselves in direct communication with her. Their blissful ecstasy climaxed through their bloodstream. They knew how much scares they had experienced over time, tracing Miss Ohara's magnetic wave form. Because they mobilized all-out technology they had, risking their lifetime career and their own life, they fully understood that they were the only people who could recognize Miss Ohara's existence.

Now, Miss Ohara was coming along to them, to Moscow and to the Kremlin, in order to deliver her pep talk directly to them. It sensationally resonated in their heart. It dramatically moved their minds. It literally vibrated the Citadel of Moscow.

One of top technocrats invited to the Kremlin, talked it over with one of his peers.

"Hey, I watched a replay of her appearance at the U.N. the other day more than a dozen times. She is beautiful Caucasian with blue eyes: very attractive lady; and very sexy wood nymph or naiad."

"Why do you refer to her through forest or river?"

Article 11: Citadel of Moscow

"Well, I think forest or river symbolizes mystic origins of fairy tales."

"Look! Miss Ohara might not be a lady, just disguising himself as a lady. Miss Ohara could be a puppet. I am still really curious about the existence behind the scenes."

"Maybe you are right. Nonetheless, today's occasion casts raptures. The occasion could have a lot of spin-offs. I hope we could derive some entrancing offsprings from today's event."

"Well, after all, I hope a pleasant upshot too."

The gathering of the technocrats to the Kremlin Hall, from a deep den of military machines and KGB network, sparked a stardom of Russia's big shots with an authentic look and shining faces reminiscent of a great war-victory party. The mood and atmosphere rose up with their stride, drifting through the hall and making the place glamorous and pleasant enough to enhance the participants' feelings up to the ceiling.

Mostly gentlemen swarmed over with a few dots of colorful ladies: wives, and typically talented female aids and agents. These people of a fine and quiet breed glittered throughout the Hall. Undulation of their movement around the Hall magnified the Hall's image to get the occasion's meaningfulness across. The top technocrats in the field of Russia's WMD considered that facing Miss Ohara directly today, even through a wireless screen, at the Kremlin Hall, would make the momentum as memorable as the World War victory.

The day's MC announced toward a bit noisy crowd of the Hall.

"Ladies and gentlemen, May I have your attention. In a couple of minutes, Miss Ohara will come to this screen from nowhere. We don't know where she is going to make this conference with us. The only thing we know is that she is going to deliver her message directly to us through the wireless screen and that she is going to conduct a question and answer herself with you in writing after this morning's event. Ladies and gentlemen, please turn off your mobile phone now, thank you!"

The MC turned his head back and looked at the big white screen hung on the wall located at the back of the lectern on the lifted stage for the various conferences and press releases. The crowd of about sixty people standing on the floor watched the screen. They hushed to a complete silence as the screen alight. Soon, Miss Ohara appeared with the upper half of her body in a comfortable smile.

"How are you? Ladies and gentlemen! I am glad to appear in front of you in this historical Hall today. All of you are very important persons not only to me, but also to the world people. I am here this morning with you to recognize your importance for stabilizing the Global Government."

Miss Ohara kept smiling, all along.

"The job of dismantling the WMD plays the crucial role in setting up the world safety, and requires time consuming efforts, outstanding expertise in its field, and compassionate political minds throughout. The Global Government needs your positive cooperation in this WMD campaign very badly because Russia has the largest piles of WMD, the largest pool of experts, and the strongest political muscles to execute the process."

"In front of you, I am honestly speaking that I am not a puppet for anybody. I am a completely independent resource working for the world people to achieve a utopia on this earth. If you believe in me, and if you follow my directions, there are going to be no threats, no nightmares, and only happy solutions for everybody."

Miss Ohara continued.

"Right now, still, many intelligence organizations are working so hard to locate me, to figure out my electro magnetic wave form, to decipher my voice and my facial structure, and to fathom the distance and angles of my moving waves. I know who they are, where they are working now, and what they are talking about now because my partners are catching every part of their work and recording the audiovisual data of their work. I am telling you that they only work in vain."

"Ladies and gentlemen, right now, I warn that those eavesdropping people must stop their fruitless hard work. Even though those people who are tracing me do not pose any harm or hindrance to my work now, but they can affect other people who work for the Global Government in a bad way. When we face any type of consequences, I am going to send the killing wave to them at anytime without any further warning. Ladies and gentlemen, thank you for listening to me today. I wish you happiness and good luck."

Miss Ohara's five-minute appearance for delivering her pep talk to the elite leaders of the Russian political powerhouse, swept away lingering doubts and anxieties of the Russian political elite over Miss Ohara's constantly posing mysteries. The Russian elite's minds pressurized by the stressful confrontation, which was amassed due to the threat of Miss Ohara's killing wave, had been driven into a corner with no way out.

Miss Ohara's appearance in front of them made sure that she was no one's puppet. Furthermore, her downright acknowledgment of the Russian elite's importance, and her explicit willingness to exercise the killing wave without any further warning, paved enough confidence and reason for the Russian elite to take action on their lingering doubts and anxieties. As a matter of fact, they knew they did not have any other choice, but they had to accept Miss Ohara's appeasing demands.

Article 12

White House

The WMD dismantling-bound citadel of Moscow levered by the high spirit of Russian politicians and technocrats, had startled Chief of Presidential Staff of the White House Edmond Murdock and National Security Advisor Steve Johnson. Both of them had been monitoring Russia's cooperative movement, and together they had also witnessed that the Global Government annexed China's sovereignty.

U.S. President's Chief of Staff Edmond Murdock called his president early in the morning at 8 a.m., six hours after Miss Ohara's appearance on the screen (10 a.m. Moscow time) in the Kremlin on October 4, 2016.

"Mr. President, good morning! I watched Miss Ohara's speech in Moscow early this morning (2 a.m. Washington, D.C. time). It was a shocking event. She spellbound the Russian WMD technocrats. Also, she issued a saber-rattling word, trying to exterminate our SSTF."

"Steve, did she mention the name of SSTF?"

"No, sir, she just made a connotation. She just said she would activate her killing wave without any further warning on those people who would lead the job of tracing her."

"Well, let's have an emergent meeting of our inner circle."

The inner circle of the White House meant Steve Johnson (National Security Advisor), Charles Manatt (Defense Secretary), Malcom Stark (Intelligence Czar), Edmund Murdock (Chief of Presidential Staff), and Clark Powell (Chairman of the Joint Chiefs of Military Staff).

On October 4, 2016, the late morning meeting of the inner circle went on at the Oval Office. The U.S. President opened the session as usual.

"This morning, Steve called me over the phone, informing that Moscow surrendered and Miss Ohara issued her last warning against our SSTF's hard work."

The President continued.

"During last four months, our special team SSTF worked hard to uncover Miss Ohara's true colors. According to the information given to me so far, I feel certain that we are closely approaching some figure where the origin of the wave is. And now, early this morning, Miss Ohara, during her appearance on a screen to the Russian WMD technocrats and Russian top politicians, issued a last warning to our effort to trace her. I am sure she will talk to me soon about the materializing matters of ten panelists' hearings of the Super Constitution held at the U.N. last June. She will probably send the Global President Mr. George Kirkman with his cabinet members over to us."

Article 12: White House

"Regarding those matters of the U.N. hearings, we could discuss in detail after we would meet them at this oval office. Right now, the urgent thing we have to clarify is what we should do about our SSTF's ongoing project of tracing Miss Ohara. I'd like to hear your straight words."

President's National Security Advisor Steve Johnson, who was in charge of the Special Secret Task Force (SSTF), initiated the response to the president's opening remark.

"Yes, Mr. President, we are closely approaching toward locating the origin of the wave. I guess Miss Ohara acknowledged our approach. Maybe, that's why she issued a warning. I think we have to brave ourselves to continue our search even though we risk our lives. I think Miss Ohara is using a threatening tactics to stop our efforts. She would not dare to kill our scientists to cause casting a chill over the people's minds. I am sure she would deploy some format of scaring tactic before taking any action of killing."

Nonetheless, Malcom Stark, the U.S. Intelligence Czar said immediately after Steve's wishful talks.

"Mr. President, we are dealing with a super genius. Miss Ohara is an extraordinary genius. Besides her technology, which our supreme science could not figure out, we could not figure out her intention and tactics. One thing I am sure of is that she would use a decisive manner to show us her determination. The technology she deploys outstretches our imagination. She is using the technology, which has made her withdrawal impossible. She knows, if her technology is exposed to us, it will mean her death. We have to assume she is much smarter than us. She won't leave things alone. I am sure she is in measuring the progress in our tracing her without any mistake. I think we should not commit any foolish action."

Super Constitution

And Charles Manet, the Defense Secretary, a hawkish man took the baton of Malcom's careful approach-borne stance.

"Of course, we are in danger at this moment. We have to measure our symmetrical points against her taking her own measure on our points as for an objective logic. Frankly speaking, we are far more inferior to Miss Ohara, in terms of powerful brainstorming capability on reading ahead of the developing situations or hypothetical scenarios, but looking at the shape of our political circumstance that plays a crucial role model to the world, killing is not a cure-all, and not a final answer either."

"So far we have felt a lot of threats, and also, we could interpret Miss Ohara's behavior as inerratic. Miss Ohara has consistency in directing her ideas or target. I am not telling that she is not going to use that horrible killing wave, but I am telling that she is not going to use that wave by digressing from a line of our thought or reasoning. In other words, we still have a space and time to maneuver our SSTF's advance."

The President nodded several times in a serious posture, and asked Clark Powell for his stance on addressing the SSTF's line of march in this urgent juncture of Miss Ohara's daunt demand which made their action crawl.

Clark Powell opened his mouth.

"Well, Mr. President, the situation is developing into the bare crescent which every corner can watch our movement. I think our move is drifting toward a wide-open space that everybody can measure our intention. We have, I assume, no choice, but to take an action whether we are going to take the course originally intended by our SSTF's effort or not. In the intended movement, therefore, we could not raise the curtain for the continued action. It is nonsense, I think, Mr. President, for us to continue SSTF's headstrong advance disregarding

Article 12: White House

Miss Ohara's raising alarm. We know her power. We heard her intention. Mr. President, it is also nonsense for us to surrender without protruding our fine sensible insistence on the global matters. We have great ideas and achievements for human political freedom, well-stabilized social organizations, abundant high technology, and rich human resources. I think, Mr. President, this is, maybe, a great moment for us to try to insert our country's vital strength into the global matters."

Edmund Murdock, the Chief of Staff, came to the line to catch the president's eyes to speak out on the situation.

"Well, gentlemen, and Mr. President, I helped Steve to organize the SSTF, and I have closely watched, deeply thought about, and carefully calculated the SSTF's start and advance. The job has been great. The advance is clear. Nevertheless, we have been on the tight rope. We may be clowns to Miss Ohara as though we dared to embark upon a touchy adventure. I have been constantly worried about for the case where we would arrive at the point which Miss Ohara could not leave things alone."

"Approaching her mechanism means a total destruction. Anyway, we will meet a total destruction before we will arrive at her nest. If this is the destiny of the SSTF, then why should we get on our nerves ourselves for nothing? Instead, maybe, it is more constructive, more realistic, and more logical for us to negotiate with the Global Government. Fortunately, the top managers of the Global Government hold Ph.D. degrees, which mean more academic and less muscular character that prefers subtlety and grace rather than forceful performance. In other words, they wield high spirit but they command weak action. They need us, and we could help them."

President of the U.S. Mr. John Garfield respected human dignity and he valued human life much more than avoiding humiliation. He sensed the inevitable and inexorable situation surging into his office. He made a decision: not to provoke the situation any further for the time being. After listening to everyone's opinions, the U.S. President opened his heart as the following:

"Gentlemen, you guys take a pretty much serious attitude towards the matter of our SSTF, and also, towards China's division and Russia's fall. I think so far Miss Ohara rolls without any major impediment because the history in making has been directed in accordance to people's basic wishful breeze. I agree with her general vision over the undulation of the globalizing movement. The free flow of the commercial commodities, the drastic savings on the military build-ups, and the ironclad security measurements against criminals, terrorists, swindlers, disease, poverty and stress would bring the end of endless wars to the human civilization."

The U.S. President continued.

"It is, definitely, a great human history, for us to experience only one constitution in the world. As a matter of fact, even a few hundreds years back, we did not have anything like the modern communication and transportation, and no WMD, and no precision weapons. Many empires and super powers, however, have tried to conquer the whole world. No matter who rules, if the ruling machinery goes by the spirit of justice, who does care who is going to be the ruler? China? Japan? Russia? America? I indeed don't care. I mean it. As long as we enjoy the new world order, who would care going against it?"

"In fact, I used to feel helpless so many times in our governing power even though it looked so powerful because of two reasons: One is that I feel I have a limit in my grip of intelligence on figuring out our developing situations, and what solution would bring the best result for that developing situation; The other one is that our so powerful governing

Article 12: White House

power is actually nothing but a joke or childish mischief or a toy of a house because we don't simply have enough power to crush over all the opposing sphere of interests. We know that the build-up of WMD only entails danger to human world. We know that the balance of power runs on a collision course with war. We know that power struggles lead us to an eventual collapse of our mutual stands."

The President kept going.

"We fight until we are exhausted, until one party collapses, but the survived one will be collapsed by another challenger or some challenging event. After all, just because of no one's dominant-crushing force, we exhaust ourselves in vain and we stress ourselves sacrificing our happy lives. Maybe, that is the mode of life. I have longed for, and you have longed for the outstanding power to be able to control everything and to be able to flatten every opposing, formidable challenge in order to dispatch business at full speed the best way of the justice you think absolutely right."

U.S. President John Garfield uttered his feelings of endless frustrations, which ensued in running world-class affairs. Now, all of a sudden, he faced an epoch-making historical technology: the absolute crushing force, which he used to pipedream time to time.

The inner circle of the White House listened to the President's thoughts on the SSTF's job. The President wanted to stop the SSTF's spearheaded drive for locating Miss Ohara's wave origin. The President did not want to have talented people get hurt for nothing. John Garfield knew what he was gambling on and understood that he depended lots on guts rather than an irresistible logic of facts. He knew courage and fortitude could not win over science. The U.S. President summed up the agenda for the coming meeting with the Global Government's President George Kirkman, as follows:

Super Constitution

"Gentlemen, we have to understand clearly where George Kirkman's Global Government is trying to lead us. In order to lead us to the destination they want, what measures do they intend to take politically, economically, militarily and socially? Large scale of social change and drastically developing phenomena would necessitate confusion or even chaos for all walks of life. It could impair the new social order. It could create continuing internecine arguments and blaming each other in the developing processes for the new social order. Maybe, it would render only bluff and bluster to the developing processes.

John Garfield, the U.S. President, continued.

"Even though George Kirkman's Cabinet has been empowered by Miss Ohara with the killing power and communicating devices which enabled the Cabinet's omnipotent listening and telling prowess, and even though they have comprehended they could exercise almightily, they will never try to use that force. Instead, they will prefer reasoning. They will choose, instead, to buy the intelligentsia's mind. They will favor an amenable leadership."

This was what the U.S. President concluded. To establish a measure minimizing the rapid disintegration of the existing social order, the U.S. President made a decision to hold the SSTF's further advancement, for the time being. He wanted to wait until he would finish the talk with the Global Government's top officials on the matter of the role of the U.S. in the course of materializing the U.N. hearings' ideas of ten panelists for the Super Constitution.

According to the U.S. President's last-minute decision on the SSTF's further advancement, George Kirkman and his Cabinet could make an appointment with the U.S. President

Article 12: White House

and his inner circle at the White House Oval Office at 10 a.m., on October 6, 2016.

Ever since three nations of Russia, China, and the U.S. failed on presenting serious candidacies for the Global Government officials (according to promulgation #2: p. 130), and accordingly, since Miss Ohara's actual in-person appearance for the second time on August 15, 2016, announcing her choice of the Global Government's officials, the modern world experienced most sensational events in a headlong thrust such as the Global Government emergence, China's division into twenty nations, and Russia's determination for the downright initiative on dismantling the WMD; and now, George Kirkman's Cabinet into the Oval Office of the White House to discuss the establishment of agenda running the new global order.

Since the U.S. presidential inner circle's meeting on the matter of SSTF on October 4, 2016, Steve Johnson, the National Security Advisor, who was in charge of the SSTF's activity, and Edmond Murdock, the Chief of Presidential Staff, were too busy in preparing for the meeting with the Global Government's top officials set for October 6th.

Johnson and Murdock played the major architect to frame the organization of the SSTF. Even though the U.S. President made a decision to hold off further activities of the SSTF to trace Miss Ohara until the October 6th meeting would be over, the two guys, Johnson and Murdock had to manipulate many things on top of the subjects of running the global order: such as unusual incoming waves activated by Miss Ohara for listening and watching the White House; and deciphering the wave behaviors, and fathoming the wave's timing and angles, and analyzing the gathered data through electronic devices. All of these activities required a lot of communicating jobs, which could have been intercepted by Miss Ohara's network.

Super Constitution

The Global Government's Intelligence Minister Andrei Milovanov utilized his two biggest advantages for the effort to organize the most efficient intelligence network of the world: one advantage of the Global Government's omniscient political power, and the other one of mysteriously transcending capability for communication–two devices of fixed and mobile equipments which encompassed a radius of 1,000 and fifty miles, respectively, for listening and watching. Milovanov's incorporation of his worldwide intelligence network, especially in Beijing, Moskow, and Washington, D.C., had loomed on the horizon as a glaring, monumental deity.

The biological world moves through a spontaneous process, borne destined to stick to superior power. Human being, as the lord of all creations, acts superbly to which one they should stick for their survival and prosperity. Intelligent guys, professionals, high performers and shrewd businessmen usually make much faster headway to become a member of the super power. In this way, Milovanov managed his humongous scale of espionage to grow in snowballing. Milovanov stood in the intelligence society as a clearly visible and formidable giant. He was getting a note of important talks and topics done inside the Kremlin, Beijing's governments, and the White House.

On October 5, 2016, the day before the Oval Office meeting with the U.S. President, the Global President George Kirkman had a meeting with his cabinet members to have a general report concerning vital information on what the White House thought, talked, and set up to gauge Ohara's interception. Intelligence Czar Andrei Milovanov distributed two pages of confidential papers pertaining to major movements of the White House on the subjects of global matters along with the White House's basic strategy on their SSTF's activities.

Article 12: White House

George Kirkman's Cabinet of Wang Yen-Jee (Military Minister), Jay Kim (Minister of Economics), Toro Yono (Minister of Politics), and Wolfgang Thierse (Minister of Sociology) glanced at the two-page papers, which Milovanov would be briefing for the Cabinet's discussion preparing for the White House meeting. Milovanov explained in detail about what the White House wanted in the area of ten panelist's indications at the U.N. hearings on the Super Constitution (p. 119–128), and about how the White House moved for the tracing job on Miss Ohara.

First, the ten subjects covered by the ten panelists were explained: religion, economic paradigm, politics, language, military power, moral fiber on fair play and criminal treatment, education, public enterprise and administration, and free trade (p. 116–125). The White House wanted to be involved in organizing ad hoc commissions for fact finding and to establish suggestions on those matters of the Global Government. In other words, the White House desired to take, at least, some portion in forming leadership of the new world order as the foremost super power on the earth.

Moscow forcedly took some important steps by making determination for grabbing initiative in dismantling job of the WMD. China collaborated with the Global Government in coordinating the new world's political reshuffle grudgingly. The U.S. had to do something. The White House figured that it could, must, and should make contributions to the new leadership of the world by providing something valuable with the Global Government. The U.S. had immense resources in information, technology, science and management for establishing a right leadership on those above ten subjects. The U.S. could bring forth the best source in every field. The White House thought so. George Kirkman's Cabinet thought so too.

Super Constitution

Second, the tracing job of the White House was explained: The White House's basic strategy on its SSTF's activities had changed from its "dynamic wedging into interception" to a dormant "wait and see" situation by the U.S. President. However, Steve Johnson (U.S. National Security Advisor and prime manager of the SSTF) and Edmund Murdock (Chief of Presidential Staff) had to monitor and manage overall stuff of blipping radarscope and intercepting devices and results. Even though they had an order to stop all activities of the SSTF from the President, they had to take care of the closures of the ongoing things. They happened to get in touch with many of the remains.

While Kirkman Cabinet was talking about the ten subjects and learning about the status quo of the White House's tracing job, John of the troika was in the middle of checking the antenna array to change from ground to satellite (according to the decision made on page of 99&100), and happened to listen to the conversation between Steve and Edmund.

Steve spoke to Edmund.

"Hay, Edmund, it looks to me that our SSTF is closing the gap between the fogy situation and clear vision on the matter of locating the origin of the wave Miss Ohara is sending."

Edmund gave his advice.

"However, we'd better stop here for the time being until the White House meeting with George Kirkman's Cabinet would get over."

Steve made a ready reply on Edmund's advice.

"But, Edmund, you know, I think it's maybe a little bit of a chicken to throw in the towel on the remnant job of a trivial butt. Don't you think so?"

Article 12: White House

"Well," Edmund hesitated in a little for the right word.

"I think, Steve, that even though it is a remnant thing of an ending job, you'd better ignore the situation and leave it alone because it is a matter of extremely sensitive trigger."

But Steve Johnson, as the U.S. National Security Advisor and the Directorate of operation of the SSTF could not leave it alone, or could not speak up either for shutting off the final job of the five-member team's analysis of laser beam for locating the origin of the wave. And, he could not resist his itching curiosity. Steve did not take care to stop the laser beam's continuous finishing job, which continued to intercept incoming waves and fathom the length of the waves.

While John Smith was checking the maneuvering device for the Joshua tree National Park's antenna in order to change the hooked-up mechanism from the ground to one of satellites, he happened to listen to the conversation between Steve and Edmund. He then sensed an intercepting wave from outside which the SSTF's busy trials had generated. John immediately turned around toward James who was watching John's job and discussed the disturbing matter. James looked up at John and talked to him calmly.

"You see? We have been talking about this quite a time. The SSTF is coming faster than we thought. Let's stop all wave patterns until we finish the change of the hook-up from ground to satellite. How long it was going to take did you say the other day? A couple of days you said, didn't you?"

"Yup James, just two days we need to change up. Let's talk about this incident with your father and Brenda."

Michael Leigh, Brenda Chen, John Smith, and James Leigh got together as usual in the vault room to discuss the matter of the SSTF's close approach while George Kirkman's Cabinet did get together to discuss the matter of the White House meeting.

Michael opened the meeting session.

"I heard from John about the change of the hooked-up mechanism to satellite, along with the SSTF's dangerous approach. I am sure we came to the point whether we are going to activate the killing wave to tell the world that we are not joking with our awesome technology. Once we issued a word, the word must be followed through. Otherwise we are going to face too many obstacles or difficulties in the process of setting up the new world order."

"I totally agree with Dad."

Brenda asserted her strong opinion with clear brevity. Then she continued.

I gave a clear warning notation through the appearance on a screen in the Kremlin Hall meeting the other day. We have to give an example to those powerful apparatus in real life. We have been in tacit understanding among us to try our best not to have anybody fall under our killing wave. But I guess we have to activate it now, to minimize future victims."

James also expressed his firm opinion.

"I have been thinking about this unavoidable incident time to time. Now a grim potentiality of applying our killing wave translates into reality. We can't help but have to act now to prevent further agitation."

John concluded the decision.

"We cannot avoid some sacrifices in the job of establishing the new world order. Through history, we have seen too many

Article 12: White House

victims, much hardship, big agonies, and endless bloodshed. I am sure that we are doing our best to save even one person as far as possible. Activating the killing wave to get rid of any impediment in achieving our goal for the Global Government, calls for the imperatives of our technology. I think we have to act now."

In this way, Brenda, John, and James together maneuvered the activating device to pin down the killing wave on Steve Johnson. He was currently in another meeting with the President along with the White House inner circle, to further discuss the detailed subjects with George Kirkman's Cabinet for the next day (October 6th).

All of a sudden, Steve fell on the floor from his chair with a whine from the pain of heart. Everybody was startled. The President called for emergency help. An emergency medical team appeared in three minutes. But Steve had already lost consciousness. The Emergency team found Steve's heart had already stopped. And then Miss Ohara's voice followed. She told to the Oval Office crowd that Steve ignored her warning. So the upshot just happened. The U.S. President, his inner circle, and the emergency team stood dumbfounded. Their face turned pale. Nobody said anything.

U.S. President John Garfield murmured a question to his chief of staff.

"What happened to my order?"

"Sir, sorry, I advised Steve to stop all actions of the SSTF. But he wouldn't stop the remaining, ending job. He considered it negligible."

The President sighed.

Super Constitution

"How could such a meticulous person like Steve Johnson ignore such a sensitive last touch? This is not his mistake. This is his destiny. He became the first victim for the new world order. The history of the earth will inscribe his name along with the incredible technology of Miss Ohara. Even while his funeral would be taking place, our debate with the Global Government's Cabinet on the matter of the new world order would take a heat."

China's Politburo and Russia's Kremlin survived any victimization of human life. However, the unfortunate incident happened at the White House. The least probability broke out in most negligible dustup without any significant result at a very normal moment: no decisive clue to locate the origin of the wave on the communications. The only thing the SSTF had achieved so far was the assurance that the wave had not originated from out of the earth but right from some place of the earth. Further a little more tracing job would have provided a chance to reveal the wave origin's whereabouts: Japan or China, or Russia. It was too bad and sorry for the SSTF.

The troika changed the hooked-up mechanism from the "Hidden Valley" of Joshua tree National Park to one of hundreds of satellites circling the earth. No one would notice small antenna attached on the other side of Joshua tree branch in the Hidden Valley's bouldered area forever. The troika would never remove it. It would be there at least for several generations.

Even though the SSTF would finally locate the origin, the origin would be one of satellites. No technology could read the incoming wave to the satellite from any part of the earth because John maneuvered the reflecting angle. So without catching an incoming wave to the spot of the satellite, which was mission impossible, nobody could figure the origin of the incoming wave to the satellite.

Article 13

Vulnerableness

On October 6, 2016, even though Steve Johnson, the National Security Advisor of the U.S., passed away by the incident of negligence right yesterday, the scheduled world affairs had to roll.

In the U.S. President's Oval Office, the President's inner circle (Charles Manatt: Defense Scretary, Malcom Stark: Intelligence Czar, Edmund Murdock: Chief of Presidential Staff, and Clark Powell: Chairman of the Joint Chiefs of Staff) took the seats the other side of the table surrounding the President in the center, and the Global Government's Cabinet (George Kirkman: Global President, Wolfgang Thierse: Sociology Minister, Jay Kim: Economy Minister, Toro Yono: Politics Minister, Wang Yen-Jee: Military Minister, and Andrei Milovanov: Intelligence Minister), six persons took seats facing the other side symmetrically by placing Kirkman in the front of U.S. President John Garfield. President Garfield opened the session.

Super Constitution

"Gentlemen, welcome to the Oval Office. I preferred having ladies as well as gentlemen. But gentlemen's club is not bad either. I discussed the order of topics we are going to talk about today with President Kirkman over the phone the other day. Also, I discussed opening up our minds for better understanding and a smoother new world order. We listed the religion as the first subject, and then language, education, criminology; then the basic economic issues: public enterprise, tax regulation, nation's borders and free trade; and the last one: armed forces in the world."

"Gentlemen, the Global Government would speak up first for the basic direction and idea, and we, the White House members will indicate something else that could be a problem, and add our creative opinion. Then, President Kirkman will give closing remarks on all subjects one by one."

George Kirkman made a pleasant smile in taking over the U.S. President's baton.

"Thank you Mr. President Garfield! For the sake of the new world order, I talked of substantial details with Miss Ohara, and sufficiently exchanged opinion with President Garfield already. Through this meeting, however, we are going to solidify for more concrete directions and ideas. Not only the first subject of religion but also the matter of language, education and criminal things, I'd like to have Dr. Wolfgang Thierse speak out."

"Dr. Thierse as a prominent, distinguished scholar of the current world plays a spiritual spokesperson of the Global Government. All crooks, criminals, corrupted bureaucrats, inefficient intellectuals, and greedy interest groups consider Dr. Wolfgang Thierse as a disgusting devil. But people who look for justice would welcome Dr. Thierse's theory passionately. Please, Dr. Thierse!"

Article 13: Vulnerableness

"Gentlemen, I would like to talk about the core of religion first. There are so many wonderful things and so much unbelievable miracles in the human mind. Billions of people were borne able to speak and think with the same organs of body structure, with the same brain cells, and with the same mechanism of the mind. However, some people believe in one God as the creator and ruler of the Universe without rejection of revelation (theism). Some believe in with rejection of revelation (deism). Some disbelieve in the existence of God (atheism), and some other people are in doubt forever."

"Socrates and Plato believed in the existence of the soul of human being by arguing that the soul has been existed somewhere and at sometime because we, human beings, have a function of recollection. We remember something if we have seen it before. We think and remember about the soul because the soul had been somewhere and in some form before it came to the human body. Most people in the ancient time used to believe in the existence of the soul of human being. We have many religions: Christianity, Catholicism, Islamism, Buddhism, Daoism, Hinduism, Confucianism, and many other forms of belief. The more modernized we become, the more people shift toward skepticism (agnosticism)."

"Human history saw that hostilities, struggles, slanders, persecutions, and wars between the disputing religions continued to occur. We have to learn and practice tolerance on the matter of our belief or disbelief. The Global Government is going to set up an absolute standard not to impose any doctrine on anybody, and an absolute arbitration on the disputes of the religious matters. This is the Global Government's basic stance. Thank you, Gentlemen!"

Dr. Thierse's talking manner was soft, but his tone firm.

George Kirkman nodded pleasantly, and asked the White House members to speak their opinion. And U.S. President

Super Constitution

John Garfield praised Dr. Thierse's basic theory as a strong demonstration of the principle of the separation between state and religion, and expressed his concern on the arbitrary decision-making process on the matters of religious disputes.

"Dr. Thierse, I am wondering what is going to happen if we face severe disputes between religions, severe enough to be unable to make them contain. I doubt the arbitration itself can solve the deeply rooted chasm between the beliefs."

President Kirkman intercepted.

"Well, President Garfield, that's why we have this conference. Of course, we could face very difficult subject to solve. But the World Government's final arbitration must come with the most appropriate persuasion. Within the Global Government, we are family: no more disputes. We will contemplate and invent the best form of compromise."

President Kirkman again asked Dr. Wolfgang Thierse to continue for the talk about the next subject: language.

Dr. Thierse got the voice again, now on the matter of language.

"Gentlemen, how many languages do you think we have on this earth? About more than six hundreds we have at the moment. The best administrative capability comes with communicating ability. Not only administration, but also any type of human activities brings better result with better communication. It is going to even ease personal life's stress if they can speak the same language. In old days, without any modern types of transportation, different languages did not matter too much. But now in the globalizing days, the efficient means of transportation and communication faces too many frustrations in the complex of languages which divide the world with high walls."

Article 13: Vulnerableness

"Unfamiliar languages could sound the same as singings of birds or strange sounds of animal worlds to the strangers. We have to unify human's languages to bring our world to a much better place to live in and enjoy. Of course, varieties of cultures, customs, and life styles create hundreds of beautiful mosaic societies which bloom human talent into an extensive boundary. However, we never saw hundreds of ethnic languages came into the mainstream of the world."

"The mainstream of the world should exercise communication with the most convenient, scientific, and easiest language. For the global affairs of human concerns, we should use only one language, not three, not even two. All elementary, middle and high schools, colleges, and special schools must use the same language. In the beginning stage, the practice using one universal language would severe the people who were not used to. It will pose a difficulty to break in or break out from the one they had been soaked in because language is not being steered up like riding a bicycle or driving a car. No matter how difficult it is, it should be done because it is going to give the greatest power to the people for the new world order. It is not a matter of having an intellectual grip, but it is a matter of willpower and a matter of forming a habit. Even morons can achieve it if they feel necessary."

Again, U.S. President Garfield, upon Dr. Thierse's curt conclusion of the one language as an unconditional downright imperative for the globalization, raised a question to Dr. Thierse.

"Dr. Thierse, what do you think about allowing each person to choose second or third language at discretion? It is going to be too bad for us to abandon valuable languages human being developed for tens of thousand years."

Super Constitution

Before Dr. Thierse answered that question, President Kirkman intercepted again.

"Gentlemen, regarding that question, I'd like to mention the following: in the matter of choice on almost anything related to the global fronts, besides the imperative, the Global Government would respect every individual's choice. If any person who speaks, reads, and writes the selected global language, can select second language or third one, even up to multiple languages, it is going to be that person's complete freedom. Allowing the maximum of individual freedom on all global fronts is Miss Ohara's unquestionable intention."

President Kirkman emphasized Miss Ohara's determination on the concept of people's freedom, and asked Dr. Thierse to continue on the next subject. Dr. Thierse drank a little from a glass of water, and then continued.

"Gentlemen, the topic of education is very universal and an often discussed subject. Nevertheless, education denotes too dynamic a quality of human civilization, ever deeply and widely. I would like to quote President Kirkman's quotation from Miss Ohara's emphasis on the spirit of education as follows":

"The number one power to change our social behavior for the better comes from the human mind, especially the educated human mind which thinks of betterment and the better off. The educated mind brings practical efficiency on all fronts. The most relevant mode of human thought plays the basic, powerful dynamism of the creative mind. Education polishes a vision of the human mind. Education enriches information into the human mind. Education finally touches the human mind to rise up for a quality upsurge in every field: social organization; technology development; economic upheaval; and political ecology." (p. 65: This quotation actually

Article 13: Vulnerableness

originated from Michael Leigh's opinion about his philosophical view on the matter of education related to his R&D institute. Brenda used Michael's view as her own one when she emphasized importance of "education matter" to George.)

"Gentlemen, education takes the role of the most crucial cornerstone in human society for change. We have to install right institute, socialized behavior and thinking stance. We are going to instill 'the principle of the right man in the right place' in our children. We are going to promote the educational environment where everyone must be educated to their mental limits by respecting everyone's in-born talent and hard work. We are going to wipe out all equalizing standards by promoting performance in every field."

Dr. Thierse continued.

"Also, we are going to foster and inculcate a moral code of honesty, creativity, hard work, punctuality and appreciation as an imperative behavior. Law alone could not contain almost unlimited variance of modern society. Education would bring not only the right behavior but also would provide the right basis to encourage personal and social productivity with the globalization."

This time, Edmund Murdock, the Chief of Presidential Staff raised a question.

"Dr. Thierse, the global drive for the best education can breed too harshly strenuous effort to the world's learning practices for a handsome success. Probably, it can cause cantankerous discontents in the process of its justification. I think, while we promote talent and performance, we should pay attention to the matter of equalizing practice for generalization of the categorical groups. Especially, the general education for the moral code requires a strong emphasis on the matter of equalization. Not only moral code, but also classification of the majority people into their different interests will require some format of solid equalization."

President Kirkman responded by a ready-made reply.

"Mr. Murdock, you indicated a right question. We had discussed that substance quite a time. The real substance of education calls for continuous advance towards desired improvement. Education trails dynamism. Education does not instigate any inertia. Education for the skill of majority people demands steady drill or training for a designated target. In this area, definitely, the feasible success needs a standardization and equalization. We are going to, of course, institutionalize something for this generalization."

President Kirkman turned his head toward Dr. Thierse and requested him to close his speech with the criminal matters in a criminological approach. Dr. Thierse, in a serious sitting posture, continued his firm and ringing low tone.

"Gentlemen, The basic idea or general thinking stance on religion, language, and education along with an applying mechanism for the justice on the criminal matter, indeed deeply affects our globalization. Economic numbers, political framework, military forces, and gargantuan intelligent activities depend on the shape of human ideology greatly. Specifically, the ideology on the matter of religion, language, education, and crimes actually dictate our political and economic life styles. They form the basic and quality resources of our life. They could make our life harsh or enjoyable, according to its application method and result."

"Especially, a handling mechanism of criminal matters, including swindlers and double crossers, should focus its solving force, at the striking point for bull's eye. We have to maximize and generalize the secret watching and listening

Article 13: Vulnerableness

capability of our spying facilities to catch criminals and proofs, along with a positive application of logical interpretation and convince in case of no proof."

"We have to start from the point of concept that no leniency would be applied to any crime. All the criminals should be separated from ordinary people who abide by the laws and moral codes the Global Government would emphasize. Any sort of anti criminal institutes should never stop hounding criminals while biological and psychological study to mitigate the criminal mind would take place vigorously. Also, heavy duty or labor should be imposed on the shoulder of the criminals to pay the cost of preventing and managing the crimes. Only the people who abide by law and moral code should prosper."

Dr. Thierse continued his speech on the criminal matter.

"In order to crush any hotbed of social evils and to root out any source of criminal weeds, we should use even military powers in addition to local police force. It would serve a decisive notice to the criminals or criminal-minded people for preventing crimes in advance. Presently, there are too many criminals everywhere, including frauds, intellectual thieves, industrial spics, and corrupted public officials, which infect social fabric like a cancer. Getting rid of criminals from the main stream of our society depends on the basic and firm way of thinking in general lifestyles. If we tolerate each other's beliefs, speak the same language, increase the value of education, respect justice, and hate crimes, then the world will go prosper and peaceful."

Again, U.S. President Garfield questioned to Dr. Thierse looking at Dr. Thierse's eyes with serious manner about the difficulty in sorting out the criminals from the massive population and the extreme complex of manifold social composite.

"Dr. Thierse, one of the biggest challenges indigenous to human life, I figure, is the criminal matter. If we could solve crimes substantially, and if we could reduce crimes efficiently, it would bring more than half the world's public works to get done, I assume. Also, on top of that problem, minimizing sacrifice for the innocent people to get hurt in the process of conducting justice, is going to be another perspiring challenge."

President Kirkman averred his opinion over the topic of the impending criminal affairs between Dr. Thierse and President Garfield.

"Well, gentlemen, the less criminal affairs we are going to have, the more successful world affairs we are going to achieve in every field. We have very confident and optimistic happenings in the making. Miss Ohara introduced several very much interesting discoveries and invention in human DNA that would change human's criminal behavior into more service-minded and more soft-minded personality. Human society suffers from innate violent-minded and deception-tended personalities."

"Also, Miss Ohara suggested us to mobilize the Global Government's omnipotent intelligence devices and military strength for the war on criminals. On top of the above, as Dr. Thierse emphasized, the Global Government's vigorous campaign for the severe punishment and the practice of moral codes will categorically hold sway over the difficulty President Garfield worried about. I think Dr. Thierse made a clear-cut road map into a wild plateau of global affairs for the Global Government's basic direction. We would like to have a topic on the economic affairs of the world now. Well, Dr. Jay Kim, please open your streamlined idea on the world's economic dynamism."

Article 13: Vulnerableness

"President Garfield, President Kirkman, and gentlemen, it is my honor and pleasure to talk about the basic direction and principle for the world's new order of our economic life. I'd like to remark the outline of the economic thought of our Global Government which the Global Government's cabinet members came to an agreement. We intend to maximize people's freedom to enjoy each one's economic life. Nobody or no institute would dictate any production of any major commodity, and any price. All the major commodities should be regulated or controlled by national authorities or the Global Government's decrees on the basis of a market economy. For example, most of natural resources, including land and space, are going to be owned by the Global Government. Most of utilities including highways and bridges are going to be owned and administered by national governments."

"We will encourage private business. However, the world and local governments will exercise an auditing power for ethical public standard. In other words, commercial activities for profit pursuit are going to be positively allowed freely for improving the quality and cost of products and services. But for the fair business practices, the observation and auditing by public organizations will be installed most efficiently. Any corruption, deception, and stealing will be prosecuted up to the hilt with heavy punishment. The Global Government and national governments will make strenuous and consistent efforts to bring optimum efficiency in fair play which will provide creative, honest, and hard working people with the best opportunities to prosper, and will wipe out injustice as well."

At this time, Edmund Murdock responded to Jay Kim's economic theory of combined doctrines of tinted capitalism and socialism.

"Dr. Kim, your ideological stance on the management of economy looks a brand of fusion food. Could you, Dr. Kim,

Super Constitution

specify the Global Government's principal tint or tinge of a certain doctrine we could hinge on?

Dr. Jay Kim explained about Global Government's ideological stance on economic policy further.

"Yes, Mr. Murdock. It is an interesting question. We are not going to adhere to any established academic doctrine. We are going to respect the reality foremost: the facts of economic situation in the resources, demands and supplies, and the human nature of self-interest. In other words, for setting up practical policies, we are going to use a method of 'inductive' which means to establish a conclusion (policy) on the basis of a number of facts of the reality, and 'deductive' which means to trace the derivation (policy) from the conclusion of the reality. We are going to set up a policy according to the reality of certain situation and to institute an approach towards the interest of people. You may say it is socialism or capitalism or fused stuff. We do not care any description or any definition."

President Kirkman interrupted Jay Kim's further talk.

"I guess Dr. Kim's explanation stresses more focus on the practical side rather than on theory or doctrine. However, we think we have a good spiritual guideline from the inspiration of the Super Constitution. From the point of interest of people's welfare, we have to start to figure out the most suitable frame for individual's maximum freedom and benefit. Of course, we are going to face some difficult situation in pros and cons at the process of making decisions for the institution of measures and a choice of measures. Fundamentally, we are going to work out with concerned professionals. Let's continue, Dr. Kim, to the topic of public enterprise and taxation."

Jay Kim resumed his talk.

Article 13: Vulnerableness

"Basically, there can be no definite line of demarcation between the private and public enterprises. In spite of that, at all events, according to the nature of the businesses and products, we could and should characterize the business and products as a public one such as gas, oil, electricity, some minerals, some housings, railroads, and etc. Simultaneously, some products go hand in hand with only incentive stimulus for its productivity, and some others depend on only market economy for its full-blown efficiency. Herewith, we are going to encourage both areas of private and public enterprises."

"For the public enterprises, we prefer national government's ownership and the most efficient administration which promote ever better quality and cost. The public enterprises shall be the main source of income for each national government's major coffers. Each nation must provide the best services with its people, like competent and competitive private business's successful operation. Global Congress will exercise the command of bigger issues of world affairs. Global Congress will define whether it is public enterprise or private one according to the spirit of the Super Constitution. However, the global Government's executive branch will make a decision and execute until the full fledged operation of Global Congress."

Jay Kim emphasized national ownership and national government's direct administration of the public enterprises in the manner of operation like private businesses, and also stressed audition by the Global Government's institute for the right price and an efficient management information system.

Dr. Kim continued for the matter of tax reform.

"The matter of taxes touches the bread and butter of all human's daily life. Tax depicts social organization's intrinsic dynamism. Without the taxation, no public organization could go. The proper tax amount and the proper choice of tax resource will make our social and political life easy for prosperity. The creator of the Global Government Miss Ohara, advised us to minimize the level of tax levy. If possible, no tax would be preferable. We are going to set up standardization for the minimum level and the least taxable items. I would like to indicate several examples of taxable items and its levying percentage as 10% to 5% only, and only two items of income and property taxes. But we are going to set up some reasonable and practical degree of low license fee and royalty to the big corporations and public enterprises for the Global Governments. We consider tax as an evil. But we have to contain it. We believe in the workable government."

Mr. Charles Manatt, the U.S. Defense Secretary, got involved in the topic.

"Dr. Jay Kim, I feel I am listening to some advocacy of socialism or anarchism. The U.S.'s annual budget amounts to around three trillion dollars out of 15 trillion GDP. 10% levy would amount only to less than one tenth of three trillion dollars. Even the present U.S.'s annual budget runs in red ink. It looks to me that the Global Government's Cabinet tries to praise a certain oligarchic process with dictatorship and socialism like former Chinese political formalities. I am getting worried about an extreme, one-sided, headlong measure of the globalization."

President Kirkman sensed that the conference ran into more confused scene rather than conciliatory persuasion to bring out the U.S. Government's positive stance. President Kirkman's Cabinet drew out China's willingness of participation in the drive for the enactment of the Super Constitution with all sorts of hardship and privation. Also, the inducement of Russia's dismantling job of the WMD reminded Kirkman of some stunt.

Article 13: Vulnerableness

Now Kirkman figured he faced the last hurdle. He must overpower the U.S.'s resistance intellectually in order to gather crushing force and dispatch business at full speed. He perceived the U.S. as a rather formidable character standing forth through the mist. Of course, he could mobilize the coercive killing power as a last resort. But his intuition on the ongoing development sent an alarm to his brainstorm to contain the vast reservoir of resources and knowledge of the U.S. The U.S. held the most powerful base of capitalism, democracy, technocrats, finances and human rights. Kirkman knew from the beginning that he had to persuade the U.S. to join the Global Government's drive to sweep away everything in its way, in order to set up the Super Constitution.

He now saw a growing difficulty to break the hard shell of stubborn adherence to the callous concept of the established kingdom. On top of that hardened concept, the leadership of the U.S. did not like to lose their grip on the political power to keep their prestige and comforts. They predicted that the implementation of the Super Constitution would degrade their dignity and perquisites. In other words, the coterie of the leadership placed their prerogatives and interests first. Instinctively, the leadership, as one of self interest groups, put a last-ditch resistance on the reform for the sake of themselves.

President Kirkman considered the above situation as a source of "vulnerableness" in his campaign for the constructive process of the globalization. The "vulnerableness" of the Global Government clearly appeared in its attempt to instill justification of the Super Constitution into the mind of the current American leaders. The vulnerableness definitely took place at this turning point as a monster.

This transient torrent of unheard-of power shift could torment the traditional leadership with suspicion and uncertainty. Also breaking off the hard shell of their protection-minded instinct required a distinct impact of a dazzling force along with black and white logic.

The lunchtime already passed. Kirkman offered the conference a break time to bite some ham and cheese sandwich, which he made an arrangement with the U.S. President the other day.

Article 14

Countdown

In the U.S. President's Oval Office, the brief lunchtime went on without cracking any joke. A heavy atmosphere settled. George Kirkman broke a silent air of the Oval Office.

"President Garfield, is this coffee Columbian or Arabic?"

"Frankly speaking, I don't know. Do you have any guess?"

"No guess either, but, upon drinking this wonderful coffee, some idea flashed through my mind that I have to break a knot of your key men's political libido."

"What do you mean by a 'knot of political libido'?"

The U.S. President made a severe countenance. Kirkman continued speaking.

"President Garfield! Some of your cabinet members do not realize what this moment of conference means. We did not come to your office as a diplomat. But we came here to let you understand a great juncture of the unprecedented revolution of human history, which will distinguish the global world from the traditional, divided sovereignties. Everyone at this conference must understand the inborn human nature of self-interest. Anyone of your Cabinet should not be affected by the general human's unconscious instinct of self-interest in discussing the matter of globalization."

"We don't care that our effort for the globalization looks like communism or democracy. This is an extraordinary revolution. Without an absolute order, and without discarding any type of personal niche, the revolution cannot go. If anyone mentions any insinuation derived from a personal libido, he could be executed by the killing wave, not by me, but by Miss Ohara. She listens to and watches our conference now. She told me to express a warning in case of anything insinuated by the personal inborn interest. I am sure you know which is which. Mr. President Garfield and gentlemen, please make it sure for you to express a constructive and objective view for our globalization. We are not here looking for any negative or any self-interested stance. Let's continue for the next topics, gentlemen. Dr. Jay Kim, please further narrate your economic policy."

George Kirkman hinted that his mission was based on explanations, and was not up for discussion.

Jay Kim continued.

"Gentlemen, I hope the U.S. Presidential Cabinet understands our difficulty for this globalization. We absolutely need your positive cooperation. Your positive stance will bring a crucial impact on moving this globalization ahead."

"We consider the matter of 'National Border and Free Trade' as one of the most critical practices the Global Government has to entail. 'National Borders' have marked the birth of chauvinism, which symbolized the ancient civilization that did

Article 14: Countdown

not master modern means of transportation and communication. Natural boundaries such as mountains, rivers, and oceans, along with lacerating natural disasters such as flood, drought, and storm, had fixed people into a collective body which had generated an inevitable culture of religion and language that encouraged promoting nationalism."

"The nationalism has built human history. The human history under the pressure of nationalism had painted a rise and fall of human's cruel ambitions and inexorable outcry over human blood and flesh. Actually, it resembles ferocious cannibals and boneheaded internecine feud. Man, who has high IQ mentality, has been historically pushed into an impossible corner to do nothing but play a moronic. The national border collectively built national security. It was its original purpose. But, ironically, the national border became an ugly obstacle to 'hogtie' people's freedom, by checking up passports in making a long line for customs inspection, and also to hurt economic benefit by shooting up prices in disturbing free flows of commodities."

"The national border now hurts a brisk process of globalization by its deeply carved stigma of jingoistic habits, concepts and practices. We are going to destroy the national borders step by step, along with a rapid increase of the sanctions for complete 'Free Trade' on the earth."

Jay Kim asked another cup of regular coffee to the Oval Office attendant and continued his talk about "Free Trade."

"Free Trade connotes no national border, no taxation, no overlapping regulations and no indirect social cost. Free Trade will slim human's economic structure from undesirable heavy fats into a splendid physique by disallowing the build-up of additives in the supply process. How much we are going to save is a big question. But Free Trade alone will cut the humongous, hidden indirect costs, on top of slashing out the acts of racketeering monopoly under the name of national interest."

"Free Trade, also, will boost the cost-efficient localizing of a product. For example, Japanese consumers will not have to pay ten times higher price for their rice than other country for the top quality one produced in California or Louisiana of the U.S. The marketplace of petroleum or natural gas managed by the Global Government will stabilize the world's energy-based economy which will have a great ripple effect on all other economic fronts too, along with a vigorous global policy of replacing the present fuel-based energy to the solar and wind and ocean-current energy. One tenth of the U.S.'s present budget will be more than enough together with one military forces of the Super Constitution that will be discussed later on by our military minister Dr. Yen-Jee Wang."

Jay Kim drank the   coffee brought by the Oval Office attendant, and continued his remark on the matter of Free Trade.

"I have an excellent idea on the global economy in terms of Free Trade. Let's look at all nation's numbers and statistics of their budget and their economic scales. The numbers and statistics dwarf our imagination. The giant scales make our brain cells stagger around. My rough figure alarms my heart. The waste of world economy by the inefficient bureaucracies, unheard-of military build-ups, non free trade items, unnecessary taxations, and the national borders altogether exceeds the amount of the gross world product."

"The Free Trade will make it possible for the world industry to kick off its economic neurons for activating its muscle power. The unbridled freedom of Free Trade will kindle the world commerce to its full extent through a much lower cost of product: it nurtures its market value, expands its marketing periphery, stimulates an upgrade of quality, and finally

Article 14: Countdown

generates a synergistic effect on all economic activities. Of course, the Free Trade causes the relocation of some industries and shifts a weak market into fade-out. But it creates new dimensions and innovative circumstances for the affected people after all."

U.S. President Garfield, seeing a sagging morale of his cabinet upon President Kirkman's thrashing over for the spirit of the Super Constitution, tried to whip up his cabinet into good cheer.

"Well, Dr. Kim, the matter of National Border and Free Trade is very exciting and impressive. The target points out an excellent attraction. But, getting there remains the prevalent concern. We have to, I think, focus our ideas on how to deliver rather than how to clarify the attractions. I think figuring out how to get there truly magnifies our concern. The imagination of the target contains no arguable stuff."

"However, the process of achieving the target has no precedent. Of course, that's why we are here. I can tell one thing sure: We cannot achieve 'no national border' and complete free trade if we have to sacrifice some humanitarian concerns and if we could break some laws under the name of revolution. I would like to suggest, gentlemen, to organize an ad hoc committee for each major topic: for example, language committee, free trade committee and military committee, and etc."

President Kirkman responded to the U.S. President's suggestion to organize the committee immediately.

"I am glad to hear Mr. President Garfield's recommendation. Actually, we came here to set up R&D for making a decision about the basic direction of the topics we are contemplating now."

Super Constitution

President Kirkman encouraged President Garfield's outspoken idea. President Kirkman thought he might have to undergo a severe backfire in his bold attempt to quell China's resistance on the division of China into 20 nations and to pacify Russia's irritation on the dismantling job of the WMD. But he maneuvered China and Russia into his arena, which solidified his standing on his entering into the pantheon of the glamorous globalization.

His motive moved in an ever-higher confidence. But he had a tedious anxiety in dealing with super powerful figures amidst his vulnerableness: to persuade the powerful figures for the change against their titanic interests. Without Miss Ohara, Kirkman was nothing but an ordinary green horn scholar. Kirkman, from the beginning, realized that he was one of puppets played by Miss Ohara. But he figured he had happened to be riding a big gunboat. He had happened to become a captain of that awesome gunboat. He had been serious about the happening. And in the other sense he could think he had been enjoying in playing with fantastic toys.

He sometimes thought he was on a long journey in a dream. Behind his audacious confidence–built along the developed incidents and conversations with Miss Ohara–he could not refuse his creeping recognition that he had no power. He just looked like exercising a great power. His innate consciousness active in his every brain cell told him that he was a man of empty hand. That recognition got on his nerves time to time, especially before and after a major event or incident. George Kirkman, through this mist of self-understanding, used to deposit his psychological irritations to the bottom of his heart.

In the meantime, after all, he had to vitalize his imagination on the shift of political power, social change, business climate, culture-revolution, managemental innovation, and others. Kirkman demonstrated bravery and intelligence at every conference even though he felt his mind toddled. He always

Article 14: Countdown

sustained a confidence over every procedure he presided. However, always, he had been uncertain over the exact consequences. We could consider this status of anxiety to be the "root of humility," which would nurture the root of smart decision because the smart decision comes from the humble stance that provides objective stance.

Kirkman acknowledged the U.S.'s military might as a foremost faculty for the symbol of the political power in terms of organization and equipment and personnel and size. And also he observed its political capacity as a dynamic energetic source for bringing an excellent wrapping power for the program he had in mind. But he worried about the U.S.'s intention to accommodate the Global Government with its giant assets.

Of course, on top of the killing power, delivering means and communicating capability, the Global Government entered into the middle of organizing a dreadful, scientific network of intelligence gathering performance hand in hand with Miss Ohara. The intelligence minister Andrei Milovanov, finished a master plan and placed the plan in the middle of implementing the worldwide network. He could catch any major organization or institution's communication by wire or wireless, or could watch and listen to any meetings or conferences open or clandestine.

Virtually, everyone on the earth would have no privacy. Any organized mutiny, rebellion and seduction plot would be watched and heard by the intelligence network. On top of the above, four critical, monopolized powers (politics, economy, military and social services) and the only one military organization of the Global Government would stabilize Global Government's governing force. Kirkman, however, had to deliver this concept to the U.S. Presidential Cabinet not as a pressure or a threat but as an amicable emergence of a favorable reality to the people. Even though Kirkman surely predicted the U.S.'s cooperation, he displayed cautious approach not to disturb the U.S. Cabinet's pride.

U.S. President and the members of his inner circle fully understood the undertone of Kirkman's soft manner of persuasion. But surrendering everything completely did not make a sense to them.

First of all, they felt shame of giving up their mighty sovereignty to an unknown handful of scholars powered by the hidden technological source. Their minds were drenched with a bitter chagrin, implicitly pitched their grumble to reticence and kept silence in a poker face.

Secondly, they tried or hoped to grab even a straw to insert any of their influence in erecting a new global policy for the world's new order. They pretended very unhappy in losing their authority, prestige, and prerogative. They poised that they should be compensated for the cooperation they might render.

Thirdly, they figured the Global Government could not actually deploy the killing power to kill innocent lives. Maybe, Kirkman Cabinet would exercise the killing wave to intimidate any nascent opposition to obliterate a wide range of upheaval. If the U.S. took an intrepid manner to resist the Global Government's indiscriminative orders, the Kirkman Cabinet would yield something as they did to China and Russia. The U.S. could contribute tremendous building blocks to the globalization.

Hereby, the U.S. and Kirkman's Cabinet started in a tug of war for a compromise of gaining more shares on the new power emergence. President Kirkman tried to secure a complete cooperation of the U.S. And the U.S. tried to get more yields from the Global Government. Over this wriggle, Garfield and Kirkman brainstormed in searching for

Article 14: Countdown

something that could bring a breakthrough to the hard feelings and refractory concepts created by their fervent insistences.

President Garfield thought about throwing an extravagant and lavish cocktail party to relax both parties so that both could mingle their feelings to make a friendly atmosphere. After all, he figured that the U.S. and Kirkman's Cabinet would have to work together on many major fronts of the globalizing process. Meanwhile, in order for the U.S. Cabinet to take it easy, Kirkman thought about giving the U.S. a job of organizing ad hoc committees for the study of feasibility to implement Global Government's intention on the matters of ten subjects: religion, language, education, criminology, economic theory, public enterprise, tax, national border, free trade, and only one military organization in the world.

Before President Kirkman would announce a plan for a breakthrough of the hard feelings and refractory concepts by actuating the job of organizing the above ad hog committees, he presided over a further talk about the final subject for the day: the military organization of the Global Government.

Dr. Yen-Jee Wang, who used to work for China's Politburo institute in charge of military matter as a chief advisor to China's Central Military Committee's Chairman (p. 143), took Kirkman's offering to talk about the Global Government's intention of military organization. Dr. Wang already had a master plan of the whole military structure and units from squads through brigadiers to divisions and corps, and its strategic posts. At this time, however, Dr. Wang would outline only the topic of the military scale, performance, and controlling mechanism.

"Gentlemen, I am glad to be able to explain the purpose of maintaining military power for the Global Government, and to define the limit of its power in addition to describing its scale, performance and controlling mechanism. I would like to tell you the purpose of a military existence primarily for the sake of establishing and maintaining the global new order."

"Mostly, the military strength of the Global Government will symbolize the Super Constitution's ownership of an overpowering clout over carrying on the legal authority of the Global Government. The executive branch of the Global Government will exercise the mandates given by the people through Congress according to the spirit of the Super Constitution. Fundamentally the executive branch's executing power of decrees will be buttressed up from overpowering armed forces only."

"In other words, governing power of any form must have clear symbol as an outstanding nemesis. Nobody can even try to emulate the executive branch's executing power of decrees authorized by Congress. Only the overpowering military strength should play an unchallenged nemesis for the Global Government, and it must also be the only one in the world controlled by the Global Government."

"In reference to the limit of military power, I would like to make sure of its existing role for the sake of existence only as a scarecrow. Global Government wishes it never exercise the military power. Of course, all military units will have maneuvers and mobile operations, and will develop special strike forces time to time according to a schedule and training purpose. Additionally, no unit of the military will ever move without the executive branch's pre-approval. All military units must keep an alert during its time on duty. The global intelligence network will work round clock to check their communications and movements, on top of political officer's vigilance in each unit from regimental headquarters up to corps' headquarters. Therefore, all units just present its existence. They move only according to the due commanding orders."

Article 14: Countdown

"Regarding the military scale, performance, and its controlling mechanism, I would like to explain in this way. In order to serve to maintain peace on this earth for more than six billion population, about one million manpower of army, navy, marine, Coast Guard, and Air Force will be enough. Each sector of the above five departments would carry its own R&D and intelligence unit to enhance its weapons systems and fact-finding performance: 400,000 manpower for army, 200,000 for navy, 100,000 for marine, 200,000 for Coast Guard, and 100,000 for Air Force."

"Military strength will be used for containing natural disasters, helping specific public works, and preventing some rampant crimes in addition to their usual practice for training and security activities. The military strength of this envisioned and organized massive manpower presents awesome threat to the people and to the government institutes if that military strength deviated from the due course of a chain of command. Therefore, we will apply a scientific internal controlling mechanism, which will work as a precision machine. Intelligence Ministry's specific overview and President's Special Security Commander's office, will check every major military units and personnel's communication by wire and wireless, and will study the behavior of major commanders. Gentlemen, if you have any doubts or questions, please do not hesitate to speak now."

Dr. Yen-Jee Wang talked for a long length of time. The U.S. President and his inner-circle members intensively listened to Dr. Wang's monumental shocking story. They expected it. But, upon hearing it directly from the man who was in charge of the military matters of the Global Government, they were astounded. They felt a sudden blowup. Now, the last day of the earth, after all, banged their ears. Finally, they were witnessing the apocalypse of the balance of their political power right in front of them. The giant U.S. military power looked a naïve cub. The formidable U.S. political machine toddled in front of this giant Dr. Wang.

The U.S. President shook his head a little to recover from that shocking story of the monstrous moment of the global power metastasis. President Garfield realized the tide flowed against the so-called super powers, including G8 nations. The globalizing movement won its momentum using Miss Ohara's mysterious technology. And, to make matters worse to the super powers, the movement happened to ride along on the prodigious group of talented Kirkman's Cabinet. President Garfield grasped the emerging reality. He had to absorb current incidents on the spur of the moment to survive. Immediately he offered his thought of a "cocktail party."

"Gentlemen, I am glad to understand Dr. Wang's concerns on one military organization on the earth. It is a fantastic idea even though it could create a cantankerous conflict among super powers of the world. I think the U.S. could make a substantial contribution to the one military matter. I am sure that all of us have tons of homework. In order to make our cooperation with President Kirkman's Cabinet more flexible, I think, we should better communicate through more familiarity, informally as well as formally. I would like to throw a cocktail party in the West Room of this White House for our members and President Kirkman's Cabinet the next week. How do you like my idea, President Kirkman?"

"Well, President Garfield, I appreciate your suggestion. I agree that an informal party would ease our tension, boost our friendship and upgrade the level of each other's understanding."

President Kirkman welcomed the party idea. Usually, a party signifies a success of certain things or reinforces a certain memorandum. Through the informal exchange of conversation, Kirkman figured that he could relay his

Article 14: Countdown

attractive offer to the U.S. Cabinet to organize the ad hoc committees to conduct a study of the feasibility, which requires vast data and an immense pool of talented professionals.

Kirkman also still worried about drawing a full scale of the U.S.'s cooperation in establishing stability of the globalizing process. Kirkman thought the real countdown for the Global Government's power initiative would start from the point of the U.S.'s complete submission to cooperation. Otherwise, Kirkman had to invoke the killing wave, which would pave a rough road that he would have to cross over to achieve his target.

Seemingly smiles prevailed in the conference. They all could not truly overlook the fact that they were actually walking around each other on eggshells. The U.S. President Garfield's suggestion of a cocktail party and Kirkman's quick response relieved everyone's profound anxiety so as to turn the conversation away from so dangerous a topic. They were imminently pushed into a dangerous corner to confront one another. Everyone felt relief. Everybody felt happy. Kirkman and Garfield smiled at each other in thanking each other. The real countdown for the Global Government's great initiative on the global governing prowess, for the time being, came to a temporary halt, allowing a deep breath right before action to take place.

Ideology constitutes the basic frame of human mentality, which exerts human energy to move on. Any leadership of any movement first must form a certain ideology on the matter intended for that leadership. A form and the content of that ideology move the person's behavior to do this or that. In order to set up the form and content of that ideology, we have to use reasoning power for the target with inescapable enforcement.

Super Constitution

In Kirkman's case, of course, he capitalized on the enforcing tool of the killing wave in the form of indirect threat. Kirkman had to implant an ideology that he could and would wield the killing power to enforce the ideal globalization. The implanted ideology would play the bottom resource of energy to move the human mind towards his target. Kirkman's whole program or effort had been focused on that implanting activity. When he finished the implanting job, literally his power initiative would roll on.

Kirkman had passed the Chinese peak and Russian valley. Now he had to pass through the gorge of the U.S. in order to materialize his governing power for the global matter of the ten subjects. If Kirkman could fix the U.S.'s main leaders into the concept that they had nothing but to accept his cabinet's idea on the ten subjects, and also into the concept that they had nothing but to carry on the orders logically derived from the spirit of the Super Constitution, then he thought he could dispatch the business in full steam ahead on all ten subjects.

The ten subjects of world affairs, however, were not a piece of cake. It is no fun to tackle a labyrinthine puzzle of human affairs. The world affairs tangled by the complexities of the human mind, truly challenged the smart mind. Kirkman threw himself into challenging the unknown world of human history without any confirmation. Without any available confirmation or diagnosis, only with his hazy preferences and his confidence on the justification of the globalization that had been supported by the technology, he took up the challenge. It was almost an impossible thing for the common sense to expect human creativity alone to make it possible to solve the ten subjects because the human mind is so fragile and uncertain to be able to be formed into a desirable shape without a long practice of habit.

Nonetheless, Kirkman took on it with mobilizing his intelligent intuition and his invincible bravery imbedded at the

Article 14: Countdown

bottom of his consciousness. Kirkman was a man of brilliance, pursuing knowledge during his age of study. He was a man of talent, chasing the unknown world with plenty of curiosity and enthusiasm. Not only his extraordinarily high intelligence, but also his passion for justice, bolstered him to engage in the seemingly bottomless pit of the ten subjects of globalization.

Now, Kirkman faced the countdown to break the concept of the U.S. Cabinet's attitude that they were the forerunners in forming the leadership to tackle world affairs. Kirkman had to switch the U.S. Cabinet's ideology from being the ones who would issue orders to the ones who would receive them. It is not easy job for the human mind to switch such stances. But one key factor to change the human mind is to let them compare which is better in the new, inexorable reality.

At this point, to the U.S. Cabinet, the Super Constitution was emerging as an unstoppable reality. In this circumstance, to survive, the U.S. Cabinet had to adopt themselves to the new environment as quickly as possible so as to insert their super assets into the process of the imminent globalization, no matter what it was going to be, and no matter how it was going to go.

Kirkman gave enough time. He provided enough leeway. He earnestly tried to protect the pride of the U.S. Cabinet. President Garfield and Kirkman thought the same thing, figured the same way, and understood the imperative almost at the same time. However, the palatable solution for the desirable breakthrough will meet a tantalizing taste of success in the next article of this chapter.

Article 15

Breakthrough

U.S. President John Garfield, and his Chief of Staff Edmund Murdock, sat together face to face in the Oval Office to talk about the cocktail party that President Garfield proposed the other day.

"Eddy, what type of cocktail party do you suggest?

"Well, Mr. President, I have an idea for the best but small and cozy one I have been thinking about."

"What is it?"

"Generally, I am thinking about a nice band of five or six best musicians in the country, along with topnotch singers, actors, actresses, and beauty queens. And about ten people from our office, and another one dozen of guests from the Global Government. Actually this party is to entertain the idea of revolutionary globalization of the Global Government under the name of the Super Constitution."

"We should engender an excellent mood and atmosphere they never imagined thus far. We don't have to mention anything

Article 15: Breakthrough

about the pending subjects. We just try to let the Kirkman Cabinet experience an unusual scene of the most luxurious entertaining evening, which distinguishes from the academic event. It is going to be a dynamic party memorable to the dry academic world. It is going to refresh their mind, tenderize their stance, and attract the hidden libido of their sexual desire."

President Garfield was impressed by his chief of staff's simple brief on the party's side effect, which could be the main payoff or outcome of the event. Usually, a high-powered exotic mood, which triggers phenomenal sentiment, could move an intelligent mind to a favorable memory for the party thrower. From Edmund Murdock's brief, President Garfield could sense some strange nook of the human mind animated by a pleasant scene which comes from the ability of recognizing thousands of natural secrets and phenomena, and also comes from each individual's understanding capacity.

No matter how wonderful scene exists or goes on, if the spectator does not have a cognitive capacity to appreciate it, it is going to be a nil. President Garfield and Edmund Murdock thought the party they were preparing would create one of the most thrilling exhilaration for the Global Government's key members. The key members must have possessed an excellent cognitive capacity, but yet they must have never experienced an informal and intimate party with those popular hot celebrities.

The White House's special party would boost closer informal relationship between the U.S. and the Kirkman's Cabinet that had clashed with each other in an effort to produce the least noise at the juncture of turbulence in the process of the greatest change of human politics: one side for creating a brand new current; and the other for trying to take a lion's share from the new current being created.

Super Constitution

Believing that the White House Cabinet folded their sovereign right, but still adhered to their innate influence in the world affairs, and maintained an unflagging faith in setting up a new world order, Kirkman put himself in their place and attempted to understand their unspoken ambition in the process of his globalization. One thing that Kirkman clearly realized about the ambition of the White House Cabinet was their positive participation, in the process of organizing ad hoc committees to establish the influential policies of the ten subjects.

Beyond that positive intention, regarding how to execute the policies, how much influence they wanted to exercise and how to pick the right people for the position managing the policies, the White House Cabinet's intentions were not clear. In other words, how much shares to take were they thinking about in running those matters? The inner circle of the White House did not reflect their real inner mind to the guesses of Kirkman's imagination. Kirkman could not fathom the exact depth of their desire. If the difference would get wider, the discord would become greater, rendering inefficient results for his achievement. While Kirkman groped for an answer himself, the inner circle of the White House vigorously searched for as many possible ways out as they could for achieving their target.

In the middle of dismissing the White House Oval Office meeting of October 6, 2016, for the party matter between President Garfield and his chief of staff Edmund Murdock, U. S. Defense Secretary Charles Manatt happened to discuss some other matters with Malcom Stark, the Intelligence Czar, in the security office. Because Manatt knew Miss Ohara checked almost every conference and conversation they conducted, he whispered to the ear of Stark.

"Malcom, since they listen to every word we talk, I'd like to discuss something that we don't want to be exposed, by writing or exchanging memos."

Article 15: Breakthrough

Stark nodded seriously expressing an agreement. The memo given by Manatt to Stark read as the following:

"Malcom, I am sure we can do a lot of things if we can avoid eavesdropping from Miss Ohara, and I am sure there are enough rooms for us to maneuver our military capability and intelligence network to steer the negotiation with Miss Ohara. I am going to talk this matter over tonight with Richard Hancock, my protégé, two-star general, 16th divisional commander. He has an appointment with me tonight. I have a plan to mobilize one battalion of air-borne troopers to arrest Kirkman's Global Government Cabinet, and from there on, we can negotiate with Miss Ohara. We have to insist that the global language must be English and the one military forces must be from the U.S."

Malcom scribbled a short sentence on his memo-pad.

"I agree. I will do whatever you need."

In this way, without the U.S. President's pre-approval, the dark clandestine plan went on between Charles Manatt and Richard Hancock, at the night of October 6th, right after the Oval Office meeting between the President and his chief of staff to plan the upcoming party.

Richard Hancock paid a visit to Manatt, his mentor, according to an appointment made the other day. Accordingly, the Global Government Intelligence network traced this general's movement and whereabouts according to the routine report they made. The unit of global covert operation followed Hancock to the defense secretary's residence and locked up a listening equipment to record all conversations done between Hancock and Manatt as usual.

Super Constitution

There were no specific warning factors in their conversations. Manatt handed some papers as usual for a reference on certain incident interested to both of them. Among the papers, Hancock could notice a special memo written by Manatt about the special maneuvering plot, which would be conducted by the general with his best unit of battalion controlled by his most trustworthy lieutenant colonel. The date, time, place, and what to do were clearly indicated. The general nodded without saying anything.

The date was set to take place two days after the White House West Room party. General Hancock wrote his own memo for his protégé Lieut. Col. and sent that detailed memo, along with the one written by Manatt, by his driver to that battalion commander. In this way, a complete and perfect covert plot was set up to arrest the Global Government Cabinet and to round them up into a specially organized interrogation room to start negotiation with Miss Ohara, under very dangerous a brinkmanship. Manatt and Stark braced up themselves and prepared some draft to talk with Miss Ohara.

At the same time, the unusually small, cozy, and yet most extravagant and star-studded White House West Room party, was being organized by Edmund Murdock. He had been busy in contacting celebrities and telling them about the party's distinctive features which not only top government officials but also world-figure celebrities should take a positive stance to affect those Kirkman guys. All of celebrities Murdock contacted understood imminent situations they had to participate, and also, they responded in an enthusiastic response because they knew that the miraculous historical revolution was looming all over the world. Those unusual circumstances made Murdock's job easy.

Murdock made a report on the progress for the party to the President. President Garfield felt confident of the party's success. He was now sure that he could conduct a study of the

Article 15: Breakthrough

feasibility the way he was thinking about: implementing the English language as the global one and American military power into the Global Government. The U.S. President thought that Kirkman Cabinet and Miss Ohara would think the same way as he would. The logic supported his way of thinking. But the decision was not his. If Miss Ohara would say China, or Russia, or even Japan or any other country in the world, he thought, he couldn't do anything else but to follow Miss Ohara's decision. That was his presumption.

Even though U.S. President Garfield presumed that the decision-making issue depended solely on Miss Ohara, the inference indicated that Miss Ohara and Kirkman Cabinet were inclined to use the English language and American military muscle. Important publications and libraries for leading intellectuals across the world undulated throughout every day in English. The efficient military operation would culminate in a homogeneous unit of communication, culture, compassion and a mental state, and not in a mixed unit of the best soldiers from hither and thither. Upon considering simple facts of human nature and current life organization, President Garfield felt confident of his inference. His feeling was elated. He thought he would enjoy the White House party. He imagined he would steer something desirable in the course of the new world order.

Now, Murdock's preparation for the White House party went on for a perfect performance. Meanwhile Manatt and Stark maneuvered a clandestine plot to arrest Kirkman Cabinet with easy. Manatt's protégé Richard Hancock and his confidant lieutenant colonel grew excited with ecstasy in waiting to get a launching signal from Manatt.

Paratroopers of the chosen battalion could fly over the New York City's East River to an empty lot of the river's east bank from Elizabeth, New Jersey in ten minutes, and another ten minutes would take the battalion to cross over the East

Super Constitution

River by speed boats, to take over the U.N. building, which housed the temporary office of Kirkman Cabinet. Miss Ohara and Kirkman Cabinet were in dark about the plot. President Garfield himself did not know about it at all. The White House party had been set at October 12th night. Manatt ordered Richard Hancock to mobilize the operations of the battalion's paratroopers at 10:30 a.m., October 14th.

The White House party had ended with a great success: everyone experienced an unusual pleasure. Especially, Kirkman cabinet enjoyed a great deal of exotic feelings with the world-class entertainers face to face in person. Kirkman cabinet felt sensational rapture on talking with the best actors and actresses, beauty queens and topnotch singers, at such a close proximity and real-life facial expressions. A substantial volume of bursting laughs and cracking jokes shuffled around in the West Room amid the party's participants.

President Garfield and President Kirkman exchanged meaningful nods and glimpse in a highly satiated level of the partygoers. Kirkman, from the bottom of his heart, appreciated President Garfield's generous and thoughtful hospitality given to his Cabinet. Kirkman truly felt close friendship with the U.S. President, who also hosted an overnight stay for Kirkman's Cabinet at the White House.

The next day, after a late morning breakfast at the White House, Kirkman's Cabinet flew to New York City, and resumed their normal work the following day, 14th, as usual. At the office, Kirkman conceived and outlined a plan of drawing the U.S.'s role in setting up the ad hoc committees which would exercise enormous influence in forming the new world order. Kirkman, also, intensively ruminated the most controversial and nerve-wracking subjects of one-world language and only one military existence of the world.

Article 15: Breakthrough

Richard Hancock and his confident lieutenant colonel appeared at the U.N. building located at 45th street and 1st avenue of Manhattan, New York City around 10:15 a.m., 14th, by Hancock's car driven by his driver. The general manager of New York City's regional headquarters Robert Lincoln, who was a close associate to the Global Government Intelligence Minister Andrei Milovanov, called Milovanov in the U.N. building around 10:30 a.m., 14th, over the mobile phone.

"Andrei, this is Bob. My secretary just informed me some suspicious movement of a two-star general, the leader of 16th division of Pennsylvania area, just arrived at the U.N. building with the commander of his battalion of paratroopers, without any report to our office. Any commander above the company grade is supposed to make a routine report about their movement. But the two-star general and his battalion leader have moved without our recognition and clearance."

"Oh! Bob, when did they arrive?"

"About fifteen minutes ago."

"Bob, please send our emergency security-crews to walk them off to my interrogation office immediately."

Andrei Milovanov called Kirkman, told him of an urgent poignancy, and advised him to contact Miss Ohara and the U.S. President immediately. Realizing a gravity of the situation, Kirkman first called Miss Ohara to inform her of the dangerous situation, and then called President Garfield.

"President Garfield, your U.S. army's 16th division leader, Richard Hancock, has come to the U.N. building with his paratroopers' battalion commander lieutenant colonel, who is stationed in Elizabeth, New Jersey, without giving their routine reports for clearance. Are you aware of the gravity of this situation? The battalion of eight hundred man-powered paratroopers can occupy the U.N. building in less than thirty minutes by just one mobile phone call if they had some plot in advance. I hope they will not commit any grave mistake. But my hunch tells me it is very serious."

"President Kirkman, I don't know anything   about this incident. Absolutely, it is no good at all. I will find out what happened immediately. President Kirkman! I will invoke my supreme commandment to stop him immediately, and please do what ever you can, and I will follow your command without any mistake."

"But President Garfield, please don't do anything until I call you again. The time is now approaching 11 o'clock."

Richard Hancock stood at the northeast corner of the U.N. plaza with his lieutenant colonel, and told his colonel to make a mobile phone call to his D-day officer to order him the airborne operations. Immediately the lieutenant colonel began to punch in the numbers, reached his D-day officer on the phone, and issued the order under the number of code as they prearranged (the clock was ticking at 10:40 a.m.).

"Henry! This is Ron."

"Yes sir, Colonel. I am ready."

"Good, Henry. You have code number ten."

"Thank you, Colonel, I understand, sir."

As soon as the lieutenant colonel finished issuing order by the name of "code number ten," four U.N. special security agents surrounded General Hancock and Colonel Ron to question them.

"Are you Mr. Hancock and Fox?"

Article 15: Breakthrough

"No. My name is Sonny Johnson and this is my friend Frank Kennedy."

"Well, I just heard this guy said, 'this is Ron', anyway you two must follow us to our office on 19th floor."

The chief of the U.N. special security team spoke Hancock and Fox in a quiet and calm voice.

"Gentlemen, we have to disarm you first. Please cooperate with us."

By the time the U.N. special security team walked the general and lieutenant colonel to the interrogation office, the clock was ticking at 10:50 a.m.

The general and lieutenant colonel realized what was going on, and made no resistance. They figured they could handle the situation after their paratroopers would take over the U.N. building in less than thirty minutes. The arrow had already left the bowstring. But the general had made a grand mistake. He had to come with the paratroopers, so that they could maneuver themselves without restricting their freedom. Now they lost their freedom to move around and they were entirely cut off from their own battalion.

The general and lieutenant colonel thought that the Kirkman Cabinet would have to negotiate with them, no matter where they were located, as long as their own men surrounded the U.N. building. But in reality, they had been separated from their real power base–their fully armed entity. The head of the battalion had been disconnected in the line of communication from the battalion's main body, which required receiving orders in order to activate its well-flexed body function. Unfortunately, the battalion's nervous system could not find any transmitted message from its head on what to do. The general and lieutenant colonel paid too naive attention to this last minute and final peripheral function.

Henry Ford, the D-day officer, felt his anxiety growing up by the minute. He had not heard anything in more than thirty minutes after he completed his mission to take over the U.N. building (at 11 a.m.). Henry Ford was supposed to see the general or the lieutenant colonel at the time he arrived at the U.N. building. But he had not even heard any word from them and any message either. Time had really dragged on. The prolonging silence looked going forever. Another half-hour passed. One hour had gone since the battalion had occupied the U.N. building. The D-day officer Ford now was getting sick and tired. His patience ran out. The situation got on his nerves. All this silence went on by the tactics Kirkman fixed with his Intelligence Minister Andrei Milovanov. Kirkman asked Miss Ohara send a message to the D-day officer after one hour of long silence. Miss Ohara then sent a message to the D-day officer.

"Major, Henry Ford! This is Miss Ohara. Do you hear me?"

Ford was startled. All of a sudden, he stiffened, expecting to hear the worst.

"Yes, ma'am, I hear you clearly!"

Ford was used to hearing about Miss Ohara, who had become a household word. He never expected a direct word from Miss Ohara to himself. He was, quite suddenly, aroused.

"You may now understand what has happened to your superior officers, Richard Hancock and Ron Fox. They are under the Global Government's custody. I order you return immediately to your barracks with your men. If you don't take action now, you are going to receive a killing wave. This is my last word, Major Ford!"

Article 15: Breakthrough

"Yes, ma'am, I understand. I will return to my base with my men immediately. Our specially arranged twenty buses are already here in the U.N. complex."

"Very well, major!"

The 16th division's special battalion returned without any hassle.

However, some unpleasant antagonism precipitated the relationship between Kirkman Cabinet and the White House to a prickly sensation, wiping out the good feelings of friendship and trust that the White House party had created.

After Kirkman settled the coup to end in smoke, he contacted President Garfield to find out the ins and outs of the matter. Upon hearing the whole story, Kirkman Cabinet assessed the current situation of the incident's before and after. The Cabinet arrived at the following conclusions:

First: to authenticate a black and white clear precedent that anyone who will be involved in any plot to impede the Global Government's processes or orders shall be punished severely.

Second: to enforce incremental steps for stronger and more scientific control for gathering intelligence.

Third: to expedite the processes of the Global Government's executive power; to reinforce the speed of organizing ad hoc committees of ten subjects.

Fourth: to institute some awarding events for the people or organizations that would cooperate with the Global Government.

Super Constitution

Fifth: to propagandize the concept that the Global Government is the real form and movement for the people.

While expediting the above five businesses, Kirkman notified President Garfield that the Global Government made a decision to set up a revolutionary tribunal which would handle emergent incidents including a coup or coup de tat against the Global Government. Until the administrative decree and prosecution functions of the Global Court would be fixed, the above revolutionary tribunal would handle the incident of General Richard Hancock and Lieut. Col. Ron Fox.

President Garfield sincerely apologized to Kirkman about what had happened by his close associates and expressed his deep regret and tried his best to repair the damaged relationship. However, unfortunately, to the U.S. President, the incident was spilt milk, which became an unpleasant burden in running cooperation with Kirkman's Cabinet. Kirkman's Cabinet worked off the effects of the incident of General Hancock by speeding up the tribunal: a capital punishment on Defense Secretary Charles Manatt, Intelligence Czar Malcom Stark, General Richard Hancock and lieutenant colonel Ron Fox; and a dishonorable discharge for the D-day officer Henry Ford, considering his cooperative behavior of returning to his barrack immediately in respecting Miss Ohara's order

Thus, the U.S. President lost two devoted secretaries plus two unknown army officers of high caliber in a short period of time. This loss, by far, made a play for a close-up of seriously warning demonstration that any hostile behavior or any clandestine treachery against the globalizing processes would be beheaded surely and promptly. This incident, actually, prompted the Global Government to be able to work at a higher plateau with better vision of their direction while dropping the U.S. President's influence on handling the ten subjects.

Article 15: Breakthrough

Kirkman conversed with President Garfield upon finishing the tribunal's judgment of punishment. The U.S. President said to President Kirkman.

"President Kirkman! I have to replace National Security Advisor, Defense Secretary, and Intelligence Minister with your advice. I would prefer to appoint your own choice in order to expedite our cooperative relationship."

Kirkman welcomed the U.S. President's offer.

"President Garfield, that's an excellent idea. I think that will melt the hard feeling crystallized between your Cabinet and mine. I appreciate you. I will notify our choice to you as soon as possible."

Kirkman Cabinet (Wolfgang Thierse, Jay Kim, Toro Yono, Yen-Jee Wang, and Andrei Milovanov) made a decision to present following persons for the posts of NSA (National Security Advisor to the President), Defense Secretary, and Intelligence Minister of the U.S.: Michelle Sequoia, 28 years old and the U.S. Army's star genius, for the post of NSA; Philip Hillman, the current Vice Chairman of the Joint Chiefs of Staff, four-star General, for the post of Defense Secretary; and Paul Evanse, Andrei Milovanov's chief assistant and once close classmate of George Kirkman while in college, for the post of Intelligence Dept.

Regarding very attractive genius graduated from the West Point with a record performance, Article Seventeen of Chapter Four, under the title of "First Chairperson of the Joint Chiefs of Staff" of the Global Government, will introduce Miss Michelle Sequoia in detail. Four-star General Philip Hillman's talent had been checked and appraised by the Global Government's human resources committee a long time ago and had been considered as one of elite generals in the world and as a valuable candidate for the military personnel of the Global Government. Paul Evanse was already working closely with Kirkman Cabinet, and had provided substantial achievements in several cases, which were appreciated by Kirkman Cabinet.

Four-star General Hillman and Miss Sequoia had been summoned to the special panel of Kirkman Cabinet some time ago and had long conversations with the panel to examine Hillman and Michelle's intelligence, caliber of performance, and their way of thought. At that time, each other sensed that their similarity of thinking would work out for better communicating capability.

The U.S. President invited key congressional leaders to his Oval Office after he was notified by Kirkman about three important, high-ranking posts, and the President informed them of stories about the White House West Room party and the incident of battalion's coup and its subsequent tribunal.

One of the key congressional leaders, John McKenzie opened his remark.

"First of all, those three posts actually take the whole responsibility for the security management of not only our nation, but also the important affairs of the world's power shift. In other words, we are giving up our interests in and concerns of the most important world affairs. And, the second thing I am concerned about, which really surprised me, is the case of young female officer, Major Michelle Sequoia. Even, the badge of her rank of major sounds unusual. How could we have thought of using her at the post of National Security Advisor with a rank of major?"

The U.S. President responded to John McKenzie with a soft but low firm voice.

Article 15: Breakthrough

"Well, ladies and gentlemen, we are losing our sovereignty and governing authority as well. As all of you already realize, our nation is going to be divided into six nations, and also the national boundary is going to mean nothing. The force of balanced interest groups and a governing authority of the public mind had handled the power of politics. But now, in the revolutionary process of globalization by the Global Government and its extraordinary hi-tech, the usual force behind the power of our politics has been disappeared."

"We have to promptly adjust ourselves to the emerging concept that only scientific rationalism plays a main role in the process of forming the basic framework of our new world order. The present world is already the age of genius, but no longer the age of a balance of power or interplay of authorities. A time makes heroes and heroines. Genius makes humanity brighter. Genius is borne, not cultured. We have to learn how to respect genius. The young major Michelle Sequoia is one of these extraordinary geniuses that our world has now."

At the U.S. President's special remarks, the congressional leaders kept silence for a while. John McKenzie broke the heavy silence of the Oval Office.

"Thank you, Mr. President. I appreciate your invitation very much. I sincerely apologize for my ignorance."

The next day, President Garfield talked to Kirkman over the phone.

"President Kirkman, my congressional leaders completely understood your three recommended candidates for the posts. I am so glad to welcome them to my camp. I am sure that now we can expedite the organization of the ad hoc committees for the ten subjects."

Super Constitution

Kirkman praised the U.S. President from the bottom of his heart.

"President Garfield, congratulations! You've done it. We now have a great breakthrough in the globalizing processes."

Inscrutable are the ways of human affairs. An evil development turns out lucky break, time to time in human history. Sometimes, we meet unexpected, unspeakable hardships. Hereby, we need bravery, sustained determination and perseverance if we believe in.

Article 16

First World Armed Forces

October 2016.

On the last part of October 2016 (10/26/2016), the ad hoc committee for the first world armed forces took off in order to finish a study of the feasibility for only one military power in the world, along with another crucial committee for one-world language. These two committees quickly went forward to solidify the Global Government's omnipotent symbol of the world's unprecedented political power.

President Garfield organized the administrative offices together with ten members of the ad hoc committee of one-world language, and another ten members of the ad hoc committee of one-world military muscle. Of course, organizations of other eight ad hoc committees and their administrative offices followed immediately.

However, the ad hoc committee of the first world armed forces played the most powerful leadership in consolidating the Global Government's governing power as if it were a super-nova in making a galaxy in the Universe.

Super Constitution

The most controversial, sensitive, and nerve-wracking issue of making a decision for the globalizing process was falling on a subject of organizing only one-world armed forces because it is going to play only one backbone of the world's political muscles. And also, one-world armed forces only can replace the current omnipotent technology when Miss Ohara returns to her home planetary, twenty-one light-years away from the earth.

Human political power had been formed since the evolution of human being from the some world as the lord of all creations. But, our imagination and human history pointed out that the earth was too big, harsh, and complicated. Human nature has been too egoistic, smart, and prolific. During the last more or less one hundred thousands of years according to modern anthropologists' inference, the human society has developed into a complex composite with multi races and tribes, in addition to more than six hundreds of languages and about 200 national sovereignties. As each person fights and competes with each other, each nation does too. Each superpower has been glaring at each other throughout our modern written history. Nobody could help but fight and destroy.

Modern civilization and intelligent people understand that we should not fight and destroy, instead, that we should create, prosper, and enjoy our only one life. But as long as human nature goes on, the ideal formula can never come. George Kirkman, the executive chief of the Global Government, acknowledged that the ten subjects would provide the ideal formula. He also acknowledged that the most difficult subject would hinge on the ad hoc committee of the first world armed forces.

George Kirkman, therefore, at the first meeting of the "committee of the world armed forces," made an opening remark as the following:

Article 16: First World Armed Forces

"Ladies and gentlemen, I sincerely congratulate you on your appointments to this committee! This ad hoc committee to study the establishment of only one military machine of the world is not created for finding out how difficult task to organize it, but how efficiently we are going to organize it. We have too many hostile suspicions from too many individuals and institutes because only one military muscle of the world provides omnipotent governing-prowess with the Super Constitution."

"No one is going to be allowed to possess any type of firearms except local police forces and the world armed forces. And only the world armed forces is going to have an organized military strength which will maintain the overwhelming fire power with a substantial number of fully armed soldiers. Therefore, no one will have even a concept to contest or encounter the Global Government's military force."

"This one-world military existence, in other words, will have no rivals at all, will exercise a monopoly in terms of physical strength, and will maintain its immense muscle power as a big tiger versus a small cat. How powerful and how efficient it should be, you have to study, and together, you have to study how to surely control it."

Listening to President Kirkman's serious remark, the members of the committee became intensified. However, Miss Michelle Sequoia who had been appointed as the new U.S. security advisor to the U.S. Presidency took the bold smile raising her hand to get a voice. President Kirkman responded pleasantly to Miss Sequoia.

"Oh, Miss Sequoia, I am glad to see your smile. You must have some good news for the committee."

Super Constitution

Miss Sequoia was one of two lady committee members appointed together with the new U.S. Defense Minister Philip Hillman (p. 241).

"President Kirkman, thank you for your serious concern to the committee. I understand that you have indicated a difficult side of the matter. But we can also see the matter through a snug side. I am sure, President Kirkman, we can present a downright paper sooner than later."

"I hope, Miss Sequoia, I could have a smile on your committee's paper."

Other members had heard a reputation about the young lady genius-militarist. They figured Miss Sequoia must have had some fantastic idea on organizing one-world military machinery and its control. As Kirkman indicated at the opening remark for the committee, the Global Government preferred a single super military strength to any existence of other symmetrical military forces. However, the only one military power itself could turn its strength against the Global Government. Hence, in addition, they needed another side of that military structure as to an internal controlling mechanism.

Of course, the one side meant consummate power structure itself. The other side they needed at the same time, naturally, pertained to a perfect controlling mechanism of that only power. To make an efficient and powerful military institute required not much labyrinthine brainstorm. But making the perfect implement of controlling that monster presented a real, ferocious snarl. On top of the above twin inscrutable sphinxes, the committee must handle the intensified concerns of other people or nations that will not be involved in setting up the only one military power in the world.

The three headaches the committee faced listed: first to bring the most efficient military organization, second to invent the

Article 16: First World Armed Forces

most perfect internal controlling mechanism, and third to lullaby complaints from non involved parties. The committee held second meeting to elect chairman and to designate a draft writer for their agenda to discuss. They elected the U.S. Defense Secretary Philip Hillman as the chairman and designated the U.S. National Security Advisor Miss Michelle Sequoia as the draft writer.

The committee chairperson Hillman announced the following business decision the committee made:

"Ladies and gentlemen, I am glad to announce the decision we made today that we designate Miss Sequoia for the draft writer for the draft we are going to discuss, and to make a final decision to present to the Global Government to implement it. Our lady militarist has such a rich knowledge on the military matters and a deep insight on the perfect controlling mechanism and a palatable idea to quench potential, uprising complaints from the so-called experts."

"She said she probably could finish the draft in a week. As soon as she is going to be ready, I will notify all of you. Please be prepared to attend our next meeting. I am sure all of you understand what you are going to juggle around for the fundamental power platform for the world's new order. Miss Sequoia, please make a remark on your job."

Miss Sequoia stood up on her feet and took a calmly tempered countenance and spoke on the subject as the following:

"My dearly respected members, I am very much honored by the job given to me. I have been dreaming of organizing a worldwide military network from my school days on, together including the appropriate weapons systems, proportionate manpower, strategic layout for geopolitics, the best fabric of team organization for every unit, and the chain of command based on a scientific internal controlling mechanism. I have used to imagine the ideal management information system of the military machines. I would like to present the scale, firepower, mobility, coordinated maneuver, and intelligence networks of the one-world military machinery as a unique symbol of overwhelming dominance for the Global Government. As Mr. Hillman mentioned, I will do my best to present the draft to you as soon as possible. Thank you, my dear members."

The members of the ad hoc committee left the meeting with a pride and confidence in Miss Sequoia's touch-up of the subject. They had heard frequent admirations on her academic works and actual service in the field with soldiers. She was only a young, twenty-eight-year-old woman. But she accumulated such fames attracting even young boys and girls' attention. One of the members threw a casual question to his next guy.

"I am wondering how the hell that pretty girl can have a concept to conquer the world with her soft fist."

The next guy quickly responded.

"You know what? I am pretty much stimulated. My body's nerve root rattles my feeling. I don't know why. But I guess she is too beautiful to talk about such a masculine stuff. How come such a young, attractive, and sexy contour could brandish such heavy a sword?"

One guy, getting more excited on the next guy's odd quip, added an additional pep.

"Well, I am so much enthralled by her foresight on the military matter. I can't help but feel more curious about her draft to be presented to us in a week. You know what? I think I, maybe, fall in love with her fame because she is attractive and yet talking about masculine things."

Article 16: First World Armed Forces

The next guy heedlessly niggled with the one guy's offhand mutter:

"You know what? It's not just you. I'm also going crazy about her. Frankly speaking, we are fantasying dummies. But, we feel great. We enjoy being with her in that committee."

One week went fast. Bubbles of suspicious glare from the concerned experts in the field of military matter intensified every day. The glares focused on the meeting of the committee for the matter of one-world armed forces. Since October 14th coup of two-star General Richard Hancock and lieutenant colonel Ron Fox, the movement for activities of ad hoc committees forwarded the agenda fast. Philip Hillman, the U.S. Defense Secretary, four-star General, summoned his committee of world armed forces, on November 2, 2016.

Miss Michelle Sequoia, now serving the U.S. President's National Security Advisor (p. 241), distributed her draft to the members of the committee and a couple of scores of major reporters from the world, pre-selected by the committee chairman Philip Hillman, the U.S. Defense Secretary. Miss Sequoia made a speech on her draft, adding some examples and some jokes. Learning by heart of her draft was a piece of cake to her. She narrated as the following:

"Ladies and gentlemen, I am honored and pleased to present this draft to our members for thorough examinations. This draft describes my personal ideas and suggestions derived from frequent conversations done with President Kirkman and his military minister Dr. Yen-Jee Wang. I took President Kirkman and Minister Wang's idea as my main source of instruction. Of course, the finalized study will be summarized through the committee's meticulous deliberation."

Super Constitution

President Kirkman, as a matter of fact, tried to have a closed study-session of the feasibility of all ad hoc committees. But to mitigate a possible shock to the public and to measure the public's response before finalizing a study of the feasibility, Kirkman Cabinet made a decision to open the committee's activities to the public through major media. Miss Sequoia continued introducing her draft.

"My deer members, I would like to introduce the major subject of the ideal military structure, divided into the following seven areas: one: weapons systems, two: manpower, three: deployment, four: chain of command, five: mobility, six: maneuver, seven: intelligence, under the guidance of principles of efficiency and accuracy."

"First, the appropriate weapons systems:

As you know, according to the Super Constitution's instruction, the special team has already done a lot in the demolishing process of the WMD under the great leadership of Russia. The global military command is going to maintain only about 20 nuclear arsenals in the world, and accommodate only a couple of military special research institutes handling nuclear and chemical and biological weapons as for a testing sample or an experimenting explore. Therefore, the WMD will have only a handful figure as a tokenism."

"Besides the WMD, the other weapons systems would keep its advancing pace to continue for upgrading. Specifically, precision-targeting explosives, speeding, and engineering will vigorously continue its strenuous effort to keep abreast with modern, high-tech advancements. As you may realize, every nation's military authorities have vast funds and research projects to commandeer the superiority among its neighbors and the whole world, tightly sealed under the highest secrecy and exclusive confidentiality."

Article 16: First World Armed Forces

"Naturally, the world has wasted too much money and too many talents, by overlapping expenditures occurring from similar research projects, and by hiding its discoveries. Now the global military concerns can not waste anymore money and talents; they will concentrate only on a few institutes in the same field, and recruit worldwide talents and let them share all their discoveries."

"Second, ideal manpower and unit:

Regarding an ideal number of manpower and units of the world's military organizations, diversified opinions and disputes would consequently spring up. I'd like to quote some figures given by Global Military Minister Dr. Yen-Jee Wang (p. 223). Those are: army: 400,000, navy: 200,000, Marine Corps: 100,000, Air Force: 100,000, Coast Guard: 200,000. I'd like to indicate an approximate manpower of each unit of each department as the following":

"Army's manpower will be organized into 20 divisions with each division having 20,000 soldiers: forty brigades with each brigade consisting of 10,000: 120 regiments with each 3,333: 360 battalions with each 1,111: 1,080 companies with each 370: 5,400 platoons with each 74: 33,333 squadrons with each 12 soldiers."

"Navy's manpower is going to be consisted of five fleets. Each fleet will have two aircraft carriers (of 8,000 soldiers), four cruisers (bigger unit of battleship: of 3,000), eight destroyers (of 2,400), fifty battleships (smaller unit of battleship: of 10,000), fifty minesweepers (of 4,000), 100 submarines (of 8,000), and other miscellaneous ships such as supply, transportation, hospital, and landing crafts or ships, etc. (of 5,000 soldiers).'

Super Constitution

"Marine Corps will have five special divisions (100,000 soldiers) which are going to focus on coastal landing jobs and to protect naval bases and important government offices."

"Air Force is going to have twelve major commands for field operations with 72,000 soldiers and 7,000 airplanes, and going to have another three special commands: Mass Air Lift Command for special air transportation; Strategic Air Command for special air campaign anywhere in the world; and Air Security Command for communication and air traffic control (each special command: 10,000 soldiers)."

"Coast Guard is going to have ten special divisions, similar to Marine Corps, but different job except in case of special military maneuver. The main job concerns on all happenings in the coast. Ladies and gentlemen! These numbers might look tasteless and meaningless. But the one million soldiers trained and drilled and organized into these special units are no waste. This one million of manpower will act as a stabilizing force in the world and provide extra tactical service to the people of the world."

"Third, the deployment of the four departments:

Laying out highly efficient armed forces, according to population and geographical need, is also a challenging subject. I'd like to suggest as the following:

Army (20 divisions) will be located in five major areas, which commanded by corps commanders (three-star General). The location of the first corps' headquarters will be in Denver, Colorado; the second corps' headquarters will be in Berlin, Germany; third one will be in Tehran of Iran; fourth one will be in Shenyang of North China; fifth one will be in Kunming of South China. For proportional scattering of the units according to the local situations, the corps leader must make decisions with his area's four division commanders."

Article 16: First World Armed Forces

"Navy is going to have its five fleets' base as the following: the first fleet called 'San Diego Fleet' at San Diego, California; the second fleet of 'Norfolk Fleet' at Norfolk, Virginia; the third one of 'Gibraltar Fleet' at Gibraltar, Spain; the fourth one of 'Bombay Fleet' at Bombay (Mumbai), India; and the fifth one of 'Hong Kong Fleet' at Hong Kong."

"The Air Forces' first field command will be based in Anchorage, Alaska; second one: Denver, Colorado; third one: Mexico City, Mexico; fourth one: Asuncion, Paraguay; fifth one: London, U. K.; sixth one: Moscow, Russia; Seventh one: Baghdad, Iraq; eighth one: Cape Town, South Africa; ninth one: Calcutta, India; tenth one: Jakarta, Indonesia; eleventh one: Harbin, North China; twelfth one: Sydney, Australia. All other three special commands will be located in Denver, Colorado."

"Coast Guard's divisions will take a location at the same place as marine. Each force's regional leaders will manage the selection of the best location of their branches, and further they will study some need of change and suggest anything valuable to its department's central office (the office of the Joint Chiefs of Staff)."

"Fourth, establishing and managing the chain of command:

Ladies and gentlemen! Our planet, the earth is not a small land. The earth is truly a behemoth. It has a beautiful landscape, countless humans, abundant natural resources, and hundreds of cultures and languages."

"We are talking about the security management of the earth with one million organized soldiers. That means 6500 people per one guard. The more number of organized soldiers can handle the more geometrical number of unorganized people for the social order. In other words, 100 organized soldiers can handle maybe 1,000 unorganized people. But 10,000 organized soldiers can handle the public order for one million populations. And one million organized soldiers might be able to handle the public peace for ten billion populations because the unorganized population has no chain of command, no massively organized transporting and communicating systems, and no sophisticated weapons and intelligence networks."

"It is no game at all. Therefore, the organized, armed forces of one million on this earth, with modernized, high-tech equipments and scientific management, along with an organized chain of command, can exercise omnipotent, global physical power that supports the backbone of global governing. The chain of command activates a series of administrative positions on which each has a direct order of power over the one below it."

"Human's concept of the order from upper position to lower one is being fixed in the human brain cells, so as human behaviors move according to preset ideology and regulations especially in the drilled officialdom. All class of large or small units in the armed forces have clear black and white understanding of an order issued by the commander. Every personnel and unit are like a tooth of cogwheels. This ideology is going to provide a main energy to move the human mind as part of a sophisticated, giant machine. The chain of command functions same as a soft ware for the machine as in the management information system."

"Fifth, mobility:

We have a subject of mobility of the armed forces. It means logistics. When a soldier officially moves, it involves in the matter of logistics. Dictionary says logistics is 'the branch of military science and operations dealing with the procurement, supply, and maintenance of equipment, with the movement, evacuation, and hospitalization of personnel with the provision

Article 16: First World Armed Forces

of facilities and services, and with related matters.' In order to maintain the best military machinery in shape, we need the best weapons, manpower, deployments, chain of command, and intelligence networks. Logistics means all the above combined."

"In other words, the most crucial job of maintaining the best military machinery in shape is the job of logistics. The best military power comes from the best logistics. Without proper logistical supplies, we cannot make a good plan of any military operation. Throughout the history of military operations, the best mind always put the matter of logistics to the forefront of their focus. From the best form of military logistics, civilians and civilization have always accordingly enjoyed a free ride. The promotional effort of this logistics for constant improvement makes a good deal of sense for not only military benefit, but also will enhance people's lifestyle."

Miss Sequoia paused in her narrative fashion of a seminar by taking a drink of water. She glanced around her audience, gave a little quiet smile, and took a moment to catch up on her thinking. She continued to the next subject of military maneuver.

"Excuse me. Ladies and gentlemen! We have two more subjects for me to introduce: the sixth one of military field operation and the seventh one of military intelligence network. Well, these two subjects magnify the military's existence and its value. The military's total and final function hinges on the field operation, which serves a political power base. The source of political power exists in its ideology, economic strength, social well-being, and a healthy military operation."

"Without any proper military function, politics could not exercise right power of the political function. In case that any type of political deviation happens, the final solution depends on a physical duel, which denotes military action. That military action implies all essential military functions of weapons, manpower, deployment, chain of command, logistics, and intelligence network. All of military elements exist for the best result of the field operation which brings down its purpose to a reality."

"A good field operation depends on a good leadership and plan and practice. A good field operation fulfills its prime responsibility in supporting the physical strength of the political power base. The field operation (maneuver) of a military power requires a well-orchestrated integration of all armed forces, its trained functions and its synchronized coordination in addition to a good leadership and plan and practice. Therefore, all units of armed forces must have an appropriate regular drill of field operation for both of the real case and its steady improvement."

"Ladies and gentlemen, I would like to conclude my introduction of the draft with the seventh subject of intelligence network. Of course, we have a ministry of intelligence headed by Dr. Andrei Milovanov. But, because global military establishment covers the global security matters, it requires its own intelligence network in order to expedite the cooperation of all armed forces and secure an unquestionable chain of command. The military's intelligence network is also going to have mobile and fixed listening devices—the same as the ones given by Miss Ohara and used by the Intelligence Ministry."

"This military's special 'Security Command' will be headed by three-star General, appointed by the Global President, and placed under his direct supervision. In other words, The Security Command is going to organize and manage the military's own intelligence network, and report directly to the President. The main job of the Security Command is to verify any movement of all units of world armed forces above the company and to record every critical officer's communication.

Article 16: First World Armed Forces

This Security Command's job will reinforce a categorical grip of the chain of command of the world armed forces, in addition to Intelligence Ministry's comprehensive and overall vigilance. Thank you very much, everyone, for your attentive listening."

After Miss Sequoia stepped down from the podium, Chairman Hillman stepped up on the podium. He praised Miss Sequoia's work and explanation on the draft directing the detailed feasibility for one-world armed forces.

"My dear members, I would like to add an additional remark on the establishment of the global military existence, in terms of how to direct human resources and how to adopt weapons systems and how to institute military academies."

"Regarding the above matters, the Global Cabinet and Miss Ohara made a decision to take over the present U.S. military personnel, weapons, equipments, and facilities. On this regard, maybe, some people might misinterpret the U.S. as a fugleman of our globalizing process. Naturally, the U.S. is going to make many contributions in the field of not only military area but also social behavior, economic paradigm, cultural pluralism, human rights and justified legitimacy."

"No matter how many contributions they may make, and no matter which country makes what classification of contributions, all of them are going to become a global property. Miss Ohara has emphasized that the globalizing process must take any extraction or any contribution from any source if that's the best for the global community. Once anything valuable becomes global property, it no longer belongs to any sourced source, but to the global community."

"In other words, the global sovereignty has the absolute right to take over anything valuable for the people and to demolish anything harmful for the people. Global Congress will make a decision to determine which is which, and the Global Executive will carry on the decision made by Global Congress. If any doubts arise or any significant dispute happens, the Global Court will interpret the decision. You may enjoy an honorable pride if you have made a valuable contribution to the global community, but you can never exercise any influence or any claim on that contribution."

On the above serious, terse, and decisive statement, the members of the committee and a throng of reporters, stood aghast at such an unheard-of claim by any event in the human history. The claim of global property for the people resonated in the audiences' heart. No one was going to raise any question about the Global Government's confiscation of the whole military establishments of the U.S., and possibly other country's partial or whole contributions as well. For the people and globalization of the world, and according to the spirit of the "Super Constitution," the Global Government is going to take over anything available as for a global property from the existing valuables on Earth.

This awesome claim of "confiscation" issued by the U.S. Defense Secretary and Chairman of the ad hoc committee of one-world armed forces, all of a sudden, quashed an ever-burning speculation on how to compose the global armed forces, in a single, chilling stroke.

Article 17

First Chairperson of the Joint Chiefs of Staff

November 9, 2016,
Global President George Kirkman announced the Global Government's official organization of the first global armed forces as the following:

"I am very much pleased to be able to, finally, formalize the existence of the world armed forces for the people of the world. Activities and appearance of only one-world armed forces will convince everyone of the real beginning of an entirely new world. It is going to not only symbolize unified globalization but also solidify the actual management of the Super Constitution's spirit."

"The formation and deployment of the world armed forces connote disarming all nations' military organizations. I, hereby, demand, as the commander in chief, that the first Chairperson of the Joint Chiefs of Staff for the incipient world armed forces must form and deploy the new world armed forces, simultaneously disarming all other existing armed forces of the world under the guidance of Global Military Minister Dr. Yen-Jee Wang, as soon as possible."

Super Constitution

"I am sure we should not use the world armed forces in the process of making a decision for the world affairs. We will create the ever-best capability for the world armed forces in terms of weapon, personnel, formation and chain of command. We will constantly develop armed format along with other civilian administrations for the people of the world. As I mentioned, however, I hope we will never use military power for solutions in any dispute. We are going to positively use military institutes as help for civilian's constructive campaigns or for meandering any disaster. The world armed forces must act as a friendly machine for the people and governments."

President Kirkman continued.

"In this regard, I would like to announce an appointment of the first Chairperson of the Joint Chiefs of Staff for the World Armed Forces. I am very much pleased to appoint Miss Michelle Sequoia for the post. She has an extraordinary memorizing power. Maybe, she could memorize all officers' names and their brief careers in addition to countless historical events of world military matters. She also has a preeminent mathematical brainpower to analyze logical development of academic theory and real practices. What's more, she has an excellent faculty in digging out human behaviors to locate its hidden motive on a psychological approach. I surely admire the prodigious caliber of her talent. It's truly fortunate for us to have such an oddity in the moment of one of the most complicated changeover in the current world. Ladies and gentlemen! Thank you!"

President Kirkman appointed Miss Sequoia to the post of Chairperson of the Joint Chiefs of Staff of the World Armed Forces to erect monumental world armed forces, and disarm each nation's monstrous military power. He knew, however, the job could be brutal to a young prodigy. She is only 28 years old and already a controversial figure, promoted in a lightning speed. Even though she had had an unprecedented

Article 17: The Joint Chiefs

record of achievements in the history of the West Point, her incredible, overnight debut surprised everyone.

Now, the appointment of her to the post of "Chairperson of the Joint Chiefs of Staff" indeed lacerated everyone's common speculation in terms of lifting ranks, and shook ordinary norms of military practice. It was like a tremendous trembler or tsunami of which shockwave reverberated endlessly and overwhelmed everyone's expectation.

Throughout human history, we have seen a very unusual rise of certain genius not only in the military profession but also in politics, not by nepotism but by talent and achievement. In the case of Miss Sequoia, the event generated widespread discussion, criticism, and hard feelings, especially among chauvinists of noninvolved countries in the matter of military formation. These complaints happened inevitably.

Most of the so-called experts and current military leaders in active duty of noninvolved countries fumed in their fretful irritation and anger. However, no one made any seductive insinuation or cynical sneer openly. No one could even imply any upheaval against the Global Government because they knew the Global Government had blanket coverage in every corner and nook of the world by its Intelligence Ministry.

What's more, they knew the Super Constitution rode on an enthusiastic support of the general people of the world. They realized the leading figures of the global executives were all extraordinary prodigies, hand-picked by Miss Ohara. And they were experiencing that the cluster of those essential, leading figures were performing a consummate and impeccable job. And now, the head of the executive body proudly selected and announced his favorite appointment for the job of Chairperson of the Joint Chiefs of Staff in a dignified manner. No mutiny-minded group of individuals could take any action or any conspiracy. They were enraged, but they had to stay exasperated. They were embittered, but they could not help anything else but excruciatingly watch the parade.

In the middle part of November 2016,

Miss Sequoia took the appointment for the post of Chairperson of the Joint Chiefs of Staff. At the ceremony of her appointment, she stepped up to the podium and delivered a brief acceptance speech, as follows:

"Ladies and gentlemen, respectable Global President Kirkman and Dr. Yen-Jee Wang, and honorable global cabinet members, I am honored to humbly accept Mr. President's appointment for the job of Chairperson of the Joint Chiefs of Staff for the world armed forces."

"I know this post is very important, as a job and the time wise. This post symbolizes a grand new beginning of an official performance of the Global Government under the auspices of the Super Constitution. I am going to work as a front man in the field, to organize the world armed forces under the best form while disarming all nations' military institutes all over the world."

"I am determined to work hard, to the best of my biological limit, to find the most reliable road map for the formation and deployment of the world armed forces in a very formidable structure, well balanced proportion and efficient mobility. I am gong to organize 'a coterie of the best study,' composed of about twenty young military academics: These intellectual talents will unravel the labyrinthine military tangles to find solutions."

"I am also going to set up a body for consultation, made up of five or six veteran generals to reflect deeply embedded military experiences. Presently, the U.S.'s weapons systems far exceed any other one in the world, able to completely,

Article 17: The Joint Chiefs

precisely and devastatingly hit any target. U.S. soldiers are equipped with a vernacular faculty of English language and with a high quality of teamwork which will breed latent resources to maximize the existing value of the armed forces."

"We have a lot of true-life ideas, abundant examples, and a good deal of experts in every field. Ladies and gentlemen, I am very proud of having so many talents and excellent human resources ubiquitously in our time. Please expect exceptional upshot in a short period of time. You will see a big difference not only in military appearance but also in a palpable substance on economic, political, and social front too. I believe in the Global Government's incipient campaign of the globalization. We are for the people, for individual happiness, and for the freedom of all. Thank you!"

Miss Sequoia asked Philip Hillman, the U.S. Defense Secretary, four-star General, to take a charge of the head of consultative body for her chairmanship and she picked up other five four-star generals as advisors of the consultative body, with Hillman's recommendations. She also appointed three other four-star generals in the position of vice chairman to consult with Hillman in various areas: strategic command in charge of deployment and logistics; training command in charge of personnel and maneuver; and weapons command in charge of research and weapons system. And each command will have one two-star general as a special assistant.

Therefore, the total number of generals came to thirteen in the office of Chairperson of the Joint Chiefs of Staff in the U.N. building of New York City: total number of stars in that office alone showed ninety-two, including four stars on each of Miss Sequoia's shoulders, following her special promotion at the ceremony for her appointment.

President Kirkman picked up one three-star and two one-star generals to manage the Military Security Command

Super Constitution

supervised directly by the Global Presidency. The first world armed forces started its business on a full scale: Formation, Deployment, and Disarming.

Twenty-five divisions of the army and marines would contain 41,666 units of squadrons, 130 generals, about more than 12,000 officers, and more than a half-million soldiers. Fifteen commands of Air Force would manage 7,000 airplanes, with more than 100,000 professional soldiers, forty-five generals, and about fifty thousands of civil servants. The world naval force would command ten aircraft carriers, thirty cruisers, sixty destroyers, 250 smaller battleships, 250 minesweepers, and 500 submarines. It would also include another few hundred miscellaneous ships, along with 16, 200 of the Coast Guard's speedboats, which would roam coastal areas to keep an eye on any illegal conduct.

Chairperson Sequoia summoned seventy major commanders (army: twenty-five, including five corps commanders; Marine Corps: five; Coast Guard: ten; Air Force: fifteen; navy: fifteen of five fleet commanders and ten aircraft carrier commanders), in addition to 12 generals from the office of the Joint Chiefs. She summoned them in order to have a special meeting for giving general directions on the critical matters of deployment of the world armed forces (p. 253). Eighty-two generals of top echelon of the first world armed forces gathered in a small auditorium of the U.N. building. The head of consultative body for Chairperson of the Joint Chiefs, presently the U.S. Defense Secretary four-star General Philip Hillman introduced the Chairperson, for the first time, as "Madam Michelle Sequoia."

Madam Sequoia, again, took the podium. In this time, not as a draft introducer, but as the supreme field commander of the first world armed forces, her majestic appearance absolutely overwhelmed an aura of the auditorium. An attractive, young, confident and friendly appearance alone cast a great pleasure

Article 17: The Joint Chiefs

to the mind-set of generals for the day's conference. The generals were already well charmed by her charisma and intelligence. Her sharp, quick judgment on many decisive decision-making incidents spilled over in many areas and fields. Her reputation as an outstanding genius and strikingly charming beauty queen, with her unexpectedly protruding odd behavior, entailed a lot of palatable responses from her surroundings.

Her intriguing talent actually started way before her West Point days. Throughout her junior and senior high school days, her positive and pleasant attitude comprehending her environment and the interests of other people excited others.

During her teenage years, she developed a peculiar physical characteristic in her muscle and nervous system. Her muscle power steadily grew, up to her senior year of high school, and bestowed upon her bewildered strength; it much surpassed her male peers' muscle power, allowing her to weight-lift more than 400 lbs. Not only that, she also never got tired. She always won all the competitions in the "triathlon" of combining swimming, bicycling, and distance running.

She checked with her family medical practitioner and further consulted a specialist in neurology. They were surprised by their findings; she surely had female body organs, and even her skin had the same soft tissue as her female peers. Nevertheless, the queer development of her muscle power continued, as if from body building practice. And she also realized her body's nervous system continually surged with energy, energizing ever more vitality with her body and preventing her from getting fatigue.

We sometimes hear about a female character wielding swords or spears in old days' battlefield as fiercely as a conspicuously famed knight. She felt she had a warrior-like vigor. Maybe, that's why she took the West Point.

Super Constitution

All the high-powered military experts erratically puzzled at the emerging scene of Miss Sequoia in the beginning. They observed a rapidly changing image on every phenomenal event involved in her advent, which worked out as a vital catalyst to upgrade her impression. All the high-handed top brass remembered their first reception of Miss Sequoia as a big joke or laughing stock. Then suddenly they encountered a heavy impact ringing their heart by her rich source of an intrinsic military knowledge.

On the continued events of her imposing appearance, they began to notice they forgot that she had such a charming beauty. They began to wonder how come such a young pretty girl could exercise such a quick judgment they had been looking for their professionalism. She also truly impressed the high-caliber generals in terms of logical expression on the military strategies.

They now considered her as a nymph. They now felt pleasure in expecting a meeting with her. In this way, so quickly, she became the palpable, supreme field commander under Military Minister, Dr. Yen-Jee Wang.

Now, Madam Sequoia behind the podium issued the general guidelines for the deployment of their armed forces and for the disarmament of all former nations' armed forces. Also, she made a note of the chain of command, logistics, maneuvers, intelligence and overall administrative organizations.

"Gentlemen, I appreciate everyone's attendance. Actually, I thought I am going to miss several absences. But now I am actually going to miss a several love-calls–drawing a lot of smiles from audiences. Gentlemen! Regarding intelligence activities, please feel at ease. President's Security Command and Intelligence Ministry will take care of everything. They

Article 17: The Joint Chiefs

will provide every need of intelligence work and every necessary cooperative requests you may have."

"Military Ministry will take care of almost every administrative job, including research, pension, procurement, and tribunals. Three vice chairpersons will take care of final approvals and decision-making jobs on deployments, logistics, personnel, maneuvers, field research, and weapons management. And marine division leaders will work with army corps commanders. The Coast Guard's division leaders will receive orders from each area's navy fleet's commander."

"Gentlemen, therefore, we have a final total of twenty-five field commanders, consisting of five army corps, five navy fleets, and fifteen Air Force command groups. All twenty-five final field commanders will get their orders and make reports through the three vice chairpersons: for the matters of deployments and logistics through first vice chairperson, for the matters of personnel and maneuvers through second vice chairperson, and for the matters of research and weapons through third vice chairperson."

Madam Sequoia emphasized further.

"Gentlemen, this formula is, of course, for normal cases. The final twenty-five field commanders will always communicate with me directly without any limits. Please remember that I can and will conduct any communications with even a soldier. I am determined to have a smooth flow of communication in our world armed forces."

"Gentlemen, that is all. It is clear and distinct. I wish you a lot of lucks. All of you are going to have a high sense of honor in managing world affairs. There are going to be a lot of challenges. Without a challenge, it won't breed any sense of achievement. Please be mindful of Miss Ohara's technology. Thank you!"

Super Constitution

The most noticeable, concerned, and anxiety-producing subject among the ten ad hoc committees' topics naturally came to the one of the committee of the world armed forces, which finished the job way ahead of the general schedule. And it made the initial process of deployment start earlier. Also the activities of the deployment took an unusually fast pace because the American military organization had a vast worldwide bases and experiences.

The processes of practicing the deployment according to the drawn plan of the committee went on in a perfect order and dispatched the business at full steam. George Kirkman thought it would help other pending jobs of other ad hoc committees in a great deal. All the jobs involved a lot of subtleties in or with various interests. The consequences of its performance emerged from its obscurity very fast towards a clear appearance, so they had to be prepared to move and judge fast for earlier advancement.

President Kirkman and Dr Yen-Jee Wang pushed Miss Sequoia to rush the movement of the world armed forces more vigorously and more visibly. The military matter looked like a formidable fortress not to be conquered easily. But it, actually, was a brittle giant tree. It was a piece of cake to Miss Sequoia. She had the courage of her convictions. She understood the mighty technology. She exercised decisive judgments. She believed in Kirkman Cabinet. She knew she could mobilize a humongous pool of topnotch human resources beside military.

In the territory of military, she also realized she could command superb generals, terrific officers, and excellent soldiers. She believed she could enjoy herself. She respected Kirkman, and actually she loved him. And Kirkman trusted her capability to handle the first world armed forces. He often felt a flirting sensation from her. Both guessed each other's

Article 17: The Joint Chiefs

feeling. In the rapid process of deployment and disarming, they began to feel more love for each other.

Deployment of the world armed forces, according to the original draft, did not have any problem. The main side-problems happened during the process of deployment, which was caused by small groups of extreme nationalists in Japan, North Korea, and Thailand: suicide cases by burning themselves in protesting disarming of their country's military institutes and the practice of English as the official world language in every nation of the world.

Every nation on Earth, including G8 nations and other smaller countries, followed the new global order set up by the executive team. No major figures of any country raised questions about materializing the new world order of the Super Constitution.

All the nations of the world rode on a wave of the new global order. It was a history. No one could move against it. It was a destiny formed by an "extraterrestrial being" people believed. The universe moves according to the universal laws. The earth circles the sun on its orbit with the same speed of eighty thousand miles per hour by spinning itself without changing its speed.

All the creatures on the earth live its own lifestyles according to the given dynamism. Human was borne by not its choice but by a natural dynamism we cannot control. Nobody made the Super Constitution. No one tried to figure out how the Super Constitution was borne. Now, no leadership of the nations of the world tried to go against the wave of the globalization of the Super Constitution. Even though some big grievous mumblings bubbled around every corner, no one could ever utter anything about overthrowing any new global order implicitly or explicitly. Madam Michelle Sequoia ordered her generals not to be bothered by any type of suicidal cases, and just to move forward without any comment. Silence was gold: the key to quell complaints.

The killing wave displayed some awesome mystery. No one argued about it. It invoked an embodiment of the spirit of the Super Constitution. The world armed forces presented the spirit's indisputable delegation. Yet, the killing wave alone could not master the creeping and whimsical human mind. The world armed forces alone could not disarm those monstrous giants without any fastidious hassle. The world armed forces was equipped with a backup of the Super Constitution's spirit, the favorable globalizing trend, and the peerless intelligence networks that were put through with Miss Ohara'a omnipotent communicating capability.

People believed that the Global Government prescribed an epochal network to catch up to the wishes and welfare of people. A science of neurology was now trying to take picture of a human's brain to read all of the brain's memory. If that neurological technology would be materialized soon, anyone no longer could lie. Now, the intelligence network of Andrei Milovanov could listen to and watch any suspicious words or behavior. In other words, any influential figures or any substantial power holders or any group of extreme activists could not try to plot any intriguing movement without avoiding the intelligence network's eyes and ears.

The organized government agencies and military personnel, in particular, became fish living in a fish bowl. In addition to watching and listening capability, the typical radar beacon the troika engineered later on–for checking on explosive materials anywhere in a radius of 50 miles–was another marvelous technology. Even an ounce of explosive materials would appear as a small dot on its radarscope. Therefore, the intelligence network could trace any suspicious concentration of explosive materials. Any suicidal bombing-action or hidden

Article 17: The Joint Chiefs

explosive trap became a "once upon a time" topic of a conversation.

Under the circumstances of such an intelligence network, no one could ever dream of any illegal conspiracy. No one could hide anywhere in the world. No violence could happen. The demolishing process of the WMD led by Russia and managed by the WMD Decommission Committee composed of five nations sped toward the finish line in a fully plumped sail. The work of deployment of the Global Armed Forces went on in a great festival mood while dejecting every nation's top brass. Disarming job of every nation's tigerish military machines challenged every soldier of the world armed forces in every field.

Nevertheless, every nation's gloomy soldiers never explicitly made any temperamental chagrin. They, rather, proceeded into every action of disarming their unit and delegating their weapons systems to the newly deployed global unit without any harassment. They figured their sullen process as a harbinger of demise of their nation's national authority. They realized a global authority replacing their old pride. They apprehended the new world order approaching ever faster than their assessment.

When Miss Sequoia started her directing job while consulting with her top advisor Philip Hillman, he initiated addressing Miss Sequoia as "Madam Chairperson." Since then, everybody called her "Madam Chairperson." She made a grand schedule: the grand ceremony for reviewing her troops of the global military in the month of May 2017, after completing deployment of the first world armed forces.

In the early part of December 2016,
Miss Sequoia and General Philip Hillman discussed her upcoming trip round the world to review her troops around May 2017. General Hillman suggested.

Super Constitution

"Madam Sequoia, I guess that the next five months will bring forth entirely different vision on the new world order. Decommissioning activities of the WMD, setting up formidable deployment of the world armed forces, liquidating every nation's military machines, and establishing a perfect worldwide network of intelligence gathering knack, will make the world look entirely different one. On top of the above, outstanding world economic policies, and social fabric and behavior that would conform to social justice, will make the image of the Global Government ever more magnificent. In other words, the impression of globalization will loom up as a giant snow-clad peak. That will be the time for us to go for a grand show of the global military review."

"General Hillman, I absolutely agree with you. President Kirkman told me about materializing social justice to establish a healthy social fabric that could create ideal behaviors for the world to achieve Utopia. He emphasized a moral code that honest, creative, and hard working people must get right reward. Dr. Walfgang Thierse is working hard to institute the appropriate principles and measurements through dealing with matters of religion, language, education and criminal affairs for the right moral code. He, further, told me that the best economic polices, along with social and political justice, will finally make a Utopia possible."

General Hillman added some additional thoughts.

"I understand President Kirkman's theory. His vision is absolutely on point. I think that those matters of concerned economic and social and political justice will appear in better visibility in the next five months. That is why, as you have been already thinking, I am talking about that the grand ceremony of our global military review should be done around May 2017, and the best weather of the earth is around May too."

Article 17: The Joint Chiefs

Sequoia spoke up again.

"My plan for reviewing the global military is as follows:
I'd like to have the first stop at the headquarters of the first corps, along having an air show performed by the nearby air force command: the five corps' headquarters and the five fleets' bases, the marine going with the army, the Coast Guard going with the navy: total five locations round the world. The global armed forces' spectacular scene of the five locations will have the same theme of a military muscle power. But different angles and forms of each review will single out a unique feature, eventually covering every major facet of the global military's integrated circuit."

Sequoia continued on.

"The army's five corps and the navy's five fleets will coordinate each show. They will maximize every facet's powerful appearance, its own unique dexterity, functional shift, and fantastic character: weapons systems, various types of soldiers, stunning practices, marvelous accuracies, zipping speed and fabulous strategies. It will have to have a big show. Surely, it will display a colorful demonstration. It will really pull off a distinctive picture of the new world. It will definitely pump up an ever-higher audience-rating. The Global Government will sweep an unheard-of success in solidifying and symbolizing its globalization's muscle power. I am certain that people will enjoy a thrilling sensation."

Chairperson Sequoia wanted to describe her idea of the true character of the civilized modern military image, which needs smart brain rather than brawny muscle, dexterous software rather than sublime hardware, and delicate technology rather than awe-inspiring rigidity.

Super Constitution

General Hillman inserted his opinion on a modern military framework before Miss Sequoia tried to convey her idea to him.

"Madam Chairperson, I think the navigation of military strength requires a good deal of tactics, visualization, coordination, and vast human memory capacity. Young, vigilant, comprehensive, systematic and energetic lady like you could produce a paramount charisma to a great deal of common soldiers and all of logistics-minded generals. You will definitely be able to upgrade the traditional military mind to a first-class status of the skillful management."

"Thank you, General Hillman! Now, the world armed forces should symbolize not only the firepower of the Super Constitution but also an indigenous subtlety of law and order. The unseen, true backbone of the ruling power of law and order comes from a raw physical strength. The roots of the power to subdue a rebellious mind and to stand behind the frame of support for law and order, can be traced up to the overwhelming pool of military power."

General Hillman confirmed a confidence in Miss Sequoia upon hearing her stance on her job. Miss Sequoia, the field-managing director of the world armed forces, secured her advisor's confidence in mounting a consolidating campaign to make the monstrous military institute take off for becoming a smart machine. Not only had she acquired General Hillman's confidence but also that of all of President Kirkman's cabinet members.

Article 18

World Trade

In another early part of December 2016 (first one: p. 273), other significant discussions transpired.

While Miss Sequoia was setting up the schedule for grand ceremonies to review her new global military establishment with her advisor General Hillman, Global President George Kirkman was tackling the finishing touches of his government's major policies on economic substances and social behaviors. George Kirkman sat together with Dr. Jay Kim to discuss the world economic matters, face-to-face.

"How is everything going on with your home work, Dr. Kim? Do you think the world economic matters as a piece of cake or a puzzled headache?"

"Well, President Kirkman, I have enjoyed a lot on this project. It casts a challenge. It has intensified my interesting. Economic matters have always driven me enthusiastic along a whimsical human mind. The human mind looks so simple, yet it leads me to a puzzle at the end. Economics itself poses as a science. But economy mysteriously moves according to the zigzagging human mind, which not only pursues making money but also straddles two opposite sides. I have many subjects and issues to clear with you for our general direction."

"What would you like to discuss, Dr. Kim?"

"President Kirkman, first, I'd like to talk about a controlled currency: Money concerns everybody's everyday life. Second, GDP: gross domestic product of one nation or the world; Third, import and export: commercial flow and movement of major commodity or all daily products; Fourth, tax and duty: financing public works which provide economic help with people; Fifth, distribution of wealth: Well organized distribution of wealth makes a rich social fabric, providing balanced economic growth; Sixth, industrial relationship: Good coordination among industries enhances overall productivity."

"Dr. Kim, they all sound like very dry subjects."

"Not at all President Kirkman, they're actually amusing issues because all of subjects touch everyone's interest in their happiness and freedom. The subjects aren't boring or difficult to understand. They, as a matter of fact, bring forth quite a stimulus to our life because they navigate people's own lifeblood and narrate everyone's life style."

"Well, Dr. Kim, I am very glad to hear that these subjects will describe such urgent, interesting points with easy understanding. Well, easy does it. Let's proceed to discuss them."

George Kirkman and Jay Kim understood each other in terms of personality and professional background (p. 142&144).

Article 18: World Trade

Both of them had focused their sharp interest on the mathematical economic movement, integrated with a capricious human mind and an unpredictable social change. Over this matter, they talked about palpable economic phenomena with plain language that people who have not had any formal economic education could understand. Dr. Kim initiated the plain economic topics.

"Well, as I indicated a little while ago, I would like to talk about the currency. You and I could discuss monetary theory using technical terminology. Nevertheless, by talking in common people's shoes, we may understand common people's economic situation in better shape."

"People say 'money talks.' We should encourage people respect money. Money circumvents people who run after only money itself while also distancing people who neglect or look down on it. Money sticks with people who take risks or chance ventures with the right virtues. Money respects smart people who could figure out well what people want. Money loves people who love hard work, honesty, creativity, punctuality, and appreciation. If someone does not understand the value of hard work, money will escape him. Money reveres the above virtues."

"Further euphemizing, I am sure money has an intellectual mind. If you pursue only money itself, money may despise you. Money wants matured behavior and well-balanced temperance. Money does not care who you are. Money cares only what you are doing and how you are doing. If you cheated and manipulated to reap a success, then you would be surprised later on to find you're in trouble because you did not realize where the money would eventually move on."

Jay Kim continued on the subject of currency.

Super Constitution

"Money never gives any warning. Money never predestines its course. You can't predict its behavior. You can't analyze its true color because the money does not have any color, smell, and shape. President Kirkman, I study many economic formulas in depth and quite in detail. The more I study and the more I learn, the more confused I become. The matters of currency, such as how much paper money would be needed to function the most efficiently for its social flow, what rate of interest would kick the money flow in the most appropriate stimulation, and how fast money flow could effectively satisfy commercial activity, have surprised me with its odd variations."

"Sometimes, the currency looks like an exorcist or magician. People say honesty is the best policy. I agree with it. The word may appear simple and clear. But neither simple nor sophisticated minds can fathom the depth of the simple word's real meaning. The matters of currency certainly belong to a 'Land of Oz.' I could not help but revere the role of currency whatever we set up. We have to do our best for the currency's function to exercise its innate, mighty performance. Along with currency's function, we have to pay a similar attention to the right management to tackle credit risk. On this regard I'd like to mention in other time."

Jay Kim presented some statistics of the major industrialized country's volume of paper money printed for the best quantity, which would bring the best quality of the money flow. However, Jay concluded as the following:

"President Kirkman, right now, the world's currencies interact each other on the basis of political events, economic environment, trade wars, economic cycles, and many other incidents for each nation's national interest, in addition to speculative attacks from large international banks, multinational big corporations, hedge funds, and wealthy individuals. The above phenomena cause major disturbances

Article 18: World Trade

on the world's economic health by producing unpredictable crises in the voracious, whirlwind greed on the paper profit. Of course, every nation including the U.S. committed, time and again, a grave mistake in managing credit risks interrelated with multiple currencies to cause tremendous economic bubbles. President Kirkman, I would like to emphasize that the world's only one-currency measure would wipe out all the financial diseases brought about by the multiple currencies."

Kirkman felt a delectable conversation between him and Dr. Kim in the plain talk on the heavy economic subject. Kirkman's interest in the topic grew on intensely as they conversed. Dr. Kim also felt animated in talking with Kirkman on this official discussion. Dr. Kim moved on the next subject: a topic of gross domestic product of one nation.

"As you know well, President Kirkman, GDP pinpoints a nation's wealth. Let's talk about the rich and the poor. Everyone wants to be rich. But ironically we have only a few rich people. Outstanding majority of people struggle to enjoy the status of the rich. I think, one of our urgent and imminent jobs fallen in on our hands, is the increment of GDP. Shooting up GDP high into the sky for the majority people of the world will make the most fantastic firework for everyone."

"Right now, most populations of each industrialized nation can enjoy the freedom of the rich. In order to upgrade poor nations' GDP to the level of industrialized nations, we have to think many things that will play crucial roles in enhancing the wealth of the poor countries, and also enlarge the marketable quantity and quality of the industrialized nations. One nation's growth pushes its growing power outward towards enhancing other nation's market value. Balanced economic growth of the world will stimulate synergistic effect, causing to boom the economic growing power. In order to help pull up the industry of the poor countries, we have to attack the following problems."

Super Constitution

Dr. Kim had again brought up related topics to GDP. In order to increase one nation's GDP up to the substantial level, we have to revolutionize several areas of the nation, such as education campaigning, housing drives, setting up key industries, constructing highways and paved roads, and exploring its strongest asset or advantage. Dr. Kim continued talking.

"President Kirkman, if we train or educate right people of a nation in the public administration, they can lead the nation efficiently, including general job such as computer skill, agricultural production, basic machine operation, and etc. The Global Government can make a list outlining the order for which country should start first after another nation according to the available financial strength. One more nation's take-off would add more available fund. One more nation's take-off would add more power to the world market."

"Right now, there is no order. And with everyone trying to go first, it just causes chaos. What's more, no poor country has the funds or leadership to initiate action. It could go forever like a vicious circle. But now, we can help them take action."

Jay Kim presented another remarkable statistics of the world's GDP. During the period of industrial revolution of the world in 1870 to 1913, the average growth rate of the world's GDP indicates 1.3 %; during 1950 to 1973 of the rebuilding period of Europe and Japan after Second World War, the world economy has the record of 2.9% growth rate; and the growth rate of 2006 shows robust 5.4%. The more globalized the world became, the more growth rate the world economy produced.

"I am sure, if we can increase the world's GDP more than 10% a year, we can wipe out world's poverty and lead prosperity in a short length of time. I am confident we can

Article 18: World Trade

increase the world's GDP more than 13% a year during the next 20 years if we can combine good policies in the six areas I am talking about now."

President Kirkman spoke to Dr. Kim with enthusiasm on the subject, and President Kirkman encouraged Dr. Kim to continue talking about the Global Government's economic policy. Dr. Kim continued.

"President Kirkman, let's talk about the next subject on the matter of a flow of commodity: third subject: import and export."

"Right now, free trade agreements between nations and blocks of certain groups of nations spring out sporadically here and there. But its scale and degree of reduced tariff dwarf the expected effect of full-fledged flows of commodity which could push the present economy toward a giant monument."

"Free flow of commodity between and among the nations in the world will change the economic face of our world to an entirely different appearance. We will not recognize and apprehend the different appearance because the free trade's ripple effect will mount beyond our mathematical calculation. Until the free trade reaches the saturation point of zero effect, none can measure it. Disappeared amount of duty and deregulated import-prohibit will play their synergistic effects for the time being of which result we cannot estimate exactly."

Jay Kim continued after a little pause.

"Free flow of commodity, naturally, creates some problem to the special interest groups that enjoy unfair preferential treatment. This preferential treatment, definitely, engenders a big disadvantage to the absolute majority of people and hampers the overall growth of nations and the world. However, the profit-seeking actions of those special interest groups with the vested power base, usually exercise an influential protectionism. This rampant protectionism breeds social and political instability, and ultimately brings nations into conflict. By eradicating this cancerous cell from our society, we can manage the most productive measurement for free trade between and among nations of the world."

George Kirkman understood the magnitude of the full-grown effect of a complete free trade together with some consequences of its chaos caused by the negative side. It would dislocate those special interest groups as inferior units in terms of productivity and cost-effectiveness. They would need time and some help for their units to adjust and change. Kirkman questioned Kim to that regard. Kim answered on that question as follows:

"Yes, President Kirkman. That is a problem and a challenge. Nevertheless, I am sure I can solve that problem in two ways. One solution can come from a special educational program to prepare to face the problem, and the other one: changing our concept on a 'home turf.' "

"Regarding the educational program, we have to set basic directions for them to understand the on-coming reality of an economic environment which describes a law of survival of the fittest and natural selection; they have to study what type of strong points they can set up to develop. These procreative brainstorming activities will engender new ideas to help turn their misfortune into blessing: Brainstorming for restructure always brings better opportunities in human life."

"Regarding the other one for changing concept on one's 'home turf,' we can see so many examples of human history. If we think we have strong points in the know-how or some technicality or adaptability, we can bring our innate advantage to a better environment or to an appropriate niche by moving our 'home turf.' "

Article 18: World Trade

"As for an example, we can take Napa Valley of California for winery. Italian and Spanish winegrowers carved out that area and developed into famous production regions for winemaking. The Italian and Spanish winemakers, who had developed their best know-how and technology for winery, had observed their homeland's cost of labor and land went upward in gyration beyond their control. They started moving their home turf from their country to Napa Valley of California, which had land in even better condition, of almost unlimited size with unbelievably low price, and with abundant, cheap labors. Napa Valley made 'wine-drinking-habit' possible as a popular culture also for ordinary people, not only for rich people."

Kirkman was captivated by Kim's simple story.

"Dr. Kim! I am so glad to hear the story. Well, we have to break our surroundings time to time in order to create something desirable or to find a new challenge. Our conception provides us with a jump pad to leap forward. But time and again, we must exert a bravery to smash the jump pad to change our current conception for the new one."

"Yes, President Kirkman! Our globe is big enough, and it has more than enough space to reshuffle the world population according to the need for people's welfare."

Jay Kim drank another cup of coffee just brought by one of his secretaries and continued to the fourth subject: a matter of tax.

"Well, President Kirkman, I contemplated the matter of tax over a substantial amount of time. Basically, taxes were borne to fulfill the need to finance governing activities of human society from the beginning of organized, collective life. The best mode of collective life requires the best form of governing structure, which depends on the money coming from taxation. The best form of governing structure has been mandated for people's security and prosperity."

"But the governing structure has been creating a lot of problems, inefficiencies, and tax burdens. Undue and too heavy tax burdens are actually killing potential resources of economic prosperity. How much of a tax burden is, then, necessary? I would say that no tax at all would be my ideal answer. But that does not conform to reality. The lightest possible burden should of course be the ideal conclusion."

"Right now, the average tax burden has passed about 20% of the average income and approaches toward 30% in worldwide trend. For example, France's tax burden of 1975 was 35% but it went up to 45% in 2006. The U.S.'s one in 1975 was 25% and it rose to 28% in 2006. And South Korea's one in 1975 was 15% but now in 2006 it shows 27%. I would like to bring the rate of tax burden down to below 10%. Last year (2015), the world's total GDP hung around seventy-five trillion U.S. dollars. This GDP means $1,200.00 per capita income for the world's average population, which indicates not enough for the average lifestyle. If we reduce tax burden below 10% along with a completely free trade arrangement and other programs that we are now contemplating, within the next 10 years, we can promote the global economic growth at least 10% every year."

Jay Kim continued on the taxation.

"An increase of 10% every year, in ten years, is 2.6 times the present GDP of seventy-five trillion dollars—resulting in about 200 trillion dollars. Reducing governments' exorbitant indirect social expenses due to the wrong criminal policy and mismanaged welfare work and others, and promoting mass creativity and efficiency stimulated by people's new lifestyles based on our global government's sweeping campaigns, we can estimate our global economy will move forward towards

Article 18: World Trade

600 or even 800 trillion dollars, for an economic utopia within 20 years."

George Kirkman, literally, became bewildered at the numbers Jay Kim simply cited. Kirkman excited.

"Dr. Kim! Fantastic! It really sounds like a pipedream. But I guess it is a possible reality, isn't it?"

"Absolutely, President Kirkman, I am not talking about a fantasy here. It comes from simple arithmetic figures. And also, for example, we have three tiered government structure: the Global Government, National Governments and local Governments. The Global Government and National Governments will share half and half on an 8% flat income tax from personal lives and businesses and public profits of public enterprises such as utilities, natural resources, and other public concerns. Local Governments will rely on local property tax. There are going to be only two taxes in the world: a flat 8% income tax and a 1% property tax for local Governments."

"Local Governments will, naturally, have a surplus on their coffers deluged with an inflow of the 1% property tax. Local Governments will continually look for every direction to provide ever better services with local concerns. The 8% income tax from 200 trillion dollars' economy, in addition to the incomes from world's utilities and natural resources, will amount to astronomical numbers of around at least 20 trillion dollars."

"One trillion dollars will heed enough financial strength for the world armed forces, and a half trillion dollars will cover all types of the global government's expenses. And fifteen trillion dollars will go for the world national governments' expenses. With the rest of the three & half trillion dollars, we can expedite our global programs to root out poverty from the world and spontaneously upgrade our global prosperity ever more dynamically."

Jay Kim continued to the fifth subject: the distribution of wealth.

"President Kirkman! Definitely and absolutely, I consider that an effective presiding over the distribution of wealth will not only make a good deal of contributions to balanced social development, but also build a strong fundamental and healthy economic structure which will enhance our global economic growth."

"Dr. Kim, what breed of policy or strategy do you think now, for ideal measurements of the distribution of wealth? How do you think we could transfer the excessive money the rich earn to the poor?"

Kim took a momentary silence in order to straighten his logical order of his thoughts on the matter of the distribution of wealth.

"President Kirkman, we don't have to worry about touching any excessive money the rich earn. Principally, the rich cannot make too much excess money anyway. The political structure of every nation has similar limit and balance. Every nation and global government already have direct or indirect control on the major public businesses and natural resources that are major sources for profiteering, as well as the regulatory statutes that can control excessive profiteering activities or possibilities. Therefore, there is no space for anyone to manipulate any excess profiteering."

"The market economy and economic statutes we are setting up will prevent juggling or tampering with rules for any type of monopolizing or profiteering. In other words, we won't allow any leeway for anyone to squeeze or exploit people while we

Article 18: World Trade

maximize individual's incentive for creativity and hard work: public concept on land, air, and water; public ownership on most natural resources; and public enterprises on such as highway, utilities, some housings, mass transit, and etc. These proper measures alone will make a great deal of functions to distribute the wealth on Earth evenly to all walks of life."

Kim continued after a short period of time taking some pause for a deep breath to give a break to his body's composure.

"President Kirkman, as you have often said, I believe in capitalism for promoting general economic growth and for inspiring people's productivity because human's nature, to begin with, has been set in the formula of self interest and survival. No one can change this formula because it is a part of natural law. To twist or distort that part of natural law has been failed throughout human history: feudalism, tenant farming system, communism, etc."

"I believe in fair competition on consumers' free market under the frame of public concept on land, air, water, natural resources, and public enterprises. The national and local governments have tremendous leeway to provide social services with people for various valuable wealth to share. The global government has the greatest share of financial power to exercise immense leverage for the distribution of wealth. This will be accomplished by providing global fiscal policies, special arrangements for bank loan, and global projects that will create jobs and markets for small businesses."

Kim continued without a break.

"Our whole global economic structure–its policy, its statutes, and technology–will boost paradigms that have hinged on an ideal distribution in engineering the total world wealth. Absolutely, the engineering works of distribution of the world wealth must demonstrate that creativity, hard work, and honesty constitute the real source for winning success and making money."

"I, especially, prepare to set up the most efficient small business administration office directly under my ministry. All the private and government major businesses must have a rule of procurement that at least 10% of its contract or purchase should be done to the small business entity. This small business administration would not only provide special bank loans to the small businesses, but also help small businesses in the area of professional consultation, R&D fund, allocation of procurement from government and big businesses, small businessman's training center, and establishment of one million small business associations' own internal banking institutes that will help finance the associating member's business development."

"This small business administration will make a major seismic contribution to fair distribution of the world wealth absolutely different from a traditional tokenism of the past. Taking away another's money under the name of tax and giving away to other as a free lunch or a free ride under the name of the distribution of wealth will kill both party's inspiration and social constructive dynamism. The inspiration, built upon hard work and creativity and honesty, will bring real dynamism and will move our globe towards a real utopianism."

"Well, Dr. Kim, I absolutely agree with you."

George Kirkman truly moved. He asked Jay Kim to elaborate the sixth one, the last subject: industrial relationship.

"On the subject of industrial relationships, President Kirkman, I would like to mention another miraculous factor in productivity, which would stimulate synergistic compounds to upgrade economic velocity. At a micro view on this subject, the interpretation of meaning or effect of the 'industrial

Article 18: World Trade

relationship' comes to a simple action of one industry's help to other one's development: Computer science helps machine-tooled industry's automatic system which helps manufacturing industry that helps the development of consumer goods and parts of machine. All types of services and products depend on the upgrades of its related industries, for their own upgrades. The effect of an overflow of one industry's innovation spreads into all directions at a geometric pace, along with nonstop energy."

"This simple meaning of the 'industrial relationship' alone explains how much and how far the industrial relationship can create a chain of synergistic, reciprocal reaction. If a number of factors in the industrial relationships, let's say, hundreds or thousands, not one or two, will interact each other, then the upshots of development will ride on a compound function which will engender a thunderous roll of industrial spark: a big boom such as a miraculous rise of Japan, South Korea, Taiwan, Hong Kong, and Singapore. Now, the above five economic wonders as a compound function and as a multiple cluster of industrial relationships, have been pushing China's open market towards the glaring skyscrapers."

Jay Kim continued without a pause.

"At a macro view on these industrial relationships, the meaning of the 'industrial relationship' comes down to multiple, worldwide economic booms. The chain reaction of different companies in cost reduction causes expansion and growth of the market. One company's innovation in machinery or raw materials will bring a great positive impact for its costs and quality. The chain reaction of the improvement among industries will create new skills, new products, and new markets."

"If we can manage the interaction of the world's industries with each other on one currency without heavy tax, the chain reaction of all industries for better prices and quality will expedite an ever-faster pace for the world's economic growth. If one nation's industrial relationships can be connected to another country's good industrial relationships, not only between firms or products, but between nations and regions, the whole world's industrial mechanism will run on the double."

George Kirkman excited. He felt ecstasy. Feeling extra confidence, he praised Jay Kim's vision on the world's economic outlook under his global government's stewardship.

"Dr. Kim, you've really touched my heart. I am so happy to hear your basic ideas, which confirm my ideas identically. I wish you further study for a detailed consequence and streamlined policies. I have talked with Miss Ohara about the event of Miss Sequoia's grand ceremony of our global military review around May of the next year. Right after her reviewing ceremony, we are going to announce major policies that our Global Government is going to launch on the ten subjects officially. That announcement is going to make the greatest landmark in human history and on the earth. I am going to inform you the date for meeting to discuss about the announcement with our cabinet members, along with Miss Sequoia and General Philip Hillman of her advisor."

The unconditional, supreme command given to the Global Government subsists in achieving more freedom and happiness for more people on Earth: an absolute target. In order to accomplish this absolute target, the most mysterious technology of Miss Ohara had emerged, and the Global Government was borne.

To get there, the Global Government needed the most efficient and effective economic formula. To carry out the formula without fail, the Global Government necessitated two pillars bolstering the ideal economic actions Jay Kim presented.

Article 18: World Trade

One of those two pillars is a formation of ideally behaved mentality which Dr, Wolfgang Thierse now contemplates and meditates in the matters of education, one-world language, religions, crimes and social services.

The other pillar exists in the area of political justice and military muscle. Dr. Toro Yono now concentrates on steering the right political circumstances in reshuffling the unit of nation of the world while Dr. Yen-Jee Wang and Dr. Andrei Milovanov work on the military affairs with Miss Michelle Sequoia and General Philip Hillman.

George Kirkman arranged enough manpower and basic organizations to achieve the supreme order given to him. In the following last article, we will see whether Kirkman Cabinet is going to touch Utopia or not.

Article 19

Utopia

Not only anthropologists, but also psychologists, neuroscientists, litterateurs and people of all walks of life ponder and pound out what the human mind truly is, how it actually functions and how come it behaves mysteriously. The human mind works wonder. Smart brain figures it better than ordinary one. And yet even smart people miss it too much too often. People who can read the human mind better form better leadership, achieve better, and invent more.

Humans make a society: family, town, nation and the world. Humans create culture, religion, language, history, law and order. Humans pursue money, power, freedom and happiness. Humans suffer from fighting each other, cheating one another. In a micro view, humans behave friendly while in a macro view humans move like other animals according to the law of jungle, which is different from the law and order of a civilized human society.

Esoteric scholars endlessly debate about instincts, the unconscious substances such as id, an innate energy of behaviors and chemical reactions of brain cells. Actually, even those professionals cannot catch the real essence of the human

Article 19: Utopia

mind because they only face a meaningless atom when they analyze a molecule or a certain thinking mechanism. When they dig out the human desires and its activities down to the rock bottom, they only find a piece of different fragments, which has no pertinent relationship to the action that they have tried to identify.

These days, however, with a great deal of helps from nanotechnology and computer science, neuroscientists approached very closely to the real stuff of the seemingly ghost-like thinking mechanism of the human mind. Even though humans have struggled to clarify the inner most source of instinct of the human mind, it always looked like a mirage. Nevertheless, the human knowledge has progressed in a big stride, especially in the modern civilization, along with other technologies.

Even though humans used to have guesswork on their decision-making issues for managing or governing the world affairs, sometimes, with an army of smart advisors, they have made many monumental accomplishments throughout histories along with many failures. The human affairs have become entangled with human desires and physical consequences of human environments. The physical human environments of natural phenomena and human's historical realities have existed there predictably. But the liquid human mind has always existed there at best as the unpredictables of life. In this juncture, too many unpredictable variations have made significant impacts on the human history.

Maybe, under these circumstances, humans have never achieved one dominant crushing power in the world. But now the big hindrances of natural infrastructures of the world such as vast land, mountains, rivers and oceans came under the control of modern technology of transportation and communication.

Super Constitution

The troika had established one dominant technology, enabling the establishment of the Global Government, and now the Global Government had to acquire two pillars to support its commanding activities for materializing the most ideal economic policies, which would bring forth Utopia first time in the human history. One of two pillars came from the well-established military institute under the political justice, but the other meant the appropriate mentality for the people's way of thought.

Dr. Wolfgang Thierse was supposed to handle the formation of ideally behaved mentality, constructing the most valuable support that would make the Global Government's commanding activities possible. The commanding activities of the Global Government needed the most suitable social-fabric in order to maximize the effectiveness of its actions. People's morale, satisfaction, positive attitude on honesty and hard work would be an absolute catalyst for governing power. If the government would make a success in establishing the right mentality for the people's way of thought on its social life, the government would already have achieved the most of its target. If not, even the God would not be able to achieve it.

For the successful governmental activities, President Kirkman understood that he absolutely needed the most appropriate function of the social fabric for the people's right way of thought.

In the middle of January 2017,

While Military Minister Dr. Yen-Jee Wang and Chairperson of the Joint Chiefs Sequoia were solidifying the global military power for the base of the global politics, Jay Kim had fully inspired George Kirkman with his monumental idea of a 13% growth rate of the world's GDP. Now, President Kirkman badly needed an assurance of success in establishing the right mentality for the people's way of thought.

Article 19: Utopia

President Kirkman sat at his office facing Dr. Wolfgang Thierse at around 10 a.m. on cold morning, in the middle of January 2017 in New York City.

"Good morning, Dr. Thierse! How is everything these days?"

"Very well, President Kirkman, happy New Year! How is Miss Ohara?"

"Happy New Year to you too. It is already the middle of January now. Miss Ohara is happy these days. Nobody bothers her. No incident has gone against her will, either. Actually, all the global affairs—the setup of the intelligence network, deploying the world armed forces, reshuffling the world's national units, establishing global economic policies and revolutionary transformation of people's basic attitudes–have flowed in favor of Global Government. Miss Ohara did a great job. Her killing wave and communicating capability have worked wonder. Also, her perfect arrangement of intelligence network, I, still, cannot figure out. And again, I am yet in the dark about her whereabouts. She talks to me just as if she's at my left or right side in a close proximity."

"Well, President Kirkman, maybe, that's why we are able to run global affairs without any resistance or hindrance at lightning speed. I guess you're constantly in touch with Miss Ohara these days."

"Of course, I talk with her almost every other day. Sometimes, we talk more than one hour. I feel she actually lives in this town, New York City."

"Really?"

"I think so, Dr. Thierse. Anyhow, I'd like to discuss the social matters we have to lay down to set social ethics."

Super Constitution

President Kirkman continued.

"Generally speaking, ethics means a general study of goodness, the right actions, moral psychology, and moral responsibility. But here we are talking about the social norms and fabric, which people could understand for the direction of their behavior. People must have a basic, firm frame of reference to behave as for a measuring standard. People have to have standardization or black and white instructions to guide them for a right behavior. As for an example, if they steal from or cheat somebody, they have to be prosecuted or punished including paying for all the expenses incurred in the investigation and prosecution."

"If they respect their own belief in God, they have to respect other's beliefs in different gods, or deism and even atheism."

"If somebody embezzles public funds or commits corrupt acts or intentionally violates laws, he must be investigated and heavily penalized. In other words, the belief that 'wrongdoing cannot last long and truth will win out in the long run' must be impressed on the public mind. Those immoral things will surely be exposed, and the guilty will be chastised heavily to pay back in five or even more than ten times. Honest, hard working people, we must protect from swindlers at any cost, all the way to the end."

Dr. Thierse smiled quietly at Kirkman's earnest remark for heavy penalization on all crimes.

"President Kirkman! I fully understand what you mean."

Dr. Thierse sat on his comfortable chair with relaxed composure and explained his deeply meditated idea to Kirkman, using the style of common and easy topic.

Article 19: Utopia

"President Kirkman, I know that you have often mentioned the issues of leadership, moral stand, ethical behavior, and social norm. I pretty much comprehend your mindset to provide the public's way of thinking with the frame of reference that they can depend on. The sound frame of reference which people can depend on for their judgment to take action must bear out a sound standard. These standardizations or norms must have an ironclad character in its practice and live up to action. In order to help forward the norms toward everyone's actual life, steadily and without hesitation, the norm must have, in addition to a conception of absolute practice, the soundest gravity of practicality. What is the best standardization or norm in each area of social activities? I'd like to discuss the best norm with you this morning, President Kirkman."

"Very well, Dr. Thierse, as I usually open my heart to my cabinet members, I esteem the idea of 'the right social fabric,' which is essential in staging political justice and economic advancement. Without a proper infrastructure of the right social fabric which will define and form the best norm, the Super Constitution can end up to a fallen splinter rather than a soaring rocket. The job of constructing the appropriate infrastructure for instituting the right social fabric must go along or even precede our impending job of politics and economics. Dr Thierse, please go on to your unfolding the ideas refined by your strenuous meditation."

"Thank you, President Kirkman. I do appreciate your stance on the subjects of people's way of thought and their foundations for the direction of their behavior. The other day, you suggested various subjects for me to use in creating foundations for the social policies we are going to implement for people to practice."

The two men paused momentarily to prepare to drink another fresh coffee for a moment, and then Dr. Thierse continued on.

Super Constitution

"First, President Kirkman, we have to solidify a firm program and schedule for consolidating world's more than 600 languages into one; second to practice and provide a generous tolerance to various religions and cultures; third to firmly apply heavy penalties on all crimes to lay out a maximum protection to honest and hard working people; fourth to organize an ideal people's commune for welfare recipients; fifth to have free education up to Ph.D. degree; sixth to make it free for all social services such as library, child birth, child care, institutions for the aged, consultations for positive prevention of domestic violations, and rectification for disadvantaged situations for disadvantaged people; seventh to set up all types of social ventilating countermeasures to deal with social problems such as gambling, drug abuse, drunk driving, prostituting practice and other things. All of these matters have direct interrelationship with the moral codes which conduct the behavior of the general public, providing the most influential impetus for political and economic activities."

"Dr.Thierse, please clarify the contour of the above substances so that we can contemplate the best design for engendering the most suitable social norms."

"Certainly, President Kirkman, I'd like to clarify the above seven areas for our consensus to be formed, and for our political justice and economic advance to kick off to reach our grand target."

Dr. Thierse, in a relaxed posture, felt comfortable, in delivering his refined ideas on those social fronts, which would exercise the greatest impact on the Global Government's political, economic directions and actions.

Article 19: Utopia

"I have concluded that a single sovereignty of the Global Government, consolidating a more than six billion population into about one hundred fifty units (nations), like a county of the U.S., will administer just the right touch to achieve the political justice, which will provide the most ideal and sensible economic policies."

"In order to give a right shot to the activities for political justice and economic advancement, I'd like to outline the basic policies in the seven areas as the following."

"First, language:
Man grows from infancy. Not only physical strength, but also intelligent capacity grows. The growth picks up a faculty of speech through endless practices of communication. Habitual practices of language accumulate its proficiency. Speaking the same language constitutes homogeneity and encourages gregariousness, which promotes the quality of politicking and communication, furnishing greater convenience and efficiency in life organization for the people. More varieties of languages cause more varieties of problems in the development of human culture, understanding, and intelligence without making any additional help to general human lifestyles. We should establish the most efficient measure for the world's people to speak the same language. Once they achieve, they will feel great."

"Second, religious tolerance:
Human society contains various characters, personalities and beliefs. Six billion people are not exactly same. They are all different. Their beliefs and religions and perspectives reflect their own angles. If you respect your perspective, at least, you need to have grace and generosity to acquiesce to those of others. The tolerant mind-set for other religions and beliefs will reduce substantial elements of the social conflicts which undermine people's productivity and harmony."

Super Constitution

"Third, severe penalization on all crimes:
Applying human rights to criminals and penalizing crimes to its severity must be distinguished. Crimes are a noxious part in human behavior which everyone has some portion. But everyone has a basic understanding or intelligence about the poisonous substance: conscience. Some people have stronger desire not able to listen to its conscience while others have a stronger conscience able to control its desire. Established and generalized moral code, steady and intensive education, and clear recognition of a severe penalization, and some hormone treatment could reduce an excessive desire, to make the person able to control the criminal impulse. Our legal frame of reference must set up a standard to emphasize a clear understanding of severe penalization."

"Fourth, an ideal people's commune:
Homogeneity of a society caters a better environment for the people of the same category. Not only welfare recipients but also terminal patients, handicapped people, and repeating criminals will feel better and behave better when they live collectively. They don't have to see, feel, or recognize discriminatory appearances, which create guilty feelings or anxiety. Each nation will provide a decent living environment that people can enjoy minimum standard of living, without worrying about income or expenses for their health care and maintenance of their ordinary lifestyle."

"Fifth, a free education paid up to Ph.D. degree:
Education should not cost any money to the young before they enter sociality. The appropriate education according to each person's ability and talents will help them contribute productive assets to society."

"Sixth, free social services:
A hotbed of social evils costs a society dearly. Providing social services to the needed actually increase our social facilities   and value which engender   indirect   social

Article 19: Utopia

productivity. It is going to enhance social stability, and stabilize social norms. Child birth and care, institutions for the elderly and disadvantaged, and prevention of domestic violations are going to greatly help social stabilization."

"Seventh, cares on social ventilation:
Human society, no matter how it refines its social fabric, suffers from indigenous indignities of innate human nature: such as kleptomania, gambling inclination, drug abuse, a matter of sexual catharsis through prostitutions, and other unusual bents. We should not allow negligence in these dark sides of minor social problems. They might look like negligible trivia. However, without being able to clear these poignant scenes in our way to Utopia, our political justice and economic advancement will be critically stained, and the poignant scenes will degrade our glorious and proud spirit of the globalization. Actually, rectifying measurements of these minor, intrinsic matters of our society will brighten our achievements as the right value of ethics and esthetics of human dignity."

"A unified communicating capability, the concept of generosity, equal opportunity of education, generalized recognition of severe penalization on crimes, positive sympathy for the disadvantaged and handicapped from the mainstream of society, and sincere cares for the dark side of our society, will create the most powerful frame of references for the greatest social norm. This frame of the norm will definitely bring forth a true social conscience. This social conscience will act on the guide for the direction of our globalizing process."

"President Kirkman, we need an omnipotent, overwhelming military power as a supporting pillar, in order for our action to achieve Utopia. At the same time, we need great social norms based on a true social conscience as another supporting pillar to convince people, as well."

Super Constitution

President Kirkman felt great on Dr. Thierse's confident thought about the social conscience. President Kirkman has constantly groped for the right frame of reference to act on an easy and common guide. Now, the word of the "true social conscience" uttered by Dr. Thierse, did strike his heart like a thunderbolt. He felt a great rapture. He beamed. He embraced Dr. Thierse, appreciating his pungent wit.

"Dr. Thierse, I recognize your right catchword for the campaign of our globalization: the social conscience. The true social conscience must embody the spirit of the most appropriate, single power word to express our philosophy of the Global Government. Let's stage an organized propaganda of the great concept of the true social conscience as our Global Government's intention. When people believe that our intention has been pegged on a simple, terse word of the greater social conscience, people will trust the Global Government. The public trust molds the most powerful engine for the human social movement. We have to have the trust from the people as well as the unquestionable loyalty from the world armed forces. Dr. Thierse, please create a theory of our leadership for our Global Government."

President Kirkman now felt relieved, for producing a clear vision of how to march to achieve Utopia. He had secured two of the most powerful pillars to support his drive to achieve Utopia: The World Armed Forces and The Concept of The Social Conscience. He had also secured the two most comprehensive roadmaps of political justice and economic policies through Dr. Yono and Dr. Kim. The only action left was to practice the proceedings according to the schedule that his cabinet had set.

In order to discuss the schedule of the review for the world armed forces deployed on Earth by the Global Government, President Kirkman summoned Chairperson of the Joint Chiefs

Article 19: Utopia

of Staff Michelle Sequoia and her chief advisor Philip Hillman to his office right after the meeting with Dr. Thierse.

"Good morning, General Hillman and Sequoia. Please have a seat. I would like to discuss the major programs of the military review for the first time. The reviewing ceremony is going to attract greatly intensified interests from the world as the foremost global event, symbolizing a majestic splendor of the united, global super-sovereignty derived from the Super Constitution. I'd like to review our Global Government's first establishment of the world armed forces with our cabinet members and all the important military brass, demonstrating to the world that the grand Global Government has been borne. This presentation of the military review is going to mark the most exciting human history on Earth, and we intend to maximize our propagandizing of the Global Government's philosophy of social conscience. Please state your plan for the show, General Sequoia."

"Of course, President Kirkman, I understand the immense magnitude of this first military review. This ceremony is going to implant acknowledgement of the Global Government's authenticity on Earth and provide a crucial momentum to magnify the spiritual stance of Global Government on social conscience. Bearing those two points in mind, General Hillman and I have made a plan as follows":

"First, we'd like to demonstrate our armed forces' maneuverability in field operations which may include helping any area in the world in case any local armed unit needs the massive support of extra armed forces. This demonstration will be done in a classification between battalions, regiments, brigades, divisions and the corps. The movement of a different scale of armed forces will present a different magnitude of functions and appearances. People will enjoy each one's significance and nimbleness."

Super Constitution

Second, we will use a form of briefing on the logistical readiness of a unit of one corps; this will be implemented through a thirty-minute motion picture, together with the actual performance of certain portions. We will spotlight all types of transportation, warehousing systems, and communications dealing with various issues: the procurement, supply, and maintenance of equipment; with the movement, evacuation, and hospitalization of personnel; with the provision of facilities and services, and with other related matters. Logistically strategic, overall plan for the successful military campaign will impress people."

"Third, we will operate first-class fireworks on Earth: shooting rockets and missiles from ground, ocean surface, under water and in the air; dropping smart bombs in exploding targets with super accuracy; and performing dexterous wielding of automatic guns, which will discharge three thousand rounds of bullets a minute to cover certain area without any missing like torrential raindrops. People will be surprised to see the awesome effect of our modernized fire power."

"Fourth, we'd like to dramatize a teamwork in the armed forces to bring forth maximization of organized armed power with coordinated efficiency. The team spirit in the interests of a common cause acts as a main booster for the organized armed forces' morale. Like a synchronized game, the coordinated movement of the various armed forces through various channels of communications, the use of the same language, and the agile manipulation of technology will impress people across the world and assure their belief in the armed forces' professionalism. It is going to be another wonderful show."

"Fifth, we'd like to exhibit a magnificent appearance of the massive airlift operation of our idolized Air Force. The swift and deft air power will secure the command of the air with dominant speed and accuracy across the world under the excellent conditions of our perfect air-traffic control. It will

Article 19: Utopia

cover an intensive communicating capability through its local air commands (twelve commands throughout the world), five army corps' headquarters, and the navy's five on-duty fleets' commands."

"General Sequoia, it sounds like the greatest show ever done on the earth."

President Kirkman truly felt proud of Chairperson of the Joint Chiefs, looking at General Hillman expecting some comment from him. General Hillman opened his mouth to speak with a confidant countenance.

"Yes, President Kirkman, since human's written history started, the world has the most powerful military strength. Nevertheless, that is also only a single existence. And I worry a little that it might overshadow politics."

President Kirkman smiled, and gave a ready response to General Hillman's concern.

"I understand some people's concern on a single, dominant muscle power of our military organization. But I feel different way. Actually, our military strength consists of three different organs: army, navy, and Air Force. These three organs have different functions and their own chain of commands. What's more, each organ of army and navy has five units with its own top boss, in addition to twelve units of Air Force. Also, we have an omnipotent intelligence network of the Ministry of Intelligence. On top of the above, we have intensified a surveillant function of the 'Security Command' under the global presidency. Our capability of listening and watching is almost perfect to be able to use even for crimes. Even the more powerful element far superior to all of the above is the concept of our 'social conscience.' We can think of even more powerful element than the concept: the economic stabilization based on political justice. I think we have all of those in our hands."

General Sequoia and Hillman had been impressed by the quiet words of President Kirkman. Three of them set the schedule for the grand ceremony of the formal reviews. Throughout five consecutive days, about one hour of each review, will be held in different locations. Each area's commanders will establish a detailed time schedule to fit their plans.

May 5, 2017

The first formal review of the world armed forces, according to a detailed schedule set by each area's responsible commanders, had exhibited an unheard-of historical appearance of the armed forces' stark, unique landscape, which, of course, was only an emerged tip of floated giant iceberg. The spectacular scene had captured and impressed the minds of the people, inspiring them to fantasize about the world's monstrous power. One hour's panoramic parade of the armed forces' maneuverability in a different scale of each echelon had produced a topnotch entertainment for the world.

The five days of consecutive, grand shows of the armed forces' various, brilliant facets had brought a striking effect on the favorable understanding of the people for realizing the unprecedented towering power of the Global Government.

People felt a solid sense of the Global Government's power that will promote global economic prosperity along with the protective spirit of "social conscience." People felt at ease and comfortable about the global spirit, as the magnificent military reviews went on under the banners of social conscience. The military reviews confirmed and consolidated the trust of the people.

Article 19: Utopia

THREE YEARS AFTER THE FIRST FORMAL REVIEWS
OF THE WORLD ARMED FORCES,

Around the first part of May 2020,

The troika of Brenda, John, and James got together at their usual den of the vault room to discuss the matter of their formal and complete return to their private lives: Miss Ohara's return to her home star, twenty-one light-years away from the earth.

Brenda had used a "virtual image" of her home star as "Ohara," in order to impress the sudden appearance of the troika's enigmatic technology on the world. (Actually, around April 2007, astronomers of the current world had found a potentially habitable planet about 1.5 times larger in diameter than Earth, orbiting the star Gliese 581 c, located 20.5 light-years away in the constellation Libra.) Now, the troika had acknowledged that their idea of the "Super Constitution" had worked out for the wonderful result.

During the last three years, Global Congress had organized its best niche for its legislature business and the Global Supreme Court had consolidated various undertakings for the most ideal legitimacy in the world.

George Kirkman's Cabinet had striven for the successful operation of the Global Government's target, managing more than 13% growth a year of the world's GDP while achieving greater strides in social services to the disadvantaged and the needed, and covering complete medical benefits for every walk of life under the banner of social conscience.

As usual, Brenda initiated the talks.

Super Constitution

"John and James, I am very happy to see the current development of the world political situation overall. I am sure that the Global Government is thoroughly managing sophisticated world affairs to achieve Utopia on Earth. Also, I am so happy for us able to return to our private lives to concentrate our research, and devote decent attention to raising our kids. I'd like to continue to study the human cell-organism, to enable humans to live up to 120 years without major diseases."

During the last six years, Brenda had given birth to one daughter with John and one son with James—a pretty girl of five years old and a cute boy of three years old. The kids were growing, in healthy development physically and mentally.

John spoke next.

"I feel great too. I'd like to focus my study on nano-technology, along with ultra short, electromagnetic wave-behavior. I hope to pin down the mechanism and dynamism of human brain cell's neuron, which can provide an insight into the innermost essence of the faculties of human memory, emotion, and desire. If successful, we can control or manage the phenomena of melancholy, agony, bad feelings, euphoria, orgasms, and ecstasy."

James, smiling, touched on the subject of their remarks in leaving the scene of the globalized earth for which the troika had played up the main instrument vigorously.

"You guys are going to make even greater contributions to the world after leaving the scene. For my part, I am determined to invent a 'reverse gravity engine' which can propel flying objects ten thousand miles per hour in the atmosphere (two times faster than the speed of a bullet) and half a million miles per hour in the vacuum space. I am also going to find one of the universe's laws spanning the expansion of the universe by the speed of hundred times faster than the speed of light. Presently, humans figure that humans can fathom the universe up to the size of one billion light-years diameter which represents only a tiny part of the whole universe like the size of a human cell versus a human body."

Brenda concluded.

"Well, James's world is much bigger than I thought, and John's world is penetrating into even much smaller unit. I am sure we will see a different world soon. Sooner or later, I am going to meet face to face with George Kirkman as an unknown scientist, after we give him an eternal 'farewell.' When I meet him in person, I am sure, that, even though I say I am the Miss Ohara, he won't believe it; he will smile at me, and probably say, 'That's a good joke.' "

THE END.

Super Constitution

Introducing Charles Kim

Borne in 1937 in Korea, immigrated to New York City

1964, right after graduating Graduate School of Public

Administration of Seoul National University.

Since 1964 to present, being engaged in wholesale and

Manufacturing business in high fashion costume jewelry.

For contacting:

Charlestone Int'l, Inc.

18009 Adria Maru Lane, Carson, CA. 90746

Tel. No. : 310 965 0048

Mobile : 310 702 2290 & 310 702 2251